Stevenson, D. E.
   Mrs. Tim flies home

DATE DUE

JUN 3	AUG 2 5		
JUL 31	APR 11		
AUG 21	JUN 14		
FEB 16	OCT 26		
OCT 7	JUN 5		
OCT 14			
OCT 28			
NOV 17			
JAN 18			
SEP 6			
DEC 24			
AUG 2 1			

Mrs. Tim
Flies Home

Books by D. E. Stevenson

Mrs. Tim Flies Home
Mrs. Tim Gets a Job
Mrs. Tim Carries On
Mrs. Tim Christie
Smouldering Fire
Victoria Cottage
Music in the Hills
The House of the Deer
The Young Clementina
Gerald and Elizabeth
Sarah's Cottage
Sarah Morris Remembers
The House on the Cliff
The Marriage of Katherine
Katherine Wentworth
The Blue Sapphire
Fletchers End
Bel Lamington
The Misgraves
Still Glides the Stream
Anna and Her Daughters
The Tall Stranger
Summerhills
Amberwell

Blow The Wind Southerly
Five Windows
Young Mrs. Savage
Kate Hardy
The Four Graces
Listening Valley
The Two Mrs. Abbotts
Celia's House
Spring Magic
Rochester's Wife
Alister & Co.
The English Air
The Green Money
A World in Spell
The Story of Rosabelle Shaw
The Baker's Daughter
Crooked Adam

Omnibus Volume
Miss Buncle *containing*
　Miss Buncle's Book *and*
　Miss Buncle Married

Mrs. Tim
Flies Home

D. E. STEVENSON

HOLT, RINEHART and WINSTON
New York • Chicago • San Francisco

Copyright, 1952, by Dorothy Emily Peploe
All rights reserved, including the right to
reproduce this book or portions thereof in
any form.
First published in 1952
New edition 1974

Library of Congress Cataloging in Publication Data
Stevenson, Dorothy Emily, 1892–1973
   Mrs. Tim flies home.
   I.   Title.
PZ3.S8472Moc5 [PR6037.T458] 823'.9'12 74-4807
ISBN 0-03-013171-5

Printed in the United States of America: 067

Author's Foreword
to the Story of the Christie Family

by D. E. STEVENSON

The four books about Mrs. Tim and her family are being re-published during 1973 and early 1974, and the author has been asked to write a foreword.

The books consist of:

1. *Mrs. Tim Christie*
2. *Mrs. Tim Carries On*
3. *Mrs. Tim Gets a Job*
4. *Mrs. Tim Flies Home*

The first "Mrs. Tim" was written many years ago (in 1934). It was written at the request of the wife of a professor of English history in a well-known university who was a personal friend. Their daughter was engaged to be married to an officer in a Highland Regiment. Naturally enough they wanted to know what it would be like and what she would be expected to do.

There was nothing secret in my diary so I gave it to Mrs. Ford to read. When she handed it back, Mrs. Ford was smiling. She said, "I read it aloud to Rupert and we laughed till we cried. You could make this into a very amusing book and call it *Leaves from the Diary of an Officer's Wife*. It just needs to be expanded, and you could pep it up a little, couldn't you?"

At first I was doubtful (it was not my idea of a book), but she was so persuasive that I decided to have a try. The result was *Mrs. Tim of the Regiment* (recently reissued as *Mrs. Tim*

Christie). By this time I had got into the swing of the story and had become so interested in Hester that I gave her a holiday in the Scottish Highlands with her friend Mrs. London and called it *Golden Days*.

The two books were accepted by a publisher and published in an omnibus volume. It was surprisingly successful. It was well reviewed and the sales were eminently satisfactory; the fan-mail was astonishing. People wrote from near and far saying that Mrs. Tim was a real live person; they had enjoyed her adventures immensely—and they wanted more.

But it was not until the outbreak of the Second World War in 1939 that I felt the urge to write another book about Hester Christie.

Mrs. Tim Carries On was easily written, for it is just a day-to-day account of what happened and what we did—and said and felt. The book was a comfort to me in those dark days; it helped me to carry on, and a sort of pattern emerged from the chaos.

Like its predecessor, the book was written from my own personal diary but this time there was no need to expand the story nor to "pep it up" for there was enough pep already in my diary for half a dozen books.

It is all true. It is true that a German plane came down on the moor in the middle of a shooting party and the two airmen were captured. It is true that German planes came down to low level in Norfolk, and elsewhere, and used machine guns to kill pedestrians on the roads. Sometimes they circled over the harvest fields and killed a few farm labourers and horses. Why they did so is a mystery. There could not have been any military objective in these maneuvers. People soon got used to it and were not even seriously alarmed but just took cover in a convenient ditch like dear old Uncle Joe. Perhaps the German airmen did it for fun? Perhaps it amused them to see old gentlemen rolling into ditches?

An American friend wrote to me as follows: "Your Mrs. Tim has made us *think*. We have been trying to imagine what it would be like to have a man-eating tiger prowling around in *our* backyard."

She had hit the nail on the head for, alas, the strip of water which had kept Britain safe from her enemies for hundreds of years had become too narrow: The tiger was in our backyard.

To me this book brings back the past so vividly that even now —thirty years later—I cannot read it without laughter and tears. Laughter? Yes, for in spite of the sadness and badness of Total War, the miseries we suffered, and the awful anxieties we endured, cheerfulness broke through at unexpected moments— and we laughed.

When they were first published, these four books about Mrs. Tim were all very popular. Everybody loved Mrs. Tim (everybody except the good citizens of Westburgh who disliked her intensely). Everybody wanted to know more about her and her friends. But the books have been out of print and unobtainable for years. I was pleased to hear that they were to be republished and that they would all be available again. I was particularly glad because together they contain the whole history of the Christie family and its friends. Taken in their proper sequence, readers will be able to appreciate the gradual development of Hester's character and the more rapid development of Tim's. As the years pass by there is a difference in the children; Annie and Fred Bollings become more adult; Jack and Grace McDougall, having weathered serious trouble, settle down peacefully together. The Christies' friends are very varied but all are interesting and unusual. We are introduced to the dignified Mrs. London; we meet Pinkie, an attractive young lady whose secret trouble is that (although seventeen years old) she does not feel "properly grown up, inside." But, in spite of this, Pinkie makes friends wherever she goes. Her circle of friends includes all the young officers who are quartered at the depot and is enlarged by the arrival of Polish officers who have escaped from their war-shattered country and are billeted in Donford while they reorganise their forces and learn the language. There is a mysterious lady, swathed in Egyptian scarves, who is convinced that in a previous existence she helped to build the Great Pyramid. There is Erica Clutterbuck whose rude manners conceal a heart of gold, and two elegant American ladies who endeavour to persuade Mrs. Tim to go home with them to America so that they may exhibit her to their friends as "The Spirit of English Womanhood."

But the chief interest is to be found in the curious character of Tony Morley and his relationship with the Christie family. At first he seems to Tim and Hester a somewhat alarming personage. (To Tim, because he is a senior officer and fabulously wealthy: he drives a large and powerful car, owns a string of racehorses, and hunts several days a week. To Hester, because he talks irresponsibly and displays an impish sense of humour so that she never knows whether or not he means what he says.) Soon, however, they discover that beneath the surface he is a true friend and can be relied upon whenever the services of a friend are urgently needed. We find out how he uses his tact and diplomacy to smooth the feathers of a disgruntled cook and show her how to measure out the ingredients for a cake with insufficient weights. We learn how he helps Hester to save a naval officer from making a disastrous marriage and how he consoles and advises a young husband whose wife has deserted him. We are told of Colonel Morley's success with a battalion of raw recruits, how he wins their devotion, licks them into shape, and welds them into a satisfactory fighting machine by imbuing them with the necessary esprit de corps. We see him salute smartly and march off at the head of his battalion en route for the Middle East. Knowing his reputation for reckless courage,

Hester wonders sadly if she will ever see him again. But apparently Tony is indestructible. He has survived countless dangers and seems none the worse. He pops in, out of the blue, in Rome (where Hester, on her way home from Africa, is seriously embarrassed by her ignorance of the language). Tony Morley arrives in his usual sudden and unexpected manner. By this time he has become a full-blown general and, having learnt to speak Italian from an obliging enemy, is able to deal adequately with the situation. He also deals adequately with a little misunderstanding at the War Office where he sees a friend and pulls a string or two for Tim.

Meanwhile the Christie children, Bryan and Betty, are growing up rapidly. In fact they are "almost grown up," and, although they are still amusing and full of high spirits, it is obvious that they will soon become useful members of the post-war world.

We meet them at Old Quinings where their mother has managed to find a small house for the summer holidays. Here, also, we meet Annie and Fred Bollings, Grace McDougall and her boys, an old-fashioned squire with a pretty daughter, a schoolteacher whose unconventional views about free love are somewhat alarming, and a very good-looking young man who is studying medicine but is not too busy to open gates for a fair equestrienne. We meet the amiable Mrs. Daulkes and the far from amiable Miss Crease whose sharp eyes and caustic tongue cause a good deal of trouble to her neighbours. Another unpleasant visitor is Hester Christie's landlady, the wily Miss Stroude, who tries to bounce Hester and almost succeeds, but once again Tony comes to the rescue in the nick of time to defeat Miss Stroude and send her away "with her tail between her legs."

Betty says, joyfully, "This is the best holidays, ever" but Hester's pleasure is not complete until the arrival of Colonel Tim

Mrs. Tim
Flies Home

Part I

Flying Above the Clouds

Wednesday, 13th June

THE BEGINNING of a journey by air is the moment when you emerge from the air-station and see before you a large flat plain and your aeroplane waiting for you. There it stands, a huge ungainly monster, with a silver body and wings and two enormous wheels. The fact that it possesses both wheels and wings is symbolic, showing it to be a monster of earth and air—just as a frog is a monster of earth and water. (We call the frog an amphibian but as far as I know there is no proper word for a creature having seizin of earth and air.)

If you are at all like me, your first thought on beholding the silver monster will be: Can it possibly fly? Can that man-made contraption soar into the air like a bird? Your second will be that it looks extremely unsafe—a gimcrack sort of monster—and (again if you are like me) you will feel a strange reluctance to climb the ladder which is placed so conveniently against the monster's side and enter the small dark aperture in its ribs; but if you are reluctant to embark you are even more reluctant to brand yourself a coward (and, incidentally, you have made all your plans and paid the earth for your ticket) so you exclaim with false assurance, "Ah, there's my plane!" and march forward to your fate.

All these curious ideas sweep through my mind in a moment, and this reminds me that a drowning man sees his whole life pass before his eyes before he sinks to the bottom for the last time (though how we know that it does so I cannot imagine). In some ways I am like that drowning man, that man who will clutch at a straw, but it is not my whole life which passes before my eyes—merely the last eighteen months, which I have spent in Kenya living in the lap of luxury and doing my best to sustain the part of Colonel's Wife with reasonable dignity. This last eighteen months has been a happy time—a time of sunshine and gaiety—and now I am leaving it all behind. I am leaving the large airy bungalow with the chintz curtains, leaving the garden with its gorgeous array of tropical plants; worst of all, I am leaving Tim.

Tim has come to see me off, of course, and at this very moment is walking with me towards the plane. Suddenly he grabs my arm and says in beseeching accents, "Hester, don't go!"

"Don't go!" I echo, standing still and looking at him in amazement.

"I don't want you to go in that thing," explains Tim in rapid undertones. "I mean, not alone. It wouldn't be so bad if I were coming too. Of course I've flown a lot myself and thought nothing of it, but that's quite different. I mean it's a bit terrifying at first—and anyhow the children don't need you nearly as much as I do. Bryan is grown up."

"But, Tim, we talked it all over and agreed—"

"It was crazy," he declares. "I must have been mad to agree. Don't go, Hester."

"Tim! I've got to go!"

"But I can't bear it!" cries Tim.

4

During this impassioned appeal the other passengers are streaming past, climbing the silver steps and disappearing one by one into the monster's belly.

"But it's all fixed!" I exclaim. "You know quite well I must go. It's all fixed."

"We can unfix it," Tim declares. "It isn't too late."

But of course it is too late for at this moment a large smiling steward approaches and takes my suitcase from Tim's unwilling hand. "It's all right, Colonel," says the smiling steward. "I've kept a good seat for Mrs. Christie. I'm afraid I must ask you to go back, sir, or I'll be getting into trouble. Only passengers are allowed on the airstrip."

"Yes," says Tim. "Yes, we don't want to get you into trouble, but the fact is Mrs. Christie has changed her mind and—"

"Good-bye, Tim, darling!" I cry, throwing my arms round his neck and kissing him.

"Good-bye," says Tim miserably. "You'll cable from Rome—don't forget to cable from Rome. This is hell!" he adds in a choked voice as he squeezes my hand into pulp. "I never realised—well—good-bye."

He salutes and walks away smartly, while I, wearing a false smile, climb up the ladder and enter the plane.

I know quite well what Tim is feeling and can sympathise with him profoundly, for I have experienced the same misery a hundred times. I have said good-bye to Tim and watched him being whirled away to the ends of the earth in planes or trains or ships . . . but, looking back down the years of our married life, I cannot remember a single occasion upon which Tim saw me off and was left behind. I have always suspected it was a good deal worse for the one who was left behind and now I know. Poor Tim! But he will be all right, I tell myself firmly. People will be kind to him—for people who dwell in the far-flung outposts of the British Empire stand together and bear one another's burdens. Yes, I tell myself (as I accept the seat which the steward has reserved for me) yes, Tim will be well looked after; it's right for me to go home. . . . And the reflection that I am doing my duty comforts me considerably for, if by any chance one should be killed in the execution of one's duty, it would be a noble end.

Sometimes it is difficult to see clearly in what direction one's duty lies (and especially difficult for people like myself with a husband in one part of the world and children in another) but Tim and I, talking it over together in cold blood, decided that I ought to go home. My brother Richard and his wife have been extremely kind to Bryan and Betty but the responsibilities of parenthood cannot be delegated and although—as Tim says—Bryan is grown-up, I feel he needs me more, not less, than when he was comfortably settled at school. Betty needs me less, for Betty is a self-contained unit and is of a philosophical nature.

"You must fasten your safety-belt," says a voice in my ear, but before I can comply with the instruction two thin hands seize the belt and buckle it firmly across my waist. The owner of the voice and hands is my neighbour and as I look round at her and murmur my thanks I see a thin brown face with well-marked eyebrows and very dark brown eyes.

"It's all right," she says. "Perhaps you haven't flown before. We always have to fasten our safety-belts going up and coming down."

By this time the plane has taxied out to the far end of the airstrip and halted there. The engines are going like mad and the monster is quivering in every strut, panting to be off but held back from this laudable desire by some unseen force. It is like a greyhound straining at the slips—or so I feel. Then suddenly the slips are loosed and away goes the monster tearing down the field faster and faster. The buildings approach rapidly and for a few brief moments I have a horrible suspicion that something has gone wrong and the monster will not rise . . . but lo, we are above the buildings and all is well; the monster is air-borne!

"I've flown a lot," says my neighbour comfortingly, "but it's always a little nerve-wracking going up and coming down. You can unfasten yourself now, and smoke if you want to," and she points out a notice in red lights to that effect.

Having broken the ice we begin to chat. She asks if I am flying straight home and I reply that I intend to break my journey at Rome and stay there two nights, Tim having insisted that this will be less tiring. My neighbour announces that she is staying in Rome for a week with an old schoolfriend. She then goes on to tell me that she has been visiting a friend (whose husband is a District Commissioner near Lake Victoria) and is on her way home to see her son. Her name, she tells me, is Rosa Alston, which sounds pleasant in my ears, but Mrs. Alston is dissatisfied with it and explains that many people refer to her as "Roseralston."

"It can't be helped, of course," says Mrs. Alston. "My name was Rosa Burton before I married and that sounds good."

"So you can't blame your parents!"

"Oh, I don't," replies Mrs. Alston unsmilingly.

The joke was feeble, it is true, but I am a trifle disappointed that it did not obtain recognition from Mrs. Alston.

She continues: "As a matter of fact the habit of putting an R in the wrong place is quite modern. I hate it, don't you?"

"Yes, it certainly is very ugly."

"Even the B.B.C. announcers do it sometimes," adds Mrs. Alston with a sigh.

I am now too interested in my surroundings to continue the conversation, for we are mounting higher every moment. Above us is the blue, blue sky with the sun blazing in it like a golden fire. There is no feeling of rushing through the air, no feeling of speed, the plane seems to be floating along peacefully in space. The cloud formations are magnificent and somehow they look much more solid than they do from the ground. Below are patches of fleecy cloud which move along slowly in the wind and between them there are glimpses of land (like a carpet, perfectly flat, with a curious pattern upon it). Away on the horizon there are banks of cloud which might be snow-covered mountains; there are clouds which tower up, hundreds of feet high, and look like fairy palaces of pink and white marble, and there are clouds which look like icebergs and glisten in the sun.

All this is wonderful to behold; so wonderful and so unlike anything that I have seen before that I forget to be frightened and I feel as if my eyes were getting bigger and bigger, trying to see it all at once.

Presently the cloud below us thickens into a solid blanket, blotting out every sign of the world. It is a very queer feeling to be high up in the sky with clouds all round us and clouds below, with no land in sight—with nothing in sight but blue sky and clouds and golden sunshine. It is a strange lonely feeling. The known world has vanished and there is nothing in the universe but one little aeroplane. My imagination gets out of control and I begin to wonder if the world is still there. Shall we find our way back to it again or are we doomed to wander about forever in this vast spacious universe—like some modern version of the Flying Dutchman?

When I mention these thoughts to my neighbour she looks at me pityingly and says all modern planes are equipped with instruments which show the pilot exactly where he is, so there is no need to worry.

Night falls suddenly, as is its habit in equatorial countries, the sun sinks into a bank of cloud and is gone. Now there is no more to see and the little window beside me acts as a mirror reflecting the lighted interior of the plane and its varied assortment of passengers.

Opposite to me sits a Dutch lady with a beautiful face, smoothly moulded and saintly, like the face of a Madonna in an old Dutch painting. It would be pleasant to talk to her but she cannot speak English nor French, and I know not a single word of Dutch, so all we can do about it is to smile at one another and make friendly signs; but this is unsatisfactory and I am delighted when she shuts her eyes and goes to sleep for now I can look at her as much as I like—and to look at her is a pleasure.

Just across the passageway which runs down the centre of the cabin there is a Lancashire woman with two children; the elder, a boy of seven, is restless and discontented; his mother spends most of her time trying to keep him in order. "Don't do that, 'Arry!" she says. " 'Arry you're not to pinch 'Ilda." " 'Arry, I told you not to touch that 'andle," and of course 'Arry does all the things he is told not to do, straight off. 'Arry would be much better if his mother would leave him alone, but apparently this does not occur to her.

Mrs. Alston has been reading her book, but presently she puts it aside and says, "Tell me what you're going to do when you get home, or would you rather read?"

I reply that I would rather talk (and this is true for talking prevents me from listening to the beat of the engines and wondering whether it is merely imagination that one of them is not firing very well) and as I feel it is my turn to talk I proceed to explain that I have temporarily deserted my husband and am returning home to my children. I tell her that Bryan is at Cambridge, studying agriculture, and Betty is at school near Edinburgh, and I have taken a furnished house in a little village not far from London so they will be able to spend their holidays with me.

Mrs. Alston says how frightfully lucky to have got a house. She is obliged to stay with relations and friends, which, although pleasant in some ways, is rather a strain. "Always being on one's best behaviour," says Mrs. Alston with a sigh. "Helping to wash the dishes and not knowing where anything is kept. And then, although Edmond is a dear and I understand him perfectly, he's just a little bit . . . well, a little bit *difficult* at times. Edmond is my son, of course. I wish I could have arranged to have a house. How did you manage?"

It is obvious that Mrs. Alston does not want to discuss her difficult son—and who can blame her—so I plunge into the long tale of the house and explain that it was discovered for us by the local innkeeper and his wife whom we have known for years. Fred Bollings was Tim's batman and Annie was Betty's nurse—and afterwards, when Betty went to school, she was cook-housekeeper and general factotum. In fact both of them were with us for so long and went through so many trials and tribulations with us that they became a part of the family. I further explain that two years ago, when Bollings left the Army, Tim and I decided it was high time they settled down together and had a life of their own and as we had just received a totally unexpected legacy from a distant cousin of Tim's (whom neither of us had ever seen) we were able to lend Bollings the wherewithal to buy a small inn and thereby attain his heart's desire.

"How nice!" says Mrs. Alston.

"Yes, it was very lucky. The inn is at a little village called Old Quinings and—"

"Goodness, not the Bull and Bush!" exclaims Mrs. Alston. "I know it well. I used to stay with an aunt at Old Quinings when I was a girl."

10

Wednesday, 13th June

This odd coincidence surprises us; though why it should surprise us it would be difficult to say. Personally I have found the world exceedingly small; so small and compact that it is impossible to chat for half an hour to anyone without discovering some point of contact, some mutual friend or even some long-forgotten meeting. This phenomenon is most noticeable in the British Colonies where the white population consists almost entirely of service people like ourselves.

Mrs. Alston and I agree about the smallness of the world and mention several odd coincidences which have come our way.

"Do you know the Morleys?" enquires Mrs. Alston. "They live at Charters Towers which is quite near Old Quinings."

"Of course I do! It was Tony Morley who told us the Bull and Bush was for sale."

Mrs. Alston says she knows Freda Winthrop (Tony's sister) and adds that she used to go to dances at Charters Towers sometimes. "They were very posh dances," says Mrs. Alston reminiscently. "But as a matter of fact I didn't enjoy them much. Freda and her friends all hunted like mad, and knew one another intimately, and I never hunted in my life and knew nobody—except Freda of course—so I felt rather out of it."

I can sympathise with Mrs. Alston in this experience for, long ago, Tim and I spent a weekend at Charters Towers and felt "rather out of it."

"They're very rich of course," continues Mrs. Alston. "Everything was done on a big scale and it was all quite terrifying; Lady Morley was too grand to take the slightest interest in me and Tony was unbearable."

"Tony unbearable!" I cry in amazement. "You don't mean Tony Morley!"

"He's so stuck up," explains Mrs. Alston. "So pleased with himself. Of course he did very well in the war (he's a Major General, isn't he?) so I suppose he has a right to be pleased with himself. I daresay he would have been more human and less selfish if he had married. I remember Freda told me he had fallen hopelessly in love with a married woman and had never got over it."

This description of Tony is so untrue and unfair that it takes my breath away and it is a moment or two before I can rush to his defence. "Oh no!" I gasp. "Tony isn't like that."

Mrs. Alston looks at me in surprise.

"We've known Tony for years," I tell her. "He was in Tim's regiment. He's the kindest creature alive . . . and I don't believe it's true about him falling in love with a married woman; I never heard about it."

"Oh well," says Mrs. Alston. "I expect you know him better than I do."

This difference of opinion causes a slight rift in the lute but the advent of dinner helps to mend it. Mrs. Alston shows me how to fix the table in front of me, arranges my tray and points out to the steward that he has omitted to provide me with salt. This solicitude amuses me for Tim is wont to declare that wherever I go there is always somebody who makes it their business to look after me, some capable down-to-earth person who is eager to take me in charge. "You look helpless," said Tim on one such occasion. "You aren't the least helpless of course, but you have an appealing air. If you went to the North Pole you'd find a nice kind mug of an Eskimo who would make it his business to fend for you and bring you lovely lumps of blubber." Since then "Hester's Eskimo" has become a well-worn joke in the Christie family. Tim will laugh when I write and tell him my faithful Eskimo was waiting, ready for duty, at the equator.

12

Wednesday, 13th June

The plane roars onward through the starry night and its occupants dine in comfort. The soup is excellent (and I am glad to find it does not slosh about the bowl as it does in trains), there is tongue and green peas and potatoes, there is fruit salad and ice cream.

We are all enjoying our meal when suddenly " 'Arry's" mother gives a cry of dismay and we all look round to see what that young imp is up to now. It seems to me that he is remarkably good and peaceful but his mother thinks otherwise. " 'Arry!" she exclaims in horrified tones. " 'Arry, why can't you be'ave yourself proper! 'Ow often 'ave I told you it ain't the right thing to eat peas with your fingers! You got a knife, 'aven't you?"

After dinner has been cleared away I settle down to write my diary, but Mrs. Alston makes the task somewhat difficult, for apparently she wants to talk.

"What are you writing?" she enquires. "Are you an author, by any chance? You don't look like one, somehow."

I reply that I am not an author, merely a diarist—and *that* only at certain periods in my checkered career. When Tim and I are together I seem to have no time to record my impressions, but when we are separated by force of circumstances I keep a large notebook handy and write down all the interesting and amusing things that happen to me.

"Why don't you have a proper diary?" Mrs. Alston asks.

"Because some days are more interesting than others. Some days I write nothing and other days I write reams. I know it isn't the correct way to keep a diary, but that's how I do it."

Mrs. Alston says she doesn't know how I can be bothered. She has started a diary several times (on the first of January, which is the right day to start a diary) but she has never managed to keep it up for long.

Thursday, 14th June

*I*T IS difficult to know when one day ends and another begins. I am aware, of course, that this phenomenon occurs at midnight and I am congratulating myself that yesterday is over and commenting upon the circumstance to my companion, when she interrupts me with the information that it is not. Although my watch informs me that a new day has begun it is still yesterday evening—so Mrs. Alston says. We have almost arrived at Cairo, says Mrs. Alston, and at Cairo we shall find that it is half-past eleven—no more. I find this extraordinarily muddling (probably because I am dazed and sleepy) and although Mrs. Alston continues to explain the matter it becomes no clearer.

"When it's night-time in Italy it's Wednesday over here," I murmur helplessly.

"Fasten your safety-belt," says Mrs. Alston.

We land—whether today or yesterday I cannot tell—the door of the cabin is opened and we descend.

We have nearly two hours at Cairo while the plane is re-fuelling and, thanks to my new friend who is an experienced traveller, we get through the formalities without any trouble. Soon we are walking along a broad road lined with palm trees. Here and there I see little white bungalows with flowers in their gardens.

I was sleepy in the plane but now I feel revived and ex-

cited, for there is something exciting in the air; it is so pure
and dry . . . and there is a faint but very curious smell, the
smell of the desert! The desert is near; one cannot see it but
one can feel the strange magic of its wide spaces, its miles of
baked sand and rolling dunes. Somewhere, not far away, stand
the pyramids and the sphinx, those mysterious age-old monuments of a vanished civilisation. Somewhere in the darkness
beneath the starry sky—

"Take care!" says Mrs. Alston, seizing my arm.

"What is it?" I ask, slightly annoyed at this violent interruption to my train of thought.

"The curb—I was afraid you didn't see it," she explains.
"I was afraid you weren't looking where you were going. It's
dark, isn't it?" she continues. "What a pity there isn't a moon!
I should have liked you to see a desert moon."

She continues to talk and, although it is very kind of her
to be so solicitous of my welfare, I begin to feel I should prefer
silence.

Mrs. Alston and I find the restaurant where we are to
have our supper. We sit on the veranda—it is warm and quiet
and peaceful—and here we have our meal. Presently a camel
comes walking down the road; it is laden with sacks which,
being the same colour as itself, give it the appearance of a
huge misshapen creature from another world. It pads along
soundlessly like a monster in a dream. A few moments later a
huge Rolls Royce passes almost as soundlessly but a good deal
faster.

Here is the old way of transport and the new passing upon
the same road before my eyes.

It seems absurd that this is all I see of Cairo, but somehow, although I see so little, I seem to absorb the atmosphere
of the place and my imagination is stirred by every breath I
draw.

15

Somebody is talking and gently shaking my arm. The mists of sleep recede and I come to myself to discover that I have a splitting headache.

"It's Rome," says Mrs. Alston. "I'm sorry I had to waken you, but you'll have to fasten your safety-belt in a minute and I wanted you to see Rome from the air."

I rub my eyes and, obedient to Mrs. Alston's behest, I look out of the little window. Far below I see a toy town, a town of soft colouring and bright green trees; wandering amongst the buildings I see a river—not a very spectacular river and somewhat disappointing when one remembers the romance of its history. Old Father Tiber cannot hold a candle to Old Father Thames and the exploit of Horatius in swimming it is less heroic than I had imagined.

I am still looking at Rome, and admiring the pale golden hue of its buildings in the early morning sunshine, when suddenly without any warning Rome rises up from its proper place on the ground and looks at me . . . it looks straight in at the window in a most disconcerting manner.

"Goodness!" I exclaim.

"We're banking," says Mrs. Alston. "We're circling round and getting ready to land. I know it's rather alarming when you aren't used to it—you feel as if the ground had risen up and hung itself on the wall. Of course what *really* happens is that the plane leans over (just as you lean over when you turn a corner on a bicycle) but when you're in a plane you lose your sense of balance. For instance when you loop the loop and you're upside down in the sky you feel as if you were the right way up and everything else in the universe had suddenly gone mad. The ground seems up above and the sky down below. At least that's how I felt," says Mrs. Alston reminiscently. "You should get someone to take you up and show you."

Thursday, 14th June

"Yes—er—yes," I reply in doubtful tones.

"It's very interesting."

"I'm sure it must be."

At Rome Mrs. Alston and I are obliged to part. She is staying with a friend and I have booked a room in a pensione recommended to me by my brother and his wife who stayed here last year.

Mrs. Alston seems doubtful about my ability to look after myself in Rome. Her last words as we shake hands are to warn me of pickpockets and to remind me that the traffic comes in the opposite direction from countries under British jurisdiction, and as I sit down to fill in a form (without which formality I cannot leave the airport) I can see her hovering in the doorway and looking back at me. It is obvious that if I show signs of wanting her help she will change her plans and come with me to the pensione and see me settled in. Mrs. Alston is extremely kind and I am suitably grateful, but by this time her solicitude has become a trifle boring, so I wave to her cheerfully and complete my task.

A taxi is chartered to take me to the pensione. It careers along at high speed and, although I am aware that it is conforming to the European convention by keeping to the right, the sight of vehicles approaching at high speed on (what seems to me) the wrong side of the road fills me with anxiety. We pass the ruins of the old Roman aqueducts—a broken line of arches stretching across fields and orchards—we pass wide squares and churches built of honey-coloured stone. There are trees in their summer greenery and slopes of green grass amongst the buildings and masses of brilliant flowers. We pass old buildings and new buildings, streets wide and streets narrow, streets with shops full of all sorts of fascinating merchandise and, coming at last to the Piazza di Spagna, we discover a steep little cobbled street in which is the entrance to the Pensione Scarlatti.

The pensione consists of a large flat in an old Roman palace. It is on the third floor and is reached by a fine staircase of white marble. Probably long ago this whole building belonged to some great Roman family (it is large enough to house a regiment) and as I toil up the marble stairs, suitcase in hand, I try to imagine what it must have been like to live like a prince in magnificence and luxury and to have more servants than one could count. In those far-off days life was colourful and romantic, hospitality was on a gigantic scale; these old walls could tell of revelry, of the whisper of silken dresses and the clash of swords.

Signora Scarlatti opens the door of the flat herself and welcomes me effusively but incomprehensibly in a spate of Italian to which I reply, "Si, si, buon giorno," which is the only Italian I know. I then enquire in my own tongue whether she can speak English.

"Spika no Inglis!" she exclaims, shaking her head sadly.

Things are now at a complete standstill and we look at one another helplessly . . . until suddenly I have a brilliant inspiration and try how she reacts to French.

"Parlez-vous Français?" I ask somewhat diffidently for as I have not spoken French for years (nor even heard French spoken) I have grave doubts of my ability to sustain a conversation in that language.

"Si, si!" exclaims the Signora. "Et vous, madame? Vous parlez le Français?"

"Si, si," I reply.

"Ah, bon!" cries Signora Scarlatti, her dark eyes flashing with delight and excitement . . . and she proceeds to welcome me all over again in French. Unfortunately, however, she speaks that language with an Italian accent so I find it almost as difficult. Gesticulation helps, of course, and by dint of signs and broken phrases we manage to communicate with one another and to achieve understanding.

The flat is large and has an old-worldly air. It consists of a wide hall with a beautiful parquet floor, which stretches from the front door at one end to the kitchen at the other. This hall—or sala as the Signora calls it—is furnished with sofas and easy chairs and standard lamps with orange-coloured shades. All the rooms open off the sala, some on one side and some on the other.

Signora Scarlatti conducts me round talking volubly and pointing out the comforts and amenities of her establishment. She shows me the bathroom, a gloomy and somewhat sinister apartment with an enormous bath which looks as if it had not been used for years; she opens another door and shows me a spacious roof-garden with plants in boxes and pergolas covered with vines (here some of my fellow guests are sitting, sunning themselves in deck chairs); she shows me the dining room, with eight or ten small tables set for the mid-day meal. Finally she leads me to the room she has reserved for me, which is a pleasant room, clean and bright, with a comfortable bed. It is the bed that interests me most and I explain to the Signora in my halting French that I shall sleep all day and get up to supper.

"Vous n'avez pas faim?"

"Non," I reply shaking my head.

"Vous êtes fatiguée?"

"Oui," I reply nodding violently.

All is clearly understood. She goes away and I crawl into bed.

I awake in plenty of time to unpack and prepare myself for supper, and supper seems desirable for I am now extremely hungry. There is a fixed basin in my room, a basin with two taps upon which are inscribed CALDO and FREDDO. These words mean nothing to me so I try them both to find out which is which; but this plan though reasonable in theory gets me no further for cold water flows from both taps in a reluctant trickle. As I wait for the basin to fill I reflect upon ancient Rome and her enormous aqueducts (the ruins of which impressed me so much this morning) and come to the conclusion that the Romans of today are not so enthusiastic about their water supply as their ancestors. Fortunately it is very warm, so washing in cold water is no hardship.

I wash thoroughly and am partially dressed when there is a discreet knock on the door and a pretty girl in a black dress and white muslin apron looks in and says a long liquid rigmarole in an enquiring tone of voice. She is probably asking if I am nearly ready for supper. The girl smiles so sweetly and has such lovely dark eyes and such gleaming white teeth that I am enchanted with her and am filled with regret that I am unable to talk to her.

All I can do is to smile and nod in a friendly manner and say, "Si, si!" This obviously pleases her enormously. "Si, si, signora!" she cries, and opening the door widely ushers in a guest.

"Hullo, Hester!" exclaims the well-known voice of Tony Morley and he walks into my room.

"Tony!" I exclaim, seizing my dressing-gown and enveloping myself in its folds. "Goodness! I was washing!"

"So I see," replies Tony calmly. He takes my hand in his and smiles down at me in his usual friendly way.

"Where have you sprung from?" I cry. "What on earth are you doing in Rome? How did you know I was here?"

He laughs and says, "The same old Hester, asking three questions at once! I'll sit down and tell you all about it."

Thursday, 14th June

"But Tony, you can't. I'm awfully glad to see you, but this is my bedroom."

"I shouldn't worry about that."

"But, honestly—"

"Now don't fuss," says Tony.

It is easy for Tony to say, don't fuss, but I want to finish dressing. I explain this to him and suggest that he should go and wait in the sala until I am ready.

"But you said I could come in," says Tony in surprised accents. "That exceedingly attractive young woman asked you if she should admit me and you said, 'Si, si!' I heard you with my own ears."

"I didn't understand a word she said."

"In that case it was a little risky," declares Tony gravely. "I mean she might have been asking you . . . anything."

"I wish you would go away."

"The hall—or sala if you prefer it—is cluttered with people. It would be most embarrassing for me to hang about outside your door."

"What will they all think!" I cry.

"They'll think the worst—and love you all the better. This is Rome, not Donford, my dear."

"And I suppose you think I should do as the Romans do!"

"Within limits," he replies in judicial tones. "For instance you should look to the right rather than to the left when crossing the street, but I should hate to see you spit on the pavement."

It is useless to argue with him so I am obliged to complete my toilet in his presence. He sits on my bed and watches with interest while I brush my hair and put on my frock . . . and, seeing that the frock has fasteners up the back, he rises without comment and fastens them for me.

"There," says Tony proudly. "Quite a neat job for an old

bachelor. Just a dab of powder on your tip-tilted nose and you're ready. We'll go out and feed, shall we?"

I suggest we should feed here, but my visitor says that is *not* a good idea; he saw flocks of vultures gathering in the sala and they looked frightful. "Sitting there waiting for their food! Drooling at the mouth!" says Tony with a shudder.

This description of my fellow-guests is so alarming that I suggest we should wait until the vultures have gone to feed before leaving the shelter of my room.

Tony says, "Why? They won't eat you. It's spaghetti they want."

"But they'll see us come out of my room!"

Tony sighs and says he is hungry, but it shall be just as I please. "Of course they saw me come in," says Tony thoughtfully. "They heard me being welcomed with cries of delight; so, if it is your reputation you are worrying about, it would be almost better for them to see us both come out. I may be wrong . . ."

He is not wrong. I seize a light wrap and make for the door, but Tony is there before me.

"Wait," he says, holding me back. "Not like that, Hester."

"Not like what?"

"You look as if you had picked somebody's pocket and were making off with the swag." He laughs softly and adds, "Chin up! Shoulders back! Let there be a good entrance."

The door is opened widely and the entrance is as good as I can make it. I notice as I stroll across the sala that it is as Tony said, the long hall is full of people waiting for their meal. I notice also that they seem far too intent upon their own concerns and far too busy talking and gesticulating to one another to pay any attention to me.

It is always pleasant to go out with Tony for he is the sort of person who manages the small details of living with a

22

sure hand. Taxis are always to be had when he wants one; head-waiters conduct him to the best table and attend personally to his behests. Tonight is no exception to the rule and soon we are seated side by side upon a crimson plush sofa with a white-clothed table before us.

The restaurant is garishly decorated with crimson curtains and large shining mirrors in heavy gilt frames, and these mirrors reflect the scene backwards and forwards to infinity. It is difficult to tell which are the real people and which are their reflections but the long room seems crowded and the noise of chatter and laughter almost drowns the band. I am feeling light-headed by this time—probably for want of food —and realising this I refuse a cocktail which under the circumstances might have a disastrous effect.

My host looks at me and says, "How right you are! We'll have fizz," and goes into solemn conclave with the head-waiter about food and drink.

It surprises me a little to discover that Tony is able to converse with this important functionary in fluent Italian and as I listen admiringly I reflect that, although I have known Tony for years, there is a great deal about him that I do not know and never shall.

"A penny for your thoughts, Mrs. Tim," says Tony teasingly.

"They aren't worth a penny," I reply. "You can have one of them for a halfpenny; I was wondering how you learnt to speak Italian."

"From an enemy," says Tony promptly.

The answer has an air of finality but it has roused my curiosity and I wait for more.

"It's quite simple, really," says Tony smiling. "You are aware—unless you have forgotten—that my particular war was waged against the Italians in the desert. It seemed to me

that it would be useful to know what they were saying when
they waved their hands about and jabbered like a flock of mon-
keys. This being so I caused a prisoner to be brought to my
tent daily for twenty minutes. I could spare no more, but
Italian isn't a difficult language if you have a little Latin and
my instructor was competent. He was a schoolmaster in private
life and took a great interest in my progress; a progress which
he assured me was phenomenal; but this commendation,
gratifying though it was, gratified me less when I discovered
that his former pupils were mentally defective children—"

"Tony, it isn't true!"

"But it's *such* a good story," complains Tony, "and it's
very nearly true, and as a matter of fact I've told it so often
that I've come to believe it myself. Don't spoil it, Hester."

I promise not to spoil it and he continues:

"We were both sorry when the exigencies of war brought
the lessons to an abrupt conclusion. We parted with expressions of mutual esteem . . . and I don't mind telling you expressions of mutual esteem in Italian sound extremely fine:
Signore, la ringrazio molto della sua gentilezza," says Tony
with unction. "É un piacere per me ed un onore di poter com-
piacere ad una persona illustre quale Lei è. That sounds
better than, 'Thanks a lot, it's been nice seeing you.'"

We laugh—and at this moment two plates, piled high
with spaghetti, are placed before us, and a small dish of flaked
cheese is placed between us.

"Tonight you are going to eat as the Romans do," says
my host. "You sprinkle some cheese on the top. I hope you're
hungry."

"Yes, but not as hungry as all that," I reply, looking at
my portion in dismay.

"Do your best," he says and taking up his fork twists it
into the spaghetti and conveys it neatly to his mouth.

Thursday, 14th June

I endeavour to do likewise but without success for it appears that the absorption of spaghetti is a fine art and requires practise. All round us there are people absorbing spaghetti with speed—in fact it seems to pour upwards from plate to mouth in an unbroken stream—but my spaghetti is unmanageable and slippery and refuses to disobey the law of gravity. I twist my fork in the stuff but before I can lift it to my mouth it falls off. I poke my fork into the stuff and the stuff slides away. Sometimes I manage to spear one piece and catch it before it slips.

Tony watches anxiously. "Leave it," he says at last. "Have something else instead."

"But it's delicious!"

"Then I shall have to feed you," says Tony gravely. "It may cause a little surprise to our fellow-diners but I see nothing else for it. If you persist in eating spaghetti half an inch at a time we shall be here all night."

At this I begin to laugh and my case is worse than ever.

"Twirl your fork," says Tony. "Put your mouth nearer. Don't be so elegant about it."

Thus adjured I abandon all idea of elegance and, bending over the plate, wallow my way through. After the spaghetti we have chicken in a casserole with French beans, and small green artichokes with the choke removed, cooked in butter and deliciously tender. We drink champagne of a noble vintage and finish with fruit and coffee. It is an excellent meal; I feel much the better for it, and say so to my host.

"You look better," he replies. "I must say I like to see a woman enjoying her food, especially when she's my guest. It's no fun at all to provide a good meal and see it unappreciated."

We have talked about all sorts of things during dinner; I have given Tony our family news and he has given me his.

He has also told me about Annie and Fred Bollings and assured me that they are making good at the Bull and Bush. As
Tony helped us to put them there he is interested in them
and almost as pleased as I am that the experiment is a success.
Tony expects to be at Charters Towers most of the summer
and has promised to come over to Old Quinings and see us
as often as he can.

"I'm a farmer now," he says a trifle ruefully. "I'm trying
to be a good farmer but it isn't really my métier. The one
thing I can do really well is making men into soldiers, but they
don't want me for that; I'm too senior. They'll dig me out
again if there's a war, which God forbid there ever should be."

I make various enquiries about Old Quinings, and Tony
(serious for the nonce) gives me sensible answers. It is a quiet
little place, an old-fashioned English village with a wide High
Street and a few small shops. There is a butcher, a baker and
a candlestick-maker, says Tony; I shall be able to buy hair-
pins, aspirin tablets and ankle socks, but if I want an exotic hat
I shall have to take a bus to Wandlebury which is about ten
miles distant. There is a church and a doctor and a country
squire who lives in the Manor House, and of course—like all
proper squires—has a pretty daughter.

"I think you'll like it," says Tony, "and I'm sure you'll
like The Small House. It was lucky that Annie heard it was
to let and was able to get it for you. Mrs. Stroude was a
Trollope fan, hence The Small House!"

All these details are interesting to me and I begin to build
up a composite picture of my life at Old Quinings.

"Have I told you all you want to know?" asks Tony.

"Not nearly. You haven't told me why you're here in
Rome."

"Oh—that!" says Tony smiling. "That's quite simple.
It so happened that I was in Old Quinings and went to the

Bull and Bush for a stoup of ale and a gossip with the pro-
prietors, and while I was there your name cropped up—not
an unusual occurrence to tell you the truth. Our mutual
friend, Mrs. Bollings, was somewhat disturbed at having received the news that you were spending two days in Rome, all
by yourself. Rome, in her opinion, is a wicked city and no
place for an unprotected female. Although I did not share
her views *in toto*, I decided it would be fun to fly over and
meet you—and so it is," adds Tony cheerfully.

"But, Tony, what nonsense! I mean you didn't come all
this way just to meet me!"

"No, of course not," he replies gravely. "There must have
been some other reason. I just can't think of one at the moment."

"I suppose you mean it's a secret."

"That's it," he replies. "You've guessed it in one, but you
won't tell anybody, will you? I've been sent on a Special Mission to meet Mr. Stalin in the Colosseum at midnight."

When he is in this mood it is no use arguing with him.

We walk back to the pensione through the crowded
streets; the air is mild and balmy and although it is cloudy
overhead the street-lamps are so bright that it does not seem
dark. Huge shiny cars whirl past at speed and there are hundreds of small motor-bicycles dashing about in a reckless manner. My companion draws my hand through his arm and keeps
it there firmly and when I remonstrate with him he points
out that most of the other couples are walking arm-in-arm.

"Do as the Romans do," he reminds me. "Besides you
might get lost, or run over, or trampled underfoot." And, as
none of these fates seems unlikely, I leave my hand where it is.

All the shops are brilliantly illuminated and some of
them are still open; the pavement is thronged with people talking and laughing gaily; indeed it seems to me that the city

has been sleeping all day and has just awakened ready for social amusement. The cafés are doing a roaring trade, and the little tables which are placed outside and help to block the already crowded street, are filled with cheerful clients all talking at the top of their voices. Now and then we hear the sound of music—of the radio blaring or of a band in a dance hall—and once we stop outside a wrought-iron grille let into a wall and see a dark passage and, beyond it, a lighted garden with a little fountain. Somebody is singing here, either in the garden or in the house, somebody with a beautiful tenor is singing the well-known aria from *Il Trovatore*.

My companion is more intuitive than Mrs. Alston and does not interrupt my thoughts with ill-timed conversation. We walk in silence—probably the only silent couple abroad in Rome—and presently we pass the Spanish Steps, a great broad staircase covered from top to bottom with a dazzling mass of flowers and, turning a corner find ourselves at the outside door of the pensione.

"Good night," says Tony. "I'll come and fetch you tomorrow afternoon and show you some of the things you ought to see."

It is my intention to slip in quietly and make for the shelter of my room but this is not to be. The "vultures" have gone to bed, but one light still burns in the sala and beneath this light the Signora is seated engaged in the homely task of darning her stockings. Is she waiting for me, I wonder. Is she furious with me for my unconventional behaviour? Will she rage and storm and throw me out of her respectable establishment bag and baggage . . . and if so what on earth shall I do?

At this moment she looks round and sees me. "Ah, Madame!" she cries and, springing to her feet in joyous welcome, she enquires eagerly if I have enjoyed myself, if I have dined well, and why I have not brought my friend with me so
28

that she could offer him some wine. "Qu'il est beau, votre ami!" she exclaims raising her eyes to heaven and clasping her hands. "Qu'il est gentil! Qu'il a l'air distingué!"

These ecstasies embarrass me a good deal and I endeavour to explain in my halting French that "Monsieur le Général" is a family friend and we have known him for years, but the Signora merely says, "Oui oui, c'est entendu. Fiez en moi, Madame," and continues to praise Tony's beautiful figure and distinguished air and to assure me that I am fortunate indeed to have such a handsome admirer.

Again I try to explain but before I have found the right words she waves away the explanation. "Soyez tranquille, Madame," she says in soothing tone and then, approaching nearer and dropping her voice, she informs me that she, too, has "un ami" who adores her to distraction.

I find this news far from tranquillising.

The Signora continues the story of her love; it appears that her husband is jealous, that his temper is of the devil and it is only by subterfuge that she and her "ami" can meet.

"Votre mari est en Afrique, n'est-ce pas?" she says, implying with a sidelong glance that she wishes her husband were in Africa too.

I ignore this implication and tell her that she is mistaken in her surmise that my case and hers are alike but she cannot —or will not—understand. Love should be free, says the Signora. There should be no trammels to mar the joy and beauty of love.

With the greatest difficulty I stem the torrent and explain that these may be her views but they do not apply to my case, because "Monsieur le Général" is only a friend. Unfortunately, however, the word "ami" has only one meaning to the Signora.

"Oui, oui, c'est entendu! Il est votre ami!" she agrees.

The more we converse the further we get from under-

Friday, 15th June

*T*HE MORNING is fine and warm. I spend it lying in a deck chair upon the roof-garden writing to Tim. Although we parted only the day before yesterday it feels like months and I have all sorts of interesting and amusing things to tell him. The high spot of my letter is a detailed account of what happened last night, of Tony's visit and my battle of words with the Signora. Tim will enjoy the joke thoroughly and I cannot help smiling when I think of him chuckling over my letter.

The only other occupant of the roof-garden is a very pretty American girl; she has the friendly disposition of her nation and soon we are conversing in an agreeable manner. She has been in Rome for nearly a week and has been sightseeing earnestly. Fortunately she has a friend here and he has been taking her about in his automobile and showing her Rome. When she hears that I am going out this afternoon to see the sights of Rome she produces a list of all the interesting things that must be seen. I accept it with gratitude, but I have a feeling that it is a trifle too comprehensive. The American girl says you can see a lot in one afternoon; the secret of sightseeing is to work out a schedule and stick to it.

Tony calls for me at two o'clock in a very large car with a very small Italian chauffeur. I tell him about the American girl and he says he is quite willing to show me Rome but it will take a couple of years.

"At *least* two years," says Tony thoughtfully. "Of course I'm on for it if you are; but I thought you were supposed to be resting here, like a homing pigeon, and continuing your flight tomorrow. That being so, I have no intention of trying to 'show you Rome' but intended to give you a glimpse of two mighty monuments; one, a pagan monument dedicated to the worship of pleasure and the other a Christian monument dedicated to the worship of God. To my mind these two monuments are symbolic of Rome which is at once a pagan and a Christian city."

When I ask if Tony made up this marvellous speech beforehand, he smiles and replies, "Some of it," and hands me into the car.

It is interesting to note that Tony is even more frightened than I am, as we career madly through the crowded streets, and is quite unable to take part in rational conversation. Every few moments he grips the handle of the door, or pushes down his foot as if he were braking. Every few moments he emits an anguished exclamation. Perhaps this is because he is a very good driver himself and, all his life, has driven large, fast cars with verve and spirit.

Our first monument is the Colosseum, the great Flavian Amphitheatre where the Romans staged their circuses. From the outside it is imposing enough—an enormous oval building, partially ruined, with tiers of arched windows—but when we walk in at the arched gateway its size and grandeur are breathtaking. The enormous arena has no floor and one can see the stone passages beneath, and the dens where the lions were kept; all round are the terraces, tiers of arched galleries one above the other, massive walls of honey-coloured stone, towering so high that they cut the blue sky with their jagged outlines.

We lean upon the wall and look across the arena and the

eye travels up the tiers of terraced stone to the sky. It is very quiet here, the roar of distant traffic is the only sound.

"Can you recreate the scene?" asks Tony. "This place could seat nearly ninety thousand spectators; imagine them crowding in, chattering like starlings, excited and happy, dressed in their best and carrying baskets of food. Imagine them filling the terraces until no stones are visible but only the bright colours of their clothes and their eager faces. Imagine the huge arena—the vast empty space covered with sand."

But to me this place is dead; I cannot imagine it as Tony paints it . . . and perhaps this is just as well for the arena was not always empty; it was here that the early Christians were pulled to pieces by lions, "butchered to make a Roman Holiday." This ruin does not make me feel sad (like the ruins of a house which at one time, perhaps, was a home full of happy children); this ruin is a bad place, it is the ruin of a way of life which was wicked. Tony does not agree with this, however. He says the people who enjoyed the circuses were not wicked, for they knew no better; he adds that to his mind the modern man who calls himself a Christian but behaves in a manner unbefitting his creed is much more wicked than the circus-goer of Ancient Rome.

We walk slowly round the lowest terrace and talk about the building of the place and the thousands of wild beasts which were slain at its dedication and about its subsequent history (which, as it can be found in any guide-book, need not be detailed here).

"There was no roof, of course," explains my companion. "There *could* be no roof to such a vast building as this. There were wooden awnings to shelter the spectators from the blazing sun—or the rain—but I don't think anybody knows just how or where they were erected. It must have been some job fixing them into place."

33

Presently a party of tourists invades the solitude; they are led by a guide, talking volubly in broken English and quoting all sorts of statistics, which obviously he has learnt parrot-fashion from a guide-book. The tourists stream after him with dazed expressions and are so intent on listening, and trying to understand what he says, that they scarcely have time to look at the building they have come so far to see.

"Ten minutes to *do* the Colosseum and then into the bus and on to the catacombs," suggests Tony as they rush past. "They've got to stick to their schedule. It's wonderful, isn't it?"

St. Peter's is our other monument. It is enormous too, but in no other way does the living cathedral resemble the dead amphitheatre. We approach across a vast square, so we can see the building in proper perspective and appreciate its architecture.

St. Peter's was built between 1506 and 1626 and differs from our cathedral of St. Paul's in being the work not of one man but of many different architects. The dome was designed by Michelangelo. It was built "to enshrine the magnificence of Papal power, the Christian religion and the Latin race" which was indeed a high and mighty purpose. Beneath its tessellated pavement there are vast crypts, and here are buried the bones of early Christian martyrs, amongst them those of St. Peter (who was crucified in Rome in A.D.64) and possibly of St. Paul.

Tony's guide-book treats of the history of the cathedral at length and Tony himself knows a good deal about the excavations in the crypts, which are actually in progress at the present moment.

We walk slowly across the square, bathed in hot golden sunshine, we mount the wide steps and enter the cool dim precincts of the cathedral. One's first impression is that this is a church made for giants: the vast area of the paved floor seems

34

all the larger because it is empty of pews or chairs; the height of the domed roof is stupendous. It is a church made for giants —and the giants of St. Peter's are here, commemorated in stone. The statues of the popes, which line the walls, are much larger than life. Some of them are proud and cold, they are princes of the Church; others have a benignant air, they are fathers of their people; one or two have a crafty look, a positively Machiavellian expression, which is all the more alarming on account of their immense size. One cannot help wondering whether these statues are good likenesses of their originals or whether the sculptors tried to commemorate the characters of their models rather than the physical forms.

All round the vast building there are little chapels in alcoves guarded by wrought-iron grilles. They are full of colour and light, like brilliant gems set in the cold stone walls. We walk about quietly, looking at them . . . our eyes are drawn upward to the jewelled windows.

It is all very wonderful but to my mind some of our own cathedrals are much more beautiful—more dignified and holy. The memory of St. Peter's which I shall take away with me and treasure in my heart is a human one. It is the sturdy figure of a peasant woman with a shawl of faded blue cloth over her dark hair, a shawl which is so large that it falls over her shoulders in soft blue folds. She is kneeling upon the floor before one of the little shrines. Her baby is clasped to her bosom and her arms are folded about him protectingly. As we watch she takes her baby and holds him up as if she were dedicating the little creature to God. She is there when we go in and, when we come out, she is still in the same place, kneeling upon the stone floor, rapt in her devotions.

Saturday, 16th June

YESTERDAY I MANAGED to avoid Signora Scarlatti, and so evaded another embarrassing conversation with the lady, but this morning I am obliged to seek her out to say good-bye and to pay my bill. Fortunately for me her husband is present at the interview; he is a meek-looking man (small and insignificant with soft, brown eyes) and I find it difficult to believe in the devilish ferocity of his temper. We say good-bye in the various languages at our command and make all sorts of flowery speeches.

In the middle of this scene Tony arrives to conduct me to the aerodrome and his arrival necessitates more speeches of an even more flowery nature. The Signora is prohibited by the presence of her husband from making any allusions to the relationship which she believes to exist between Tony and me, but she rolls her eyes and purses up her mouth and makes other expressive signs to show how well she understands and how deeply she sympathises with my feelings.

All this is most exhausting and it delays our departure so that the taxi-driver has to hurry to get to the airfield in time but fortunately my plane has not gone without me. I bid Tony a hasty farewell, climb into my silver monster and set out upon the last stage of my journey.

This last stage is not as comfortable as the other stages; the monster which is to take me to Northolt is smaller and less stable than the monster that brought me to Rome and there are high mountains on our route. These obstacles create air currents and pockets and other disagreeable features of air travel and make the monster stagger and plunge and buck like a restive horse . . . but worse is to follow, for this is a French monster and the pilot conceives a sudden brilliant idea that his passengers would like to see Mont Blanc at close quarters.

Mont Blanc is the highest mountain in Europe—as everybody knows—and doubtless it is interesting in other ways as well but I am too frightened to be interested. There are peaks and valleys and great glaciers and clefts full of snow which never melts; the wind, whirling about these peaks and whistling through these crevices, catches us and tosses us about like a dry leaf in an autumn gale. The mountain itself is a horrible sight and it is much too near, for it seems to me that the monster's wing is almost touching the rocks. There are great jagged peaks with icicles dripping down them and great pockets of dirty-looking snow. Behind the mountain there is a sky full of ragged clouds, torn by the wind.

I have no idea what the other passengers are thinking about their tour of Mont Blanc but I dislike it intensely and when the air hostess approaches and says excitedly, "Madame, regardez! Voilà Mont Blanc!" I glance out of the window and reply in broken accents, "Take it away!" She does not understand of course but I am afraid she realises that my comment is not one of enthusiastic admiration for her horrible mountain. Give me Mont Blanc in the distance. Let me stand firmly with both feet upon the solid ground and look at Mont Blanc with its snow-capped peaks outlined against the blue sky and I will admire it as much as you like. This is what I should like to say to the air hostess, but I am too busy saying my prayers to translate my feelings into French.

Monday, 25th June

*T*HE LAST week has been so hectic that my diary has been completely neglected, but the curious thing is that although I have done and seen so much I can find very little to say about it. I was met at Northolt by my brother, Richard, and his wife. Since then I have been staying with them in their house in London—32 Wintringham Square— where Richard and I were born. It is a Victorian period piece, built in the days when it was possible to have a large staff of servants; but Mary is a clever housewife and manages to run it with a curious assortment of "dailies," who come in at odd hours, complete their appointed tasks and vanish into thin air.

Our life has been extremely gay. We have shopped and lunched; we have attended cocktail parties and gone to various plays and every night I have crawled into bed more dead than alive with fatigue. It is obvious that people who live in London all their lives, like Richard and Mary, must be very strong indeed for a few weeks of this would undermine my constitution.

It is the eternal "rush" that exhausts me. We rush out to do some necessary shopping; we rush back to entertain friends to lunch; we rush to tea at one place and to cocktails at another and then we rush home and change and rush out again to the theatre . . . and for all our appointments we are always a trifle late. As I am a punctual person by nature

38

this worries me and it continues to worry me even when I realise that it does not matter being late because everybody else is late too.

Mary says the reason is the traffic—it always takes longer to get there than you expect, so you can't help being late for everything. (When I suggest we should start sooner she replies that, if we did so, we should be too early.)

Richard's idea is different. He says it has nothing to do with the traffic; it is because nobody wants to arrive first at a party; and, as everybody keeps on arriving later and later, one has to arrive later and later oneself. Soon, says Richard, people won't start for a party until it's over—if we know what he means.

Mary replies that she knows exactly what he means but he's wrong. Everybody says it's the traffic so it must be. This retort is so unlike Mary, who has a particularly sweet and patient disposition, that I begin to suspect she, too, feels the stress and strain.

I had intended to spend a fortnight in London but the stress and strain is too great to be borne and my thoughts turn longingly to The Small House at Old Quinings where I shall be able to live my own life at a slower tempo. It is a little difficult to escape from my kind relations but I explain that I want to see the house and get comfortably settled in before Bryan and Betty arrive . . . and, this being so, I think I shall go down to Old Quinings tomorrow.

"Tomorrow!" exclaims Richard. "There's a whole month before the children's holidays! And anyhow it's quite ridiculous going to that place at all. It's absolutely crazy taking that house without ever having seen it. Why didn't you ask me?" Richard wants to know. "I could have told you about Old Quinings; it's a god-forsaken hole; there isn't even a golf course. What are you going to do all the summer?"

"Sit in the garden," I reply.

"Sit in the garden!" echoes Richard scornfully. "And what about the children? Are they going to sit in the garden? They'll be bored stiff. Why on earth didn't you take a flat in town?"

"Can't afford London."

"That's nonsense! If you can't afford a flat we can have you here. This house is far too big for Mary and me; we could give you the whole top floor to yourselves. What about it, Hester? Why not wash out Old Quinings and stay here with us? Bryan and Betty will be far happier here than buried in a mouldy little village."

"It's frightfully kind of you, Richard, but—but it's all arranged. And I don't think summer in London would be a good plan."

"Go to Cobstead, then," says Richard. "Tim's uncle and aunt would have you there, wouldn't they?"

"Why don't you leave Hester alone?" says Mary. "You're worrying her. The children can come to us for ten days or so and have a gay time. You know quite well they can't go to Cobstead; Mellow Lodge is let and Tim's uncle and aunt are too old to be bothered with the children for the whole summer."

"Well, it seems funny to me," declares Richard. "Hester has heaps of friends and relations who would like to see her; but off she goes to a dreary village where she won't know a soul."

"It's better to be settled somewhere," I tell him; but still he continues to argue. Richard is the kindest creature on earth but he likes to have his own way.

Tuesday, 26th June

*T*HE ARGUMENT continues (if it can be called an argument when one of the contestants talks the whole time and the other is practically silent). Richard is still trying to persuade me to change my mind when the taxi is at the door; he comes with me to the station to see me off and argues on the platform.

"You'll come back," declares Richard as the train moves off. "You won't be able to bear that ghastly hole. There'll be nothing to do and nobody to talk to, and all the chimneys will smoke . . ."

I wave to him and throw a kiss and sink onto the seat with a sigh of relief.

The only other occupant of the compartment is a tiny old lady in a large fur coat. The day is warm and sunny but the fur collar is pulled up to her ears and a fur hat is pulled down to her ears, and all that can be seen of her is a sallow little face with a crooked nose and two beady brown eyes which are fixed upon me with an unwinking stare.

"Shut the window, please," says the old lady in peremptory tones.

I comply meekly with her request.

"That's right," she says. "Now perhaps you will give me my cushion—it's on the rack—and my paper. Thank you."

I give her the cushion and the paper; I help her to find her spectacles; at her behest I close the ventilator which is above the door. The compartment is now hermetically sealed and exceedingly stuffy but no sooner have I sat down than she asks for her waterproof, and wraps it round her knees. I reflect a trifle sadly that although she looks like an Eskimo she is not behaving in proper Eskimo fashion.

"Where are you going?" she enquires. "Old Quinings? That man was right, you won't like it. What are you going there for?"

"Just to live there," I reply feebly. "I mean you must live somewhere."

"You'll find it very dull."

She is silent for a few moments and then continues, "There are no picture houses, no bus tours to Beauty Spots in the neighbourhood and nobody will ask you to cocktail parties."

Certainly this is not an Eskimo—more like a bear!

"That man was right," she repeats, opening her paper and shaking it out impatiently. "You'll be off back to London in a fortnight."

"I can always go up to London for a day's shopping."

"You can't," she snaps. "The train service to Old Quinings is deplorable. It used to be bad and now it's worse. Only the slowest trains stop at Old Quinings. In fact the place has nothing to recommend it."

"Where do you live?" I enquire, for it seems to me that it is my turn to ask questions.

"At Old Quinings of course," says the little old lady with a sudden and quite unexpected cackle of laughter.

I laugh, too, and decide she is not such a bear after all.

"Oh well," says the old lady. "Perhaps you'll be able to survive. You'll be quite comfortable—that's one thing. The Small House has been well looked after and the chimneys don't smoke. He was wrong about that. Who was he?"

"Who?" I enquire in surprise.

"That man who saw you off."

"He's my brother."

"That accounts for it. Brothers have the right to be disagreeable—or think they have. I quarrelled with mine off and on for years. Yes, I might have guessed it was your brother. Your husband is in Africa, of course."

"How did you know?"

"I know everything," she declares with a twinkle of her beady eyes. "You'd be surprised at all the things I know. It amuses me to hear all that goes on and put two and two together. I've always been good at arithmetic so I usually get the right answer. If you want any information about your neighbours just come to me: perhaps I'll tell you and perhaps I won't." She cackles again, this time so heartily that she chokes and coughs asthmatically.

"You know my name, of course," says the old lady when she has recovered from her spasms.

"No, how could I?"

She points to a green label which is dangling from a suitcase in the rack. "Use your eyes," she says. "Miss Crease, Walnut House, Old Quinings. Our gardens are back to back with a high wall between. You can have the apples and walnuts that fall into your garden, but your son is not to climb my walnut tree."

"He wouldn't dream of doing such a thing!"

"Well, he must be an odd sort of boy, that's all I can say."

She is silent for a few moments and so am I.

"It's no good your taking the huff," says Miss Crease at last. "I'm old so I can say what I like—that's one of the advantages of being old—though, to be honest with you, I've always said what I liked and done what I liked. Of course if you want to quarrel it's all one to me."

This seems a bad beginning to my new life and I reply hastily that I have no desire to quarrel—my nature is peaceable—and I promise to warn Bryan not to trespass upon Miss Crease's property.

"I never said that," she retorts. "I said he wasn't to climb my walnut tree. As a matter of fact I like boys, especially if they're good-looking. Your son is practically certain to be good-looking," adds Miss Crease, staring at me in an impersonal sort of way.

We continue to chat as the train dawdles through the country. We pass woods and streams; we see cows in meadows; we stop at little village-stations and dawdle on again. Sometimes I feel I like the old lady quite a lot, and sometimes I feel I dislike her intensely but one thing is certain: her worst enemy could not call her dull.

As we approach Old Quinings Miss Crease begins to fuss. I am kept busy, taking down her suitcase from the rack, stowing away her cushion, folding up her papers and putting them into her bag.

The train slows down and crawls into the station and I am overjoyed to see my dear Annie standing upon the platform waiting for me.

Part II

Quiet Days at The Small House

Wednesday, 27th June

I OPEN MY eyes sleepily. The sunshine is streaming through the wide-open window and making pools of yellow light upon the floor. There are sounds of movement in the house: I can hear the hum of a vacuum cleaner and the chatter of subdued voices. Outside there is the clatter of heavy boots on cobblestones and the clank of a pail.

For a few brief moments I wonder where I am (for I have been in so many places during the last fortnight that my brain is somewhat muddled) and then I remember all that has happened and realise that this pleasant apartment is the best bedroom in the Bull and Bush.

It was my intention to go straight to The Small House and settle myself there but Annie had arranged otherwise. ("You'll be tired," Annie had explained as she helped me to collect my luggage and conducted me to the taxi. "Well, of course you'll be tired after all that long journey. You're coming to the Bull for a nice rest; we've kept the best bedroom for you. There isn't any hurry about getting settled in The Small House—it won't run away.") So here I am, an honoured guest, at the old-fashioned inn.

The Bull and Bush is delightful; it is an old English hostelry standing a little way back from the village street with a cobbled space in front; and there are green tubs, full of geraniums, at either side of the door. The door opens straight into the dining room which is set with small tables and has a brick floor and a doorstep of black oak which is hollowed by the passage of many feet. This curious old room is the hub of the house, passages radiate from it and lead to other rooms and to corkscrew stairs and narrow corridors which slope up and down in a disconcerting manner. At the back of the house there is a yard, flanked with out-buildings which once were stables but now are garages.

The place, though old, has been brought up to date as much as possible; it is well-kept and the paint is in good order. In fact it gives the impression that its owners are thriving, that they are comfortably settled and doing a good trade.

How interesting it is to see old friends in new surroundings! Annie and Bollings are just the same as ever . . . but with a difference. There is a new dignity about them, a new assurance, and their characters seem more defined. I did not expect this change, but now I see that I should have expected it. Responsibility is a forcing house for human beings, it makes people grow and develop. For years Annie and Fred Bollings were looked after by us; all their problems were solved for them and they had no responsibilities. Now they are standing upon their own feet and are obliged to think for themselves. Annie has always been the stronger character and sometimes I have felt a little worried as to whether their marriage would be a success . . . but I need not have worried

46

for Annie has mellowed and Bollings has blossomed forth and the two have become partners in their new venture and are making good. I had always thought Fred Bollings a typical batman but recently he has put on a little weight and, with his round cheery face and the white apron tied firmly across his middle, he might easily play the role of "mine host" in a dramatic presentation of *The Canterbury Tales*.

I am lying in bed thinking of all this and feeling happy about it when the door opens softly and Annie peeps into the room.

"Oh, you're awake!" she says. "I hope all that noise didn't waken you. I told them to be quiet but they *will* chatter, no matter what you say, and you daren't be too hard on them or they just walk off and leave you stranded—no sense of responsibility, that's their worst fault. Now you just stay where you are and I'll bring up your breakfast."

"But, Annie—"

"It's no trouble," says Annie firmly. "It's less trouble than you coming down. The mornings are a bit of a rush and you'll be much better in bed till the place is cleaned and tidied. Later on, when I've got through, I'll take you to see the house." She hesitates and then adds, "It's small, of course," and before I can reply goes out and shuts the door.

Naturally I had expected the house to be small.

The main street of Old Quinings is wide, there are trees on either side and little old-fashioned houses, some of which have been turned into shops. There is a sleepy feeling about the place and the people we meet look pleasant and comfortable and leisurely. Annie knows most of them, and greetings are exchanged, but only greetings in passing, for now that we are actually on our way to The Small House Annie is showing signs of strain.

"Supposing you don't like it!" she says, hastening along

47

at a rapid pace which is quite out of keeping with the atmosphere.

"Of course I shall like it," I reply.

"It's here," says Annie, turning into a narrow, bumpy lane marked NO THOROUGHFARE. "Well, if you don't like it we shall have to re-let it, that's all."

Halfway down the lane we come to a holly hedge with a little green gate in it. "This is the place," says Annie in trembling tones.

Somehow I had expected The Small House to be old (perhaps because most of the houses are old in this drowsy little village) but the house certainly is not more than twenty years old. It is a white house, square and two-storied, with a red-tiled roof; there is a large double window on each side of the door and three large windows above. The front garden is gay with flowers and a flagged path leads up to the door. Annie opens the door with a key and we go in.

All houses have their own particular atmosphere which can be perceived with a sixth sense. I have lived in houses that made me happy and in houses that made me miserable. This little house is the happy kind. As I walk into the hall I feel welcomed and soothed. I feel as if I had arrived at the house of a friend and she was glad to have me.

The hall is square, and although it is not large there is a feeling of space about it; doors on the right and left lead to a small dining room and a good-sized drawing room—the latter stretches from the front to the back of the house with windows at each end and a glass door which opens into the garden. There is a brightness and airiness which comes of clean white paint and polished floors and gaily patterned cretonnes; and there is not too much furniture but just a few good pieces, pleasing to the eye.

"It's a bit bare," says Annie doubtfully.

"It's lovely!" I exclaim. "It's a perfectly lovely little house. I wonder how its owner could bear to let it!"

"She didn't really. It belonged to a Mrs. Stroude and she died quite suddenly so Miss Stroude went off for a cruise. Mrs. Stroude was a nice lady, everybody liked Mrs. Stroude. She was pretty and smiling and always said good morning when you met her in the village. It was lucky her dying like that," adds Annie cheerfully.

"Lucky!" I exclaim in surprise.

"We'd never have got the house," explains Annie.

Now that her mind is set at rest Annie takes a pleasure in showing me everything and displaying the amenities of The Small House. Everything is beautifully arranged, every detail has been carefully thought out to give the maximum of comfort and the minimum of work.

"You'll be having this room," says Annie. "At least that's what I thought . . ."

I think so too. It is a charming room with a window looking out over the garden. I can see fruit trees and flowers and a wide sloping lawn and a couple of shady beech trees. Beyond is a high brick wall and, beyond that, more trees decked in their summer greenery.

"That Miss Crease lives there," says Annie. "An old horror, she is. I wouldn't have nothing to do with *her* if I was you. She'd worm secrets out of an oyster."

"But I have no secrets," I reply, smiling at Annie's description of my travelling companion.

The rooms are all pleasant and the kitchen is no exception to the rule; there is a red-brick floor, a small Aga and a fine row of cupboards with glass doors. The sink and draining-board are of gleaming metal and the table has a plastic top.

"Oh dear," says Annie looking round. "It seems awful you being here and me at the Bull and Bush. I've got a woman to come in daily—quite nice she is—but you'll have to get your own supper. Of course you'll be staying at the Bull till the holidays begin; there's no sense in you living here alone."

But I want to live here alone. The Small House is entrancing and I want to move in tomorrow. I try to explain this to Annie and to get my way without hurting her feelings but the task is not easy.

We are still arguing (standing at the window of the room which is destined to be Betty's, and which looks out over the lane) when the noise of a motor-bicycle approaching at speed disturbs the peace of Old Quinings. The bicycle comes lurching down the lane and stops at the gate with an ear-splitting explosion, and two tall figures (clad in filthy mackintosh suits and goggles) dismount.

"It's the exhaust again," says one in a loud bass voice. "I told you it would bust if you came over those beastly bumps full speed."

The other does not reply. He pushes open the gate, removes the goggles and looks up. "Hullo!" he cries joyfully. "Hullo, Mum, it's me!"

"Bryan!" I shriek, almost falling out of the window in my excitement.

Bryan waves and dashes into the house. I rush to the door. We meet on the stairs and embrace in wild abandon.

"I had to come!" cries Bryan. "We came on Hedgehog's bike. It's sixty miles and we did it under two hours which isn't bad going for a crazy machine like that. How are you, darling? You look all right. Oh Lord, I'm afraid that smear on your blouse is oil or something! This coat is absolutely foul."

I hug him again and tell him it doesn't matter and enquire a little anxiously how they have managed to get away. I am aware that, although the Cambridge term is over, Bryan

50

and his friend are taking a course in dairy-farming and are kept hard at it from early morning to dewy eve.

Bryan does not answer directly. He says, "Sixty miles— that's all. Well, when I found it was only sixty miles—and it's eighteen months since I saw you! Oh, here's Hedgehog! You know him, don't you?"

I have known Bryan's friend for many years, partly by personal contact but more by repute. Bryan has always talked a great deal about Hedgehog and although they have quarrelled now and then their friendship has survived and they have walked shoulder to shoulder since Prep-school days. Hedgehog's parents died when he was a child and, as he has no brothers or sisters, he is rather a lonely soul. His only relation is his grandfather—a somewhat irascible old baronet—who lives in solitary state in his ancestral castle. Bryan has visited the castle several times and made the acquaintance of its owner, Sir Percy Edgeburton. I am aware of all this of course and also aware of the fact that "Hedgehog" bears the same name as his grandfather, but according to Bryan he dislikes his name so much that he is liable to become violent when addressed by it. This being so it is difficult to know how to address the tall, broad-shouldered young man who has just entered the hall.

"You can call him Perry, if you like," says Bryan who has perceived my difficulty. "Quite a lot of people do. He doesn't mind being called Perry; do you, Hedgehog?"

"It might be worse," says Hedgehog—or Perry—without enthusiasm.

As we shake hands I remember the first time I saw him. It was when he and Bryan were at Nearhampton School. In those days Perry was exceedingly small for his age and not very particular in the matter of washing his ears. I have seen him at odd times since then but, even so, it seems incredible that the small, dirty and rather pathetic child should have grown into this large, good-looking young man. Some children grow up and still look much the same, but Perry has changed out of all recognition; his face is square and determined with well-defined features and hazel eyes set unusually wide apart. His mouth is large and mobile—and at this moment it is smiling a trifle shyly.

"I hope you don't mind my coming, Mrs. Christie," he says in his deep voice (the voice which I heard at the gate, raised in tones of expostulation). "You see I thought at first I'd let Bryan come alone but the bike isn't awfully reliable and I know it better than he does."

"I get the best speed out of it, but Hedgehog is good at repairs," Bryan explains.

I assure Perry that I am delighted to see him.

"So this is The Small House!" Bryan remarks, looking round the hall. "Not very big, certainly."

"It's nice," says Perry. "Awfully pretty and cheerful. I like small houses much better than big ones."

"You're a nice one to talk of small houses!"

"I know," agrees Perry. "That's just why. Our place is far too big. Grandfather and I roll about in it like peas in a drum. This house feels like a home."

"Perhaps you'd like to come and stay," suggests Bryan. "I mean we could come over together when we've finished the course. Is there room for him, Mum?"

Fortunately there is. (Perry and Bryan can share the double-bedded room which I had intended for Betty and she can go into the smaller room next door to mine); so I second the invitation and Perry accepts with alacrity. "I can go on to Grandfather afterwards," he says.

"There won't be much to do," I warn him; for Perry's

leisure is usually spent riding and shooting on his grand-father's estate.

"Hedgehog doesn't mind," says Bryan. "He'll have his bike and we can go for picnics and play tennis—or else do nothing. Personally I'm all for doing nothing at all."

Perry says doing nothing will suit him admirably, especially after their strenuous time at Wycherley Farm. "We get up at five," says Perry. "We milk cows and clean out byres; then, when the regular farmhands go to the pictures or have a good snooze, we attend lectures on Milk Production."

"I say, Mum," says Bryan. "Is there any food going? It sounds a bit greedy but we really ought to get back. We've cut out the afternoon work and they might be a bit ratty if we didn't roll up in time for the lecture."

This is Annie's cue. She appears on the top landing and announces that there is steak-and-kidney pie for lunch at the Bull . . . so, Bryan having greeted her affectionately, we lock up The Small House and proceed to the Bull forthwith.

The steak-and-kidney pie is a masterpiece and there is cider to wash it down. Bryan and Perry and I sit at a little table in the window of the dining room which looks out onto the village street. It is lovely to see Bryan, to see him looking so fit and strong and full of good spirits, but unfortunately I cannot enjoy his visit with an easy mind. My feelings are mixed. Naturally I am only too happy to provide my guests with all that they desire, but cider is a heady drink and they have to ride sixty miles . . . and, although I am thoroughly enjoying their company, I am so afraid they may have trouble on the way back and arrive too late for the lecture that I am longing for them to go. I endeavour to disguise my inhospitable feelings but Bryan is difficult to deceive; he looks at me from time to time with a twinkle in his eye.

"Why don't you say it, Mum?" asks Bryan.

"Say what?" says Perry in surprise.

"She knows what I mean," replies Bryan smiling wickedly. "I know what she's thinking and she knows I know. It's just one of those things. Sometimes it's convenient and sometimes not. For instance it's inconvenient at poker—you see that, don't you? It cramps your style when one of your opponents knows exactly when you're bluffing and when you're onto a really good thing. And I remember once," says Bryan in reminiscent tones. "I remember making a marvellous dam. I made it on strictly scientific lines and it was a tremendous success. It was convex, you know—all dams should be convex —and it turned a horrible little drain into a beautiful pool. I wish you had seen it, Hedgehog. Unfortunately the overflow found its way into the kitchen and the cook was cross."

"But I don't see what that's got to do with—"

"You'll see if you listen," says Bryan cryptically. "The point of the story is coming. Mum knew I was the guilty party and we went out together to bust the dam. She was angry at first (and as a matter of fact I realise now that it must have been rather annoying); but when she saw the magnificent feat of engineering she was so struck by her son's ingenuity that she couldn't be angry any more."

"That's where you're wrong!" I exclaim.

"No, darling, that's where I'm right. You stopped being angry the moment you saw the dam. It was just pretence after that. And now," says Bryan gravely. "Now at last we have reached the point. I knew you had stopped being angry and everything was all right." He leans back in his chair and taking a packet of cigarettes out of his pocket he proceeds to light up.

54

For a moment I am surprised—almost dismayed—for to me Bryan is still a child . . . and then I realise my foolishness.

"You see, Hedgehog," says my wicked son. "Here is another case in point. Mum doesn't like to see me smoking. But then she suddenly remembers I'm grown up and decides to say nothing."

"But you don't smoke," says Perry in bewilderment.

"No," agrees Bryan. "I don't like smoking. It's a horrible taste and it spoils your wind. I just did it to tease my mother." He stubs out the cigarette and smiles at me affectionately.

All this chat has delayed their departure but at last I succeed in persuading them to go. They array themselves in the dirty mackintosh suits, put on the goggles and depart with a series of frightful explosions and in clouds of evil-smelling blue smoke.

Annie and Bollings have come out to wave good-bye and, as the bicycle disappears down the road, Bollings sighs and says, "It's funny. Seems only yesterday I was taking Bryan to feed the swans, and look at him now!"

Friday, 29th June

*I*T IS difficult to escape from Annie's hospitable clutches but at last I manage it. I manage to convince her that I am not frightened of being alone, that I am not likely to have a heart attack and die without benefit of doctor and clergy and that The Small House can be rendered burglar-proof by the patent fasteners upon the windows.

Annie goes home. I wave to her cheerfully from the door and repeat my promises to remember all her instructions and to "ring up the Bull" if anything goes wrong.

Odd as it may seem I have never before spent a night alone in a house and I must admit to a slightly eerie feeling, but when I have locked up securely and am safely in bed the eerie feeling leaves me and is replaced by a feeling of peace.

I lie and think about things; about Tim, so far away; about Bryan who has grown up in such a surprising fashion and yet is so young and boyish; about Betty with her sturdy independence, her straightness and honesty. How lucky I am in my family! I think about Annie and Fred Bollings and wonder why they have no child. Perhaps they do not want children—for children entail self-sacrifices—but I should be a poor thing without mine. I look back down the years of my life and see pictures; some of them are bright and clear, others dim and wraith-like . . . though even as I look at them the images take form and the colours brighten. Life has not always been easy and things are different from what

56

we hoped. Years ago Tim decided to retire from the Army so that we could live quietly and peacefully at Mellow Lodge . . . but still Tim is in the Army and still there is no real peace and Mellow Lodge keeps receding into the far-off future.

In spite of this, however, I have little to complain of, for if my life has not been altogether easy, it has been full and interesting. I should have been less than I am if I had not worked like a slave in Erica's hotel or gone with Tim to Kenya. Perhaps if we had settled at Mellow Lodge I should have become smug and lazy with a double chin and Tim would have developed a bow-window.

Tuesday, 3rd July

AFTER THE rush of London it is very pleasant to relax and for the last few days I have done nothing but rest and eat and sleep. Mrs. Daulkes, the daily-help engaged for me by Annie, is a tall woman with a strongly developed figure which is encased in old-fashioned stays. Her skin is red and brown, healthy as an apple, and her pleasant smile shows strong white teeth; her hair is thick and brown and has a slightly rough appearance as if every separate hair had a life of its own and was full of spring. Mrs. Daulkes arrives punctually at nine o'clock every morning; she cleans the house and cooks my mid-day meal, and she leaves something ready for my supper.

Anybody who earns the approbation of Annie is certain to be a good worker—Mrs. Daulkes is that. She is also a cheerful worker and enlivens the house with song. At first Mrs. Daulkes is a little shy, and unwilling to be communicative, but very soon she takes my measure and shows herself to be a true-blue Eskimo.

"I'll get your rations," says Mrs. Daulkes. "Just you give me your book and I'll see you get your fair share of what's going. Eggs!" exclaims Mrs. Daulkes. "Oh we don't need to worry about eggs. My father-in-law keeps a few 'ens ('e's the 'ead gardener at Lord Ponsonby's). I can get eggs from 'im any time. Sugar is the worst," says Mrs. Daulkes with a sigh. "I can't do nothing about sugar . . . but I tell you what: you write to your 'usband and tell 'im to send us some sugar. We'll need extra sugar when the young lady and gentleman come 'ome. I'm a great 'and at puddings," says Mrs. Daulkes smiling. "I didn't ought to say it, p'raps, but puddings is my fort. You sit down and write straight off and I'll send it air-mail on my way 'ome."

"Yes," I agree meekly. "Yes, I will." For the great thing with Eskimos is to take all the good advice they offer and act upon it promptly.

Mrs. Daulkes goes away at two o'clock precisely by which time everything is in apple-pie order and all the dishes washed up. After that I am in full possession of The Small House.

It is an unprecedented experience for me to do exactly as I please and to consider nobody's comfort but my own. I should not like this freedom to continue indefinitely but for a short time it is extremely pleasant . . . day follows day, the sunshine pours in at the windows and fills the house with light. The garden, though not large, is delightfully secluded and I spend many happy hours lying in a cane-chair beneath one of the beech trees which shades the lawn. There is a vegetable garden, screened from view by a beech hedge and a long bed of herbaceous plants; but what I like best of all in the garden of my new demesne is a large round bed of pale lilac violas, so thick that the effect is of a pale lilac cushion resting upon the grass, so fragrant in the warm sunshine that the bees make a continuous hum amongst the blossoms.

Everybody told me I should be lonely, but everybody was wrong . . . and wrong for the strange reason that I am not alone. There is a gentle Presence in The Small House, a Presence much less tenuous than a ghost and not in the least alarming. It is Mrs. Stroude—I feel certain that it is—she is glad to have me living in her house and makes me welcome.

Wednesday, 4th July

*T*HERE IS a lending library in Old Quinings; it is run by the village school-mistress and is open on Saturday mornings and Wednesday afternoons. I am directed thither by Mrs. Daulkes who assures me that there are books for all tastes.

"I'm partial to murders myself," says Mrs. Daulkes confidentially. "Miss Carlyle often tries to persuade me to take something different for a change, but murders is what I like. There's nothing as soothing as a really good murder—that's what I say—but I daresay you're a bit too 'ighbrow for murders, Mrs. Christie."

I assure her that I am not.

"Oh well," says Mrs. Daulkes. "P'raps she'll let you 'ave what you want."

This remark puzzles me a little and I brood upon it as I walk down the hill to the school-house.

There is nobody in the library when I arrive, but a moment later a door at the other end of the room opens to admit a neat little woman with fair hair and bright blue eyes. I am about to explain myself but this is unnecessary; Miss Carlyle greets me by name in a cordial manner and proceeds at once to business.

"I expect you like biography," she suggests. "Or perhaps a travel-book. It must be so interesting to read about places one has seen. What about *Darkest Africa?* It is very well-written and the photographs are really beautiful."

After this recommendation it is impossible to choose *The Body in the Cupboard* (the title has caught my eye and roused my curiosity) nor can I select a novel from the shelf marked ROMANCE. Some people could, of course. Some people could say quite firmly that they wanted something light, to read at solitary meals or to send them to sleep, but unfortunately I am not strong-minded. All I can do is to take *Darkest Africa* with a slight show of reluctance.

Miss Carlyle notices the reluctance. "Don't let me influence you," she says smilingly. "I'm afraid I'm rather apt to influence people unduly in their choice of books."

"Well, perhaps, if I could have something a little—"

"This is *fascinating!*" cries Miss Carlyle, taking down a large tome, bound in dark blue cloth. *"Landscape Gardening!* Of course it isn't everybody's meat but I know you would enjoy it. William Kent and Repton!" exclaims Miss Carlyle rapturously. "And of course Capability Brown! There are pictures and maps and sketches. Landscape Gardening revolutionised the English scene. It was an art, wasn't it? And such an unselfish art, for of course the land-owners who planned and paid for all the alterations to their property could never hope to see the results. They did it for posterity—they made hillocks and dells and laid out parks with oaks and beeches. She presses it into my hands and adds, "Be sure to tell me how you like it, won't you?"

"Yes of course," I agree. From Miss Carlyle's description the book sounds very interesting but its appearance and weight are against it. The book is not the sort of volume which could comfortably be read in bed.

"How do you like The Small House?" asks Miss Carlyle.

"I love it!"

"Oh, I'm so glad," says Miss Carlyle with absolute sincerity. "I'm *so* glad you love it. You see I was very, very fond of Mrs. Stroude."

"And of course she loved it," I add, nodding to show that I understand.

"She built it herself," explains Miss Carlyle. "She designed it. Every tiny detail was carefully thought out. To me the house always seemed part of her; it seemed to express her personality." Miss Carlyle hesitates and then adds in a low voice: "Lorna Stroude was a wonderful person, the sort of person one could talk to about—about things that matter. It was a great shock to me when she died—so—so suddenly . . ."

"Was she old?"

"No, no! Not much older than I am—and nobody knew she had a weak heart. It was terribly—unexpected," says Miss Carlyle with a little tremor in her voice.

"There is a Miss Stroude, isn't there?"

"Yes," agrees Miss Carlyle in quite a different tone. "Yes, there is."

"Her daughter?"

"Oh no! Lorna had no children. Miss Stroude is a stepdaughter, that's all. They were utterly and absolutely different. In fact it would be difficult to imagine two people more unlike." She hesitates and then adds, "One hears a great deal about cruel step-mothers, but in this case it was the stepdaughter who was unkind. Yes, really unkind, and Lorna was so gentle that it made her unhappy."

"Did they live together?"

"Off and on," replies Miss Carlyle. "Miss Stroude has money of her own and preferred to live in London. She just made use of Lorna and came here when it suited her. She didn't like The Small House—I've heard her say so time and again—and that's why it seems so odd that Lorna should

62

leave it to her. Lorna was so fond of it." Miss Carlyle gives a little gasp and turning away seizes a volume at random from the shelves. "I wonder if you would like *this*," she says in a trembling voice. "Oh no, I'm sure you wouldn't . . ."

But before she can return it to the shelf I have pounced upon it. *"The Body in the Cupboard* is the very thing," I tell her. "Just to send me to sleep, you know."

"Oh, but really—"

"Tell me more about Mrs. Stroude. I'm interested."

"Interested?"

I hesitate for a moment and then take the plunge. "Yes, you see I have an odd sort of feeling that she likes me to be there. Probably you think I'm quite mad."

"Oh!" exclaims Miss Carlyle. "Oh no, I don't think you're mad . . ."

At this point in the conversation the door opens to admit a girl and the conversation ends abruptly. In some ways I am glad of the interruption and in other ways I am sorry, but Miss Carlyle is unreservedly glad.

"Susan!" cries Miss Carlyle. "Susan, how delightful! I didn't know you had come home."

"Only yesterday," replies the girl smiling. "I remembered you did the library on Wednesday afternoons."

"This is Susan Morven, Mrs. Christie," says Miss Carlyle, making the introduction with the grave politeness of a bygone age. "Susan and I are old friends, she lives at the Manor House with her father. I expect you have seen the Manor House—a beautiful Queen Anne mansion, built of red brick and half-hidden by trees."

I am more interested in the squire's pretty daughter than in his mansion, and I decide that for once Tony used the wrong word. Susan Morven is much more than pretty; she is really lovely. She is quite young and very slender with an

63

unusually long and graceful neck, which gives her the appealing look of a madonna in a Botticelli painting. Her fair hair is in curls all over her small head, little soft fluffy curls which stray bewitchingly onto her forehead and round her ears. Her skin is pale and clear, her eyes are hazel and widely open, and although she seems full of vivacity there is a curious dignity in her manner which I find extremely attractive.

"Oh, of course!" exclaims Susan, looking at me with interest. "You've taken The Small House."

I admit that I have. It has now ceased to surprise me to discover that everybody in Old Quinings knows all about my private affairs.

"I'm glad," says Susan nodding. "It's nice that The Small House isn't empty anymore. You have a daughter, haven't you? I mean," explains Susan, "I mean somebody said you had a daughter—and—and there aren't many girls in Old Quinings."

I take the point and explain my family, adding that it would be nice for Betty and Bryan to know some young people.

"Yes," agrees Susan. "But I'm afraid there aren't many. There's me, of course, and the Mellers . . ." and she enumerates several other families whose names I cannot remember, but adds that some of them live at a distance and others are rather dull.

Miss Carlyle, who has been looking very fondly at her young friend, interrupts to say that Susan has been in Paris with her mother.

"Oh, it was lovely!" declares Susan. "We had a gorgeous time. Of course Wanda knows so many people in Paris. Then we went to Lucerne for a few days. It was very hot, but I loved it. Then Wanda went on to Vienna and I flew home."

"Susan loves travelling," puts in Miss Carlyle.

Wednesday, 4th July

"But I like coming home even better," says Susan quickly. "In fact I think the best part of travelling is coming home, don't you?"

Miss Carlyle does not reply at once and, as I catch her eye, I know exactly what she feels for the simple reason that I feel the same. (Neither she nor I have homes to come home to and her state is worse than mine. Tim is my home, and wherever he is I am sure of a welcome, but the only "home" she has is the little school-house, and her tenure of it is by no means permanent but depends entirely upon her ability to "hold down her job.")

"Yes," says Miss Carlyle after a little pause. "Yes, I can understand that, Susan dear. The Manor House is so gracious and beautiful; naturally you enjoy coming home."

Susan nods. "And there are all sorts of other nice things about home . . . tennis and picnics and riding. Did I tell you Daddy has given me a new horse for my birthday? He's such a darling. You must come and see him, Miss Carlyle."

It is arranged that Miss Carlyle shall visit the Manor and be introduced to Susan's new acquisition; and then— in case I should feel out of it—they both explain to me that Susan's old pony died. They also explain that Susan rides all over the country, usually in the early morning before breakfast, and that next winter she hopes to hunt.

"Some people find the country dull," says Susan. "Joan Meller is always grumbling about it, but I have so much to do that the days are never long enough to fit everything in."

We spend a few minutes chatting. All the correct things are said and various plans are made for picnics and junkets when Bryan and Betty return. Miss Carlyle suggests that I should write to Betty and tell her of the pleasures in store— and this I promise to do.

It is all very pleasant and I am delighted about it, but

65

as I walk home I begin to experience doubts. The fact is my family does not always share my enthusiasm for new friends and especially for new friends which are foisted upon them by their elders. I am enchanted with Susan, but supposing Bryan and Betty are not? It would have been better to let things alone, to wait and see, to allow them to make friends with Susan themselves.

I decide, a little sadly, that my impulsive nature has betrayed me again.

Thursday, 5th July

Mrs. Daulkes arrives as usual and with her the postman who hands me two letters, one from Tim and the other in an unknown hand. Tim's letter has precedence of course and although it is short it cheers me considerably. Quite obviously Tim has settled down. The other letter is from Rosa Alston, which surprises me, for so much has happened in the last fortnight that I have almost forgotten her.

> Rose Bank,
> Esher.   4th July.

Dear Mrs. Christie,

I hope you enjoyed your short visit to Rome and arrived home safely. I was sorry we did not meet in Rome. I called at your pensione on the afternoon following our arrival as we had arranged—the 15th of June to be exact—but Signora Scarlatti told me you had gone out with a friend and she did not know when you would be back. Of course it did not matter at all as our arrangement was quite vague and indefinite. It was very pleasant meeting you on the plane and our conversation whiled away the time and made the journey seem much shorter than usual . . .

I pause here and feel extremely guilty, for Mrs. Alston and I made a quite definite arrangement to go out together

67

on the afternoon following our arrival in Rome—a fact which I had completely forgotten until this moment—and instead of being annoyed at my casual behaviour, Mrs. Alston has taken it in a most Christian spirit and covered my rudeness with a layer of the best butter.

The letter continues:

Edmond and I are staying with some friends at Esher. As I told you my summer was fully planned out (we are supposed to be going to Cheltenham early in August and then on to Scotland); but Edmond has some reading to do and finds it difficult to concentrate when staying with friends. With so much going on in the house it is impossible for him to work. Edmond suggests we should find rooms in some quiet country place where he could do as he liked without upsetting other people's arrangements. I have been thinking of Old Quinings. I knew it well when I was a girl and talking to you about it made me remember it clearly. Somehow I feel it would be the right place and perhaps not as expensive as other larger places. Do you think it would be possible for us to get rooms in Old Quinings? Either the Bull and Bush or quiet lodgings would suit us. It would be very kind of you if you could find out and let me know as soon as possible. I feel I am imposing on you dreadfully but I really am rather worried.

> With kindest regards,
> Yours very sincerely,
> Rosa Alston

My first reaction to the second half of Mrs. Alston's letter is a feeling of amusement, not unmixed with annoyance; here is the reason for the butter! But second thoughts are more charitable and I decide I must help her. The letter is an S.O.S.; obviously Mrs. Alston is in desperate straits—and she was kind to me on the plane. I imagine myself in her shoes, staying in other people's houses with a "difficult" son who wants peace to work. I imagine myself a buffer, trying to behave like a perfect guest and contending with the moods of a bear. Of course I must help her, and without delay. If Annie cannot have the Alstons she will be able to advise me where lodgings can be found . . . so I arrange a few domestic matters with Mrs. Daulkes and set off to the Bull and Bush.

Annie is laying the tables in the dining room; she asks anxiously if everything is all right. "Mrs. Daulkes said you were quite cheery," declares Annie. "I meant to come along on Sunday but we had a frightful day: two buses from Birmingham and the girl laid up with a poisoned foot and of course, being Sunday, I couldn't get nobody to help. I didn't know what work *was* till I came here—neither did Fred," says Annie frankly. "*Never,* not even at Tocher House. At any rate you got your time off regularly. *Here* it's day and night and you never know from one minute to the next."

This amuses me a little for Annie often complained of her burdens in bygone days, or, if she did not exactly complain, she spoke of them as being onerous.

"But you like being here?" I enquire.

"Oh yes," nods Annie. "We're working up the place—it had been let go down a bit—and it's very interesting kind of work. Fred was saying last night we've never thanked you properly. If it hadn't of been for you and the Colonel and General Morley we'd never have had the Bull—not by a hundred miles."

I assure Annie that we want no thanks and are delighted it is such a success. Then I broach the subject of the Alstons.

"Well," says Annie thoughtfully, "I don't see why not.

Friday, 6th July

By this time I have fallen naturally into a routine. I get up at eight and have my bath and breakfast before Mrs. Daulkes arrives. I shop in the morning and sit in the garden after lunch. I sit in the shade of a magnificent old beech tree and read or knit—or merely think in a vague and idle manner. I make my tea when I feel inclined and then go out for a walk through the woods or in the fields which surround Old Quinings. After supper I write a few letters and then go off to bed.

So far none of my neighbours has called to see me (though I am informed by Mrs. Daulkes that they will do so) and to tell the truth I am not sorry for I am enjoying this spell of absolute peace. In the course of my wanderings I have started life anew in many places, and in every place the same thing happens: at first there is little to do, one knows nobody and life passes by like a pageant, then gradually the world breaks in and one becomes a part of the pageant instead of a mere spectator.

The weather is warm and sunny; it is the right sort of weather for idling in a light summer frock. Unfortunately, however, all my light summer frocks are coming by sea and will not be here for another fortnight at least. (Looking back, I remember myself sitting upon the floor of the sun-drenched bungalow surrounded with piles of garments and suitcases, large and small, and trying vainly to make up my

mind what I shall really need; which of these garments is to
come with me by air—squeezed into the limited compass of
the air-travel bag—and which is to follow by sea. The problem was complicated by the fact that it was extremely hot, by
my recollections of a cold, wet English summer, and by Tim's
advice to "take warm clothes.")

Mrs. Daulkes is sympathetic and helpful. "You could try
Miss Phipps," she suggests. "Miss Phipps would run you up
a nice summer dress in no time. She wouldn't let you
down. All the ladies round about 'ere go to Miss Phipps.
You go to Miss Phipps straight off; I'll tell you 'ow to get
there."

"Straight off" is a favourite expression. Mrs. Daulkes
likes to do everything straight off. Whether it be turning out
the drawing room (a form of employment in which she delights) or posting a letter or telephoning to the fishmonger.
Mrs. Daulkes is all for doing it straight off . . . and as I am
aware that I shall get no peace until I have visited Miss
Phipps I set off then and there.

"It's easy to find," says Mrs. Daulkes, pursuing me to
the door. "You cross the 'Igh Street and take the first to the
left—near Wiggs the baker's it is—then left again before you
get to the smithy, and down a steep 'ill. You turn right at the
bottom—or near the bottom—but I don't mean the street that
takes you into the old village, nor yet the one that takes you
to the mill—*that* would land you down near the river. You
must turn before you get there. It's a nice respectable street
and Miss Phipps is the second 'ouse on the right with geraniums in the window-boxes. It isn't far and it's quite easy to
find. You can't make a mistake."

I have a feeling Mrs. Daulkes is wrong but there is
nothing for it but to try.

Wiggs the baker is easy, of course, and as his establishment is my first landmark I make for it with all speed. The High Street is broad and open and at one end of it is the War Memorial set about with iron seats beneath shady trees. These seats are usually occupied by old men, reading their papers, and by women with shopping-baskets or perambulators, taking a rest and chatting to one another the while. All this gives Old Quinings a leisurely, friendly air and for this reason my first impression of Old Quinings was of a leisurely, friendly village; but today I am to see a different Old Quinings.

The little street near Wiggs the baker is narrow and cobbled; it winds between the houses in a perplexing manner and although there are several turns to the right there is none that turns left. Quite soon I reach the blacksmith's—which is wrong of course for I should have turned before. The only thing to do is to retrace my steps.

A forge is a fascinating place and before I retrace my steps I linger there, standing in the doorway of the dark little shed. The blacksmith is small and dirty; his face is hairy as an ape's, his arms are long and skinny but knotted with muscle. He is busily engaged in shaping a horse's shoe upon the anvil while the horse stands patiently nearby. The red-hot iron is bent like butter and twisted and hammered into shape; the fire glows and the sparks fly upward in the gloom. Presently the shoe is ready and is clamped into place upon the horse's hoof with the usual sizzling and smoking and the usual horrible smell of burning. It is difficult to believe this is not a painful process for the horse, but obviously it is not, for the horse makes no objection.

Having seen the job through, I decide it is time for me to go but unfortunately I have been so absorbed in the shoeing that I have forgotten which way I came. The blacksmith will tell me the way, of course, but the difficulty is I have no idea how to put my question; for, although Mrs. Daulkes told me exactly how to find Miss Phipps, she omitted to give me her address.

I approach the blacksmith a trifle diffidently. "Did you see me come in?" I enquire. "I mean which way did I come? Can you tell me?"

The blacksmith looks at me (his eyes are bright like the eyes of an animal in his dark, hairy face) but he makes no reply.

"Did I come this way . . . or that?" I ask him, pointing.

The blacksmith is silent. Somehow I cannot blame him for his refusal to answer my question.

Leaving the forge I turn to the right and after walking about a hundred yards I discover a turning to the left, and take it . . . but this is wrong, of course, for I am coming in the other direction. I stand still and think it out seriously. The thing to do is to go back to the forge and start afresh; so I turn and go back, but the forge seems to have vanished. By this time I am lost—mentally and physically—and I wander hopelessly up one street and down another.

This place is the old village which Mrs. Daulkes mentioned. It must be hundreds of years old. It must have been here long, long before the other Old Quinings was thought of. The streets are mere lanes, paved with cobbles, narrow and winding; the houses are small and dark with tiny windows and sagging roofs and they are huddled together in a sinister sort of fashion as if they were whispering secrets to one another and did not want to be overheard. There is an odd sort of twilight in the streets for the houses are so close that the light of day cannot penetrate, and there is a stifling feeling— as if too many people were living herded together and using up the air. In spite of this, however, there is nobody to be seen, not a creature from whom I can ask the way. Now and then I think I see a face peering out of one of the little dark windows but, before I can be certain that it really is a face, it has gone.

This maze of twisting lanes and leering houses is very small (it must be small for it lies between the broad High Street of Old Quinings and the river) and yet I am lost . . . it is quite absurd . . . it is even more absurd to be a little frightened.

When I discover that I am frightened I stand quite still and take myself to task. What is there to be frightened of? There is nothing. Obviously I have been walking round and round in a circle like a person lost in a maze and the stifling atmosphere and leaden light is due to an approaching thunderstorm. All I have to do to get out of this horrible place is to walk straight on (or as straight as the winding street permits) and turn neither to the right nor to the left . . . and of course this is the solution to the problem for after a few minutes walking I discover myself back where I started, at Wiggs, the baker's.

Mr. Wiggs is a humane man and when I explain what has happened to me he says that old village is a bad place and did ought to be pulled down, but then where are you to put the people? There's the rub. Those houses can't be pulled down until other houses are built . . . and building is a slow matter with everything so scarce.

"I don't wonder you got a bit scared," says Mr. Wiggs kindly. "Bad things used to go on down there, and bad things still go on, if all they say is true."

Mr. Wiggs is not only sympathetic but also helpful and, calling an extremely small errand boy, deputes him to lead me to Miss Phipps, to wait for me and bring me back again. He adds that I shall be quite safe with Jacky because Jacky is a Cub and this will be his Good Deed for today.

Jacky is quite willing to undertake the task so we set out

together and presently arrive safe and sound at the little house with the geraniums in the window-boxes.

Miss Phipps is a large untidy woman, dressed in a peculiar assortment of garments, but in spite of her obvious disregard of her own personal appearance she seems very competent. She shows me several dresses which are half-finished and these seem very nicely made.

"This is Mrs. Meller's old black lace," explains Miss Phipps. "She's had it for ten years to my knowledge. I'm taking it to pieces and making it into a pinafore dress that she can wear with a coatee. She's putting on weight like mad," adds Miss Phipps confidentially. "And I'm doing up Miss Carlyle's grey for the school concert. She keeps her figure well . . . and I'm altering this jade cotton frock for Miss Susan Morven; she got it in Paris but it doesn't fit well on the shoulders. Pretty, isn't it?" says Miss Phipps displaying it with pride. "Suits her, too. She is a pretty young creature, isn't she?"

"Yes indeed!"

"You haven't seen Miss Susan's mother have you?" asks Miss Phipps. "Miss Susan always calls her Wanda, which seems a bit odd to me but then I was brought up very strictly. Mrs. Morven is beautiful—really beautiful—and of course her clothes are beautiful too. She gets them all in Paris at the Very Best Places," says Miss Phipps in awed tones. "They must cost a fortune, but she's American and Americans are always rich, aren't they?"

This sounds a little sweeping to me and I suggest that some Americans may be less rich than others.

Obviously Miss Phipps does not agree, but she is too polite to say so. "She doesn't like Old Quinings," continues Miss Phipps. "You can't wonder, really. I mean it's a dull little place for a lady like Mrs. Morven. At one time there was talk of a divorce but that blew over and everything seems all right. She doesn't stay here long but just comes and goes as the fancy takes her. She thinks nothing of flying to America and back. Of course Miss Susan stays here most of the time with her father—very devoted they are. I always think Miss Susan was the one who got them to make it up."

For the last few moments I have been trying to stop this flow of indiscretions but without success; I might as well have tried to stop the torrent which rushed from Bryan's burst dam. There is nothing for it but to raise my voice and enquire loudly if Miss Phipps will make me a dress.

"A dress!" exclaims Miss Phipps stopping suddenly. "You mean a new dress, starting from scratch?"

I explain exactly what I want and the reason.

"Oh, that *will* be nice," cries Miss Phipps. "Of course I don't mind altering things for my clients—as a matter of fact most of my work is altering, because nowadays, with income tax at nine-and-sixpence in the pound, ladies can't afford new frocks, but it *is* nice to start from scratch. It gives you so much more scope. Have you brought the material?"

"No, I thought perhaps you might have some."

"I don't usually keep materials," she says. "But I'll just see . . ."

Miss Phipps hurries away and returns with a small roll of gingham. It is pale lilac, self-coloured, and the moment I see it I decide that it is exactly right. I can see myself sitting in the garden or busying myself about The Small House wearing the frock that Miss Phipps is going to make for me.

"Yes, it suits you," declares Miss Phipps, as she drapes the material over my shoulder and stands back with her head on one side to admire the effect. "I thought it would suit you. I just said to myself *that lilac gingham is the very thing*. You have the same colouring . . ."

77

"The same colouring?" I enquire.

"I mean it's the right colouring for you," explains Miss Phipps. "It's lucky, isn't it? Customers usually provide their own material, but I just happened to have this . . . and if you're in a hurry for a frock I could put aside Miss Carlyle's grey and get it done in half no time."

Somehow I have a feeling that there is some mystery about the lilac gingham (Miss Phipps has been so informative upon other matters that one would have expected her to reveal the whole story of how the roll of lilac gingham happened to be available) but that is none of my business, of course.

"Do have it, Mrs. Christie," she says. "I could make it in three days—and I'm sure you'll be pleased with it."

"I'm sure I shall," I reply, and the matter is settled forthwith.

Sunday, 8th July

M RS. DAULKES does not come on Sundays so I am entirely
on my own, but The Small House is so "labour-
saving" that this is no hardship. It is cloudy today
and just as I am starting off to church the rain comes down
in torrents. This is a little annoying in a way but in another
way it is not, for the garden needs rain badly.

The church is at the other end of the High Street and as
I hurry along beneath an umbrella I see other people doing
the same. There is a Sunday-feeling in the air and it is pleasant
to know that Tim will be enjoying a holiday; Tim will be
at church, partaking in the same service, hearing the same
words. Unfortunately the time is different (it would be even
more comfortable if I could think of him partaking in the
same service at the same moment) but one can't have everything.

The church is old and beautiful, as so many little English
parish churches are, but sad to say there are many empty pews.
I slip into a seat at the back but am moved by the verger who
explains in undertones that the vicar likes the front pews filled.
Somewhat reluctantly, I allow myself to be conducted up the
aisle and placed in a more conspicuous position. Just behind
me is a fat woman in a very tight-fitting brown coat-and-skirt
and a red hat and I take her to be Mrs. Meller the vicar's wife
(perhaps because at a casual glance she seems to be putting on
weight).

79

The service is a little dreary, or so I find; the hymns are long and dirge-like and quite unknown to me. Apparently they are unknown to most of the congregation for nobody, except Mrs. Meller, makes any attempt to sing them. Mr. Meller's sermon is entirely taken up with scolding his hearers for not coming to church; he thumps the pulpit and gets rather cross about it, but as all his hearers have come to church it seems rather pointless. I cannot help thinking some of his hearers will be bored at having to suffer for the sins of their weaker brethren; some will feel smug (as did the Pharisee) and it is just possible that some will be feeling in their secret hearts that next Sunday morning might be spent more profitably at home.

When we come out of church we discover the clouds have disappeared and the sun is shining brightly. People linger in the churchyard and chat to one another cheerfully amongst the tombstones. Perhaps tombstones are a curious environment for cheerful chat, but these are so old and mossy that they cannot arouse any sad memories. It is good that these people are cheerful and happy amongst the graves of their ancestors and perhaps it is nice for the ancestors as well.

I know nobody of course, but that is not to say that nobody knows me, and I feel that all these people are looking at me and saying, "That's Mrs. Christie. She's taken The Small House for the summer. Her husband is in Africa, you know . . ." (but perhaps I am wrong about this and they are merely commenting upon my clothes and criticising the shape of my hat). The ancestors are in a different case; they have not the slightest idea who I am. "Who is she?" they are saying. "She isn't one of mine." "What is she doing here at Old Quinings?"

This feeling of being a stranger in the land—not only amongst the living but also amongst the dead—is very dis-

turbing. I am hurrying away, skirting a plot which is surrounded by high iron railings, when I find myself pursued by
the stout lady in the brown coat-and-skirt and the red hat. Her
face is red too and she is slightly breathless owing to the swift-
ness of her pursuit.

"Mrs. Christie?" she asks. "I was sure it must be. I'm Mrs.
Meller, the vicar's wife."

We shake hands solemnly.

"I meant to call," continues Mrs. Meller. "But there's
such a lot to do. The fact is I wondered if you would do the
flowers one Sunday. There are such lovely flowers in the garden of The Small House. Mrs. Stroude used to do the flowers
sometimes and we miss her so much . . . just one Sunday in
the month," says Mrs. Meller. "It would be *such* a help."

"Yes, of course. I should like to."

"Oh good! Now let me see. Shall we say the twelfth of
August?"

We say the twelfth of August and the matter is arranged.

One of the chief joys of being alone is that there is no
need to be punctual for meals; and as it is now so fine and
sunny I decide to go for a walk before lunch. Already I have
discovered a "favourite" walk; it is a footpath through the
fields and along the river. The day is bright and sweetly
scented, there is clover in the grass and the golden buttercups
glow in the light of the golden sun. The sunshine is a soft
warm effulgence, benign and health-giving, quite different
from the baking heat of the sunshine in Africa.

The river flows slowly through the meadows and the blue
sky is reflected in its pools. There are brown-spiked reeds
growing in the water and, on the farther bank, a mass of willow herb. There are irises, a whole regiment of them, straight
and strong, gay in their uniform of green and yellow. The
green of the meadows is almost startling to one whose eye is

used to another, less fortunate, land. They are greener than ever today after the refreshing showers; the tiny raindrops hang upon the sedges and "a livelier emerald twinkles in the grass."

While I am watching, a cow blunders into the stream, breaking the reflections into shards; the ripples spread and lap against the banks and a kingfisher flies from the willow with a flash of blue. I find a fallen tree which makes a comfortable seat, and here I sit and admire the brilliant picture.

The afternoon is the right sort of Sunday afternoon for sitting in the garden and reading, but unfortunately I have nothing to read. I finished *The Body in the Cupboard* last night. It was a "good murder" (as Mrs. Daulkes would say), horrible enough to satisfy my taste for horrors but not realistic enough to give me shivers up my spine. I have read it and forgotten it which is just as it should be with this kind of tale. Now that I have nothing to read I regret that I did not borrow *Landscape Gardening* which would have lasted a good deal longer besides improving my mind. There is, however, a cupboard in the dining room which looks as if it ought to contain books and, although it is locked, the key is in a small brass bowl on the mantelpiece. For a moment I hesitate, but only for a moment. I am so comfortably at home in Mrs. Stroude's house that I know she would like me to read her books.

The cupboard is a treasure-trove; here is a splendid assortment of books—mostly books which I know already but which I am delighted to meet again: here are *Kidnapped* and *The Master of Ballantrae*, *The Wind in the Willows*, *Alice in Wonderland* and *Persuasion*, *Little Women* and *Vanity Fair*. *Redgauntlet* rubs shoulders with *The Mayor of Castorbridge* and the *Adventures of an Irish R.M.* Here are *Sanders of the River*, *The Free Fishers*, *John Splendid* and *Gaudy Night* (a catholic selection indeed and incidentally a selection which tells me a good deal about the lady to whom they belonged); and joy upon joys here is a collection of Trollope, not only the beloved Barchester novels but others such as *Miss Mackenzie* and *The Belton Estate,* with which I am unacquainted. Naturally it takes me a long time to make up my mind, but after due deliberation I decide upon *Doctor Thorne* and take him with me into the garden.

The bed of violas is looking lovelier than ever after the rain and their scent is fresher. I carry out the long wicker chair and arrange the cushions and settle down happily. Could anything be more delightful than a Sunday afternoon in the garden with *Doctor Thorne?* The fact that it is an old edition with thick paper and large print and a number of fascinating pictures heightens my pleasure in the perusal of the tale.

I am getting on famously, and already have reached that part of the story where the dear, good man is redecorating his house for the benefit of his little niece, Mary. (I might have voyaged further if I had not spent some time looking at the picture of the doctor showing Mary the glory of the new drawing room.) Unfortunately at this very moment I hear the buzz of an electric bell, and the peace of the afternoon is shattered.

But need the peace be shattered? After all it may not have been the front-door bell. How foolish it would be to disturb myself and then to find I had been mistaken! The bell rings again in a demanding fashion and I am obliged to face the fact that it is the bell of my front-door . . . but why should I answer it? Nothing urgent can have happened on a quiet Sunday afternoon and any visitor will be unwelcome. By this time the bell has ceased to ring; the matter has settled itself and whoever it was has gone away in disgust.

This deduction, though reasonable, proves to be false

and before I have time to pick up my book Susan Morven appears round the corner of the house and comes across the lawn.

"Don't move!" she cries. "Please don't move, Mrs. Christie. You look so comfortable; it's awful of me to disturb you like this."

I tell her I am very pleased to see her and this is true, for Susan is a very pleasant sight. Only a bear could fail to be pleased to see such a delightful creature.

"I'll sit on the grass," she continues, suiting the action to the word. "And I promise faithfully I shan't stay more than a few minutes. I expect you're wondering why on earth I've come, aren't you?"

"I thought perhaps you had come to see me."

Susan smiles. "You're making it more difficult, and it's difficult enough already."

"Difficult?"

"What I've come to say is very difficult," explains Susan. "So difficult that I don't know how to say it."

"Am I very alarming?"

"No!" she cries, shaking her golden curls. "It's only because you aren't alarming that I've come. You see, Mrs. Christie, when I thought about it—about what we said on Wednesday—I realised that it was rather a mistake. You haven't written to Betty, have you?"

"No, not yet."

"Don't write. I mean don't write about me and about the plans we made. It sounds awfully queer I know," says Susan hastening over what she feels to be delicate ground, "but when I thought about it I realised that if somebody made plans like that for me I should hate it and probably be prejudiced against the other person—I mean me, of course. It's all very muddly but the point is I don't want Betty to be prejudiced against me from the very beginning by hearing a lot about me." She pauses and looks at me to see how I am taking it.

"I've been thinking the same thing," I tell her.

"The same?"

"Exactly the same. I remember once hearing a great deal about a woman from some friends of hers. They told me how wonderful she was, how clever and amusing; they told me she was always perfectly dressed, that she had a gorgeous voice and played the piano divinely; they said she had naturally curly hair and was always the life and soul of the party . . ."

Susan is giggling. "Goodness, how you must have hated her!"

"M'm," I reply nodding.

"Did you ever meet the paragon?"

"Yes, and it was all true and she was a darling. Of course it took me some time to get over the bad start but eventually we became great friends. One day when we knew one another well she asked me to tell her—in confidence—what I had heard about her that made me so stand-offish."

"She thought it was something dreadful, I suppose!"

"Quite dreadful. She wouldn't believe me when I told her what I had heard."

"Oh well," says Susan. "That just shows, doesn't it? Of course I'm not a bit clever or amusing and I can't sing a note and nobody notices whether I'm at a party or not—"

"But you've got curly hair."

She looks up at me with a mischievous twinkle in her eyes. "Is Betty like you?" she asks.

"Absolutely different."

"Tell me about her," says Susan.

It is a great temptation of course but I resist it manfully and remain dumb.

"Oh!" exclaims Susan after a short pause. "Yes, I see!" and she begins to chuckle delightedly.

By this time I am more than ever enchanted with my guest and am hoping with all my heart that she and Betty will become friends, but I feel a little doubtful whether they will have much in common. Betty is a school-girl, and young for her age, whereas Susan is a finished person. There can be no harm in telling Susan this, so I tell her.

Susan smiles at my warning. "I'm old because I'm *only*," Susan explains, "and because I've been about such a lot, and because—well, because I've had some unhappy things to bear. Unhappiness is ageing isn't it? But I'm quite young inside, and very adaptable. It will be fun to have a friend younger than myself."

We are silent for a little after that; the sun is warm, the birds are singing and the garden is a peaceful spot.

Monday, 9th July

TODAY IS the one appointed for Mrs. Alston and her son to arrive at the Bull and Bush. They are expected at lunch-time so I give them the afternoon to settle down, and visit them after tea. Mrs. Alston is in the parlour, writing letters; she greets me happily and overwhelms me with gratitude for finding her the rooms.

"My room isn't very large, of course," says Mrs. Alston, "but that doesn't matter as long as Edmond is comfortable. His room is just overhead," she adds, raising her eyes to the ceiling and lowering her voice.

"The walls are very thick—" I begin.

"Oh yes! And he says this old house is conducive to study. He's working *now*. Isn't it splendid?"

I agree that it is. My slight prejudice against the studious Edmond is considerably—though somewhat unreasonably—strengthened.

"Mrs. Bollings is very kind," she continues. "We had to move the furniture in Edmond's room (he's fussy about things like that) but Mrs. Bollings didn't mind at all, and Mr. Bollings came up and helped. They *are* nice, aren't they? You don't know how grateful I am to you, Mrs. Christie. It's all your doing of course."

She has thanked me adequately already and her gratitude is beginning to bore me a little so I change the subject and apologise for my behaviour in Rome. There is nothing else for it but to tell Mrs. Alston the truth; that I quite forgot our arrangement to go out together and am very sorry about it.

"It doesn't matter at all; don't think of it," she says. "Signora Scarlatti explained."

These words, though casual and reassuring upon the surface, cause me some slight discomfort. It would be nice to know what the Signora explained and how she explained it, but it is all too difficult and the moment passes.

"Don't think of it," repeats Mrs. Alston. "I quite understand. I just thought you might like to see the catacombs and it's so difficult getting about in Rome if you can't speak Italian."

"You speak it?" I enquire.

"Oh yes, I've knocked about in Italy a lot."

This information adds to my disquietude.

Once more the subject is changed and I enquire with solicitude whether Mrs. Alston and her son had a good journey and hear a somewhat dreary recital of rude porters and slow trains. Mrs. Alston and I found plenty to talk about in the plane but today we seem to have less in common. I feel a trifle distrait and her mind is wandering; I can see her eyes turn to the ceiling every now and then. Perhaps she is listening to that Great Brain which is working so industriously in the room above.

Mrs. Alston asks if I know an old lady called Miss Crease and adds that her aunt used to know Miss Crease so she supposes she had better go and see her. I reply that Miss Crease lives next door to me and that we came down in the train together. But neither of us has much to say about my neighbour and presently the conversation becomes so barren that I decide not to prolong my visit.

Monday, 9th July

"Must you go?" says Mrs. Alston. "I thought perhaps you would stay to tea . . . and you haven't met Edmond! Shall I go and tell him you're here?"

"Oh no!" I exclaim. "We mustn't disturb him."

"Perhaps not," she agrees with a sigh of relief.

We say good-bye and she sees me off at the door.

It is unthinkable to leave the Bull and Bush without a glimpse of Annie so I make my way round to the back and through the cobbled yard. The back-door is open invitingly; it leads into the scullery and from thence to the huge raftered kitchen where I discover my old friend busy preparing dinner for her guests.

"There you are!" exclaims Annie. "You've been talking to Her, of course. I hoped you wouldn't go away without coming in to see me. I'm making puddings so I can't sit down, but you can sit down and talk to me. That old chair's more comfortable than it looks."

The chair is a period piece with a high back and carved wooden arms and is very comfortable indeed. Its owner is surprised when I tell her it is valuable and would fetch a good price in an auction room.

"I must tell Fred," says Annie, looking at it more respectfully. "Fred likes that chair to sit in, so I don't suppose he'd want to sell it, but it's nice to know we could if we wanted. There are all sorts of old things in this house; we took over most of the stuff when we bought the place, it was the easiest way."

We chat about this and that. Annie wants to know whether I like Mrs. Daulkes and how I am managing about food; she is much relieved when I assure her that everything is working out splendidly and I am enjoying myself no end. She shows surprise when I mention the Alstons and apologise for the trouble they have caused.

"Trouble!" says Annie. "There wasn't any trouble that I know of."

"Moving all the furniture," I explain.

"Oh that! That wasn't any trouble. The young gentleman wanted his table in the window to get a better light, so he and Fred moved it. I'd given him a big, heavy table for all his books. He's a very nice young gentleman. I'm not so stuck on Her," declares Annie as she seizes a large bowl and proceeds to beat her pudding with furious energy.

What with one thing and another my visit to the Bull and Bush is somewhat disturbing and I walk home to The Small House in a thoughtful mood.

Wednesday, 11th July

*I*T IS unprecedented for Mrs. Daulkes to be late in arriving at The Small House. She and the postman always meet upon the doorstep at precisely nine o'clock. This morning, however, Mrs. Daulkes is about ten minutes after schedule. She arrives breathless with haste and looking quite unlike her usual cheerful self. When I ask her if anything is the matter she bursts into sobs and rushes madly into the kitchen, banging the door behind her. I pursue her and find her dropping tears into the sink.

At first Mrs. Daulkes refuses to tell me what has befallen her but after a little persuasion I discover that her father is ill and she has been sent for. She wants to go to Stepney and see him.

"Of course you must go!" I exclaim.

Mrs. Daulkes says yes, of course she must go. Jim can say what he likes but your father's your father and they wouldn't never have sent for her if he hadn't been bad. She wouldn't never forgive herself if she didn't go. Jim doesn't understand what she feels. He never even tried to understand. Selfish, that's Jim. Spoilt, that's what Jim is. He doesn't think of nobody but himself and his own comfort. But *she* doesn't care, she's going to Stepney straight off and if Jim doesn't like it he can lump it . . .

All this time Mrs. Daulkes is washing up the breakfast dishes and sprinkling them with tears.

91

I tell her to leave them and go home at once and pack so that she can travel to London by the mid-day train.

Mrs. Daulkes sobs louder and says in blurred tones that the bus is cheaper and she would rather go by bus.

I tell her to go home and pack her suitcase and catch the bus.

Mrs. Daulkes says yes, that's right; she'll just finish washing up and then she'll go. She can't help it if there's nobody to get Jim's breakfast and see the children off to school . . . "Oh dear!" sobs Mrs. Daulkes. "Who's going to? Who's going to see to everything and look after Eric? Who's going to look after you? Who's going to sing the solo at the Women's Institute on Thursday? Well, I know who'll do *that,*" declares Mrs. Daulkes, fiercely dabbing at her poor red eyes with a ball of wet handkerchief. "Alice Seager'll be only too pleased to oblige—not 'alf she won't! But it's to be 'oped she won't go flat in the middle—and you aren't as 'elpless as you look—though 'ow I'll ever look Mrs. Bollings in the face, leaving you stranded all in a minute—but the worst is Jim and the children. Oh dear, it *is* a problem!" says poor Mrs. Daulkes dabbing her eyes and gulping. "If only it 'ad been last week I could 'ave gone quite easy, because Jim's sister was 'ere and she'd 'ave looked after things, and last week there wasn't the Institute Concert. Last week would 'ave been *easy.* But there, Dad always *was* inconsid'rate."

This seems a little unreasonable to me and I make the mistake of saying so, but Mrs. Daulkes does not listen.

"Last week would 'ave been *easy,*" she repeats. "Last week I could 'ave gone. Elsie's young but she's got 'er 'ead screwed on all right and she'd 'ave seen to things for me. She's quite good with Eric, too—Eric's my youngest and it isn't everybody can manage 'im—I could 'ave gone without any bother if it 'ad been last week."

Wednesday, 11th July

This line of thought seems unproductive and time is passing. Mrs. Daulkes will need all her time if she is going to London by the twelve o'clock bus and, as I can be no help to her without knowing a little more about the matter, I endeavour to find out from Mrs. Daulkes what news the telegram contained; whether her father is in hospital or, if still at home, whether he has anyone to look after him.

"Mother's there of course," says Mrs. Daulkes in surprise. "It was Mother that sent for me and if I know anything about Mother she wouldn't let me do a 'and's turn if I *did* go."

"But you feel it your duty to go?" I enquire.

Mrs. Daulkes considers the matter and after a few moments she replies that it's her duty to go and it's her duty to stay. She promised to obey Jim when she married him and the Bible says you should honour your father and your mother so what *are* you to do? And the last time she left home—the time Mother had her bad leg—Jim gave himself a sick attack eating things out of tins—things like crab which she doesn't hold with—and he left it in the tin for days, which is a thing you should never do, but always turn it into a glass jar with a cover. And the children were out all hours at night and stupid at their lessons next morning—Miss Carlyle said so—and if someone would tell her which is right she would do it straight off, but to be in two places at once is a thing she cannot do.

I can see Mrs. Daulkes wishes me to be arbiter in the matter but I am unwilling to advise her. All I can do is to supply her with a clean handkerchief and make her some tea —and, as I can never resist a newly made cup of tea, I sit down and have it with her. These ministrations revive Mrs. Daulkes. She begins to talk more coherently and to press me for my advice. At last I tell her I think she should go, for this is my considered opinion; not because I know much about the matter (Mrs. Daulkes, though she has talked a great deal about it, has failed to make it clear) but because her departure would inconvenience me considerably and therefore I cannot help feeling it would be the Right Thing. The Right Thing is usually the uncomfortable thing—or so I have found.

Mrs. Daulkes does not subscribe to my Edwardian viewpoint. She says why should it be the Right Thing just because you don't want to do it? There's all sorts of things she doesn't want to do which wouldn't be the Right Thing at all. And, becoming incoherent again in her excitement, she adds that Alice Seager can do it for all she cares but if the children were out till all hours—like they were before—and got run over by a bus—which they well might be—or if Jim poisoned himself, or them, she wouldn't never forgive herself if she lived to be a hundred which isn't likely with all the worries. It was all mouldy on the top, so no wonder he was sick and the only mercy was he didn't give it to the children.

It is now obvious that Mrs. Daulkes has decided not to go, so I suggest we should send a telegram to her mother, pointing out her difficulties and asking for further information. This seems good to her, so together we concoct a suitable message and I despatch it by telephone.

Mrs. Daulkes says she doesn't know how to thank me and it just shows what a mistake it is to have a Labour Government—a conclusion which puzzles me considerably. I am also considerably puzzled by the fact that she is completely satisfied; the burden drops from her back as if by magic and she worries no more.

How lucky to be Mrs. Daulkes! If I were in her shoes I should still be worrying, still wondering if I had done the Right Thing.

Now that the matter is settled Mrs. Daulkes starts her usual morning's work at top speed to make up for lost time and The Small House seems to be in the throes of a hurricane.

Wednesday, 11th July

She is here, there and everywhere; at one moment clattering pans in the kitchen, the next moment dusting the drawing room and a few moments later polishing the bathroom taps.

The hurricane is at its height when a large, shining car drives up to the gate and Tony Morley gets out of it and comes up the path.

"Hullo!" he says cheerfully. "I got home last night so I thought I'd come over. How are you getting on?"

It is a delightful surprise to see Tony; I lead him into the dining room—which is the only room available at the moment —and we sit down and talk.

Presently Tony says, "What on earth is happening overhead? It sounds like furniture movers."

"It's only Mrs. Daulkes," I reply.

"And is that Mrs. Daulkes singing?"

I listen and reply that it is. Mrs. Daulkes is singing while she works and her song is "The Holy City" which she is to render as a solo at the Women's Institute Concert on Thursday.

"It's a good voice," says Tony. "Untrained of course but also unstrained. She sounds very happy, doesn't she?"

"Yes," I reply—for although "The Holy City" is not exactly a cheerful song in itself there is a sort of buoyancy in the voice which reminds one of a blackbird in spring.

"You seem surprised, Hester. Why shouldn't the woman be happy on a lovely sunshiny morning?"

This question is not a rhetorical one. Tony wants an answer and, as he is the sort of person who, like myself, is deeply interested in the affairs of his fellows, I tell him the whole story. I even tell him Mrs. Daulkes's reference to the Labour Government and how it has puzzled me.

"Puzzled you?" says Tony smiling. "The reference is as clear as crystal. No, I'm not going to explain."

"I suppose I'm stupid!"

"Not stupid," he replies kindly. "I should describe you as an intelligent woman, but you have your blind spots."

"I don't know what you mean."

"I know," he says, nodding. "You don't know what I mean and you never will—at least I hope not. As things are it would certainly be a thousand pities if the blind spot disappeared."

"You're talking nonsense," I tell him.

"Sometimes there's quite a lot of sense in nonsense," replies Tony. "Now run along and put on your shoes, I'm taking you out for a drive."

"But, Tony—"

"We'll go to Wandlebury," says Tony. "I've got to see a man about a dog and, while I'm trying out its bark, you can do some shopping. Don't tell me you haven't any shopping to do because I shan't believe you. We'll have lunch at a nice old Inn called the Apollo and Boot and I'll bring you home to tea."

The expedition sounds delightful—and of course I have shopping to do—but I am obliged to refuse. I have promised Mrs. Daulkes to stay at home and receive the reply to the telegram and Mrs. Daulkes is to send her elder daughter when she gets home from school to get the message.

"You really *are!*" exclaims Tony—but what I really am he does not say.

"I can't help it," I tell him. "Of course I'd like to come, but I can't."

"Saturday then," says Tony. "Only it will have to be the afternoon. I'll look in at tea-time and we'll nip over to Wandlebury afterwards."

This suits me admirably and the matter is arranged.

The large, shiny car is standing outside the gate.

"Nice, isn't he?" says Tony. "I got him the other day. I'm thinking of calling him Belshazzar."

"Why?" I enquire.

"Why not?" asks Tony.

"I thought cars were usually feminine, that's all."

"Some are and some aren't," replies Tony gravely. "This one is definitely masculine—he goes like smoke."

Tony has always been fond of large, powerful cars; he drives fast but extremely well and although I am not particularly keen on speed I enjoy being driven by Tony. I remember a golden sunshiny day in the Highlands when we went across wild moors; over hills and past forests and lochs to a little bay at the edge of the Western Sea. I remember another day when we went to Inverness and had various strange adventures on the way. I remember a silver day when we took the beautiful road which runs in curves down the valley of Tweed.

Tony remembers too. "They were good days," he agrees. "But we'll have other days as good." He gets into the car and shuts the door. "This road is the end," he declares. "I never saw such a road. Can I get round or must I back over those ghastly bumps?"

"You must back," I tell him. "The road finishes abruptly twenty yards past this gate, and there's no room to turn a donkey cart, far less Belshazzar. That's why The Small House is so nice and quiet. If you go very slowly the bumps won't break your springs."

"Absolutely heartless!" declares Tony and backs his car carefully down the road.

The telegram from Mrs. Daulkes's mother arrives in the afternoon. It comes by telephone as arranged and it is so cryptic that I have a good deal of trouble taking it down; fortunately the telephone girl is patient with my stupidity and spells out the message word by word. When the message is complete it runs as follows: THOUGHT ELSIE WAS THERE OR WOULDN'T HAVE ASKED MOTHER.

At first I am completely puzzled as to what it means, but after careful thought I begin to see light. Elsie is the sister-in-law who was here last week. So far so good, but "wouldn't have asked mother" is still a problem. I read it again, trying a comma in various places, and at last I hit on the solution. Mother is the signature of the sender, of course, and if she had known that Miss Elsie Daulkes had left Old Quinings she would not have asked her daughter to come.

If I have read aright the news is reassuring; Mrs. Daulkes will be able to remain at Old Quinings and carry out her duties to her family with an easy mind.

Saturday, 14th July

MRS. ALSTON drops in to ask if I know of a dressmaker in Old Quinings, someone who could alter a frock.

"All my things are too short," says Mrs. Alston. "That's the worst of going abroad. You come home and find everyone is wearing their things longer or shorter and you feel a freak."

This is perfectly true—as I know to my cost—so I sympathise with Mrs. Alston and tell her about Miss Phipps and explain as best I can how to find the way to her dwelling-place.

"Don't worry," says Mrs. Alston. "I'll find it all right. I'm used to finding my way about in all sorts of places."

Having received the information for which she has come Mrs. Alston does not take her departure, but sits down and says in a melancholy voice that she had no idea Old Quinings would be so dull. There is nothing to do, says Mrs. Alston, absolutely nothing—not even a picture house—and of course Edmond is hard at work all the time. Even at meals Edmond is not very lively company (he can't help it, of course, because his mind is on his work). She tries to take Edmond for a short walk every day but he never seems to want to go. Quite often she finds he has gone out by himself before breakfast without telling her. She thinks it's a little unkind of Edmond when he knows perfectly well she has given up all her plans to come here with him. She doesn't see why he couldn't arrange his hours of work so that he could go out with her at a reasonable time. It wouldn't be so bad if there was anybody else to talk to—anybody staying at the Bull and Bush—but people come and go so quickly that there's no opportunity of getting to know them. The only residents are two elderly ladies; but one of them is deaf and the other reads all the time so she can't make any headway with *them*. She knows nobody in Old Quinings—nobody except Miss Crease who is a horrible old creature and (in Mrs. Alston's opinion) not quite all there. Mrs. Alston went to see her yesterday and she was ill in bed but insisted on Mrs. Alston going up to her bedroom and talking to her. The room was terribly hot and stuffy—I have no idea how hot and stuffy it was—and Miss Crease was absolutely repulsive, all wrapped up in shawls and looking exactly like a witch. She kept on asking questions about everything and everybody all the time, so it was impossible for Mrs. Alston to get up and come away without being definitely rude . . . in fact the only way Mrs. Alston could escape was by promising to go back today after tea, so she supposes she will have to.

"Why should you go and see her if you don't want to?" I enquire.

"Oh, because," says Mrs. Alston, "because—well, as a matter of fact it's better to keep on her right side. She's so—so *horrible*. You never know what she might say if she got her knife into you." Mrs. Alston pauses for a moment and sighs. "It's so awfully dull," she says. "I wish to goodness we had stayed on at Esher and then gone to Cheltenham as we arranged. Of course it's too late now. I've written and put off all our visits and people hate you to keep on changing your plans."

I feel slightly annoyed with Mrs. Alston and find it difficult to show any sympathy with her in her plight.

"Of course it isn't your fault," adds Mrs. Alston magnanimously.

100

Saturday, 14th July

Perhaps this should mollify my feeling of annoyance but it does not; in fact it has the opposite effect and I decide it is a great mistake to try to help people by interfering in their affairs. But even as I make this decision I am aware that it is useless and that I shall go on interfering in people's affairs until I die or become too old to care.

Time is passing and Mrs. Alston remains seated in her chair. I am particularly anxious for her to go away for I am expecting Tony—this being the appointed day for our expedition to Wandlebury—and, all things considered, I feel it would be a mistake for them to meet. But Mrs. Alston shows no signs of going away and at last I am obliged to ask her to stay to tea.

"Yes, I should like to," replies Mrs. Alston tepidly. "I don't suppose Edmond will notice whether I'm there or not. I'll have tea here and then go in and see Miss Crease as I promised. It's rather sickening to think of what a good time I should be having if I hadn't altered all my arrangements."

She is still talking in this plaintive manner when my other guest appears upon the scene. My worst fears are realised. Tony is annoyed at finding Mrs. Alston here and takes a dislike to her. He refuses to recognise her as a one-time dancing partner and suggests she must have mistaken him for his cousin who resembles him closely.

Mrs. Alston says, "Oh no, it was you. Of course I was Rosa Burton in those days." (But even this seems to ring no bell in Tony's memory.) "I remember a dance at Charters Towers," continues Mrs. Alston. "It was very gay and there were fireworks on the terrace."

Tony says he hopes she enjoyed it.

"Oh yes, of course," says Mrs. Alston without enthusiasm.

A short silence ensues. I plunge into this silence with a futile remark about the weather. We agree that the weather has been fine and dry. Tony says unless there is rain soon people will have to start watering their gardens. Mrs. Alston says she has no garden so she would prefer the dry weather to continue. Her statement ends the unprofitable subject. Tony asks whether Mrs. Alston has been to the Lion's Gorge and, on hearing that she knows nothing about it, he explains that it is very pretty indeed and she ought to go. The Lion's Gorge is the source of a little river which bursts out of a cliff and cascades between rocks. There are ferns and trees and the ruined remains of an old mill which used to grind corn for all the farms in the district.

"It sounds a good place for a picnic," I suggest.

"Oh, it is!" declares Tony.

Mrs. Alston says she does not care for picnics and has no car.

Tony, somewhat damped, murmurs that there are buses to the Lion's Gorge, but this information fails to interest Mrs. Alston.

It has now become obvious to me that Mrs. Alston intends to outstay her fellow-guest and evidently her fellow-guest has come to the same conclusion; he rises and says he must go. Somehow I cannot bring myself to mention the expedition to Wandlebury but I feel quite absurdly disappointed.

"Need you go? It's still quite early," I ask him.

"Sorry," replies Tony. "I've got to see a man in the village. It's about a cairn terrier."

I feel this is going a little too far and glance anxiously at Mrs. Alston to see how she is taking it . . . but Mrs. Alston has swallowed it whole. She becomes slightly more animated and says it has been a great pleasure to meet General Morley after so many years. General Morley smiles delightfully and says it is always so nice to be able to give pleasure to others. He then shakes hands with us both and adds, "Please don't bother to come to the door with me, Hester. I can find my own way quite easily."

Soon after he has gone Mrs. Alston takes her departure and, as she is going to see Miss Crease, I conduct her to the side gate which will be more convenient for her.

Mrs. Alston lingers, leaning upon the gate. "I must say General Morley is very strange," says Mrs. Alston.

It is difficult to defend Tony, because I realise that he certainly has behaved a little strangely this afternoon.

"I can't make him out at all," she adds thoughtfully.

"When you know him well . . ."

"You know him well, of course."

"Tim and I have known him for years and years."

Mrs. Alston hesitates and then says, "It was a curious coincidence that he happened to be in Rome while you were there, wasn't it?"

"He had business in Rome," I tell her firmly.

"Oh, I see," says Mrs. Alston.

As I walk back slowly to the house I decide that the afternoon has been a complete failure. Nobody has enjoyed it. Mrs. Alston is dreary beyond words; it seems incredible that I should ever have liked the woman and been amused by her conversation. Tony has gone in a huff; the visit to Wandlebury is off; the world is stale, flat and unprofitable.

Such are my feelings as I open the glass door of the drawing room, but they undergo a swift transformation when I find Tony comfortably ensconced in the largest and most comfortable chair.

"What a curious taste you have in friends," says Tony.

"She thinks so, too," I reply, smiling at him. "She thinks you're very strange. She can't make you out at all."

"Well, hurry up," says Tony. "It's no good going to Wandlebury, the shops will all be shutting, but we can go for a drive."

After the stress and strain of the afternoon it is sheer bliss to lie back in Tony's comfortable car and enjoy myself. We glide along slowly—for once Tony seems content to drive at a reasonable speed—and the pageant of the English countryside delights my eyes. It is so long since I have been in England that I had forgotten how beautiful it is. There are softly rounded hills; there are leafy woods; there are parks with great trees, standing alone in all the glory of their early summer foliage. There are little streams dawdling amongst green meadows and little villages which nestle in hollows; cosy peaceful villages, the cottages built of honey-coloured stone with moss and lichen growing on their roofs . . . and nearly every cottage has a little garden full of gay flowers. Here we see old men sitting in the doorways, enjoying the sunshine, women with pink cheeks and white aprons, gossiping to one another, and groups of children who wave to us as we pass. Here is a church with a square solid tower, there is a field of ripe hay with men and women working in it.

Presently we come to an old hump-backed bridge which spans a lazy stream. There is an old mill here, a red-roofed house surrounded by trees, and beside the mill there is a ford. A farm wagon is crossing the ford and Tony stops the car so we can watch its passage. It is very quiet—so quiet and still that we can hear the splash of the horse's hoofs and the rattle of the wheels on the pebbles.

Somehow I have the feeling that I have been here before. I have seen the old mill and the trees reflected in the calm green water; I have seen the meadows and the clouds; I have seen the farm wagon with its big wooden wheels and the man

104

in his shirt-sleeves driving it. The feeling is so strong that I break the silence with an exclamation of surprise.

"What is it?" asks Tony.

"I've been here before—but I haven't. I mean—I must have dreamt about it—even the hay-cart."

"The haywain," says Tony, turning and smiling at me. "Yes, I had the same feeling."

"You felt you had been here before? But we can't both have dreamt it!"

"We didn't," he replies. "As a matter of fact I'm no dreamer. For a few moments I was puzzled . . . and then I knew."

"I don't know what you mean, Tony."

"And yet it's quite simple. You've seen Constable's picture of 'The Haywain' and so have I."

It is true, of course. The scene is exactly like Constable's picture, a coloured photogravure of which hung in the drawing room of the little house at Donford. Whether or not this is really the exact place where the picture was painted we do not know for, as Tony says, there are thousands of fords and mills and haywains in England . . . but somehow I like to think it is.

By this time the wagon has crossed the ford and rumbled away.

Part III

The Serpent in the Garden

Monday, 16th July

MRS. DAULKES has definite ideas as to what I am to do and what I am not to do in the house. At first it was a little difficult and I found myself a frequent offender against her notions of propriety, but now I am beginning to learn the rules. I may make my bed and dust, but I must not clean the bath nor polish the furniture; if she is "in a rush" I may use the vacuum cleaner, but not on the stairs. In the kitchen it is even more complicated for I am allowed to make a cake but not a pudding and I may wash up after tea but not after any other meal. Doing the flowers is my province; Mrs. Daulkes never interferes with that.

"I'm no good with flowers," says Mrs. Daulkes. "Never 'ad a taste for arranging them. Sometimes they 'ave competitions at the Women's Institute—a bowl of spring flowers— but I never bother myself. It's ladies' work arranging flowers," adds the remarkable woman with a curious mixture of admiration and contempt.

The flowers need attention this morning so I take the basket and a pair of scissors and sally forth to cut some fresh ones for a tall glass jar. It is a pleasant task and I am taking my time about it when suddenly I am addressed by a voice which seems to come from the sky.

"Mrs. Christie!" says the voice in peremptory tones.

I turn and look up and behold the small, sallow face of Miss Crease above the garden wall. This wall is at least six feet high and nothing of Miss Crease is visible except her queer little face and her fur hat and her two little claw-like hands gripping the ivy with which the wall is covered. She looks like a sort of wizened Humpty Dumpty and, if I had not seen her before, I should be considerably alarmed.

"I suppose you're annoyed because I haven't been to see you," says Miss Crease in complaining tones. "I've had a chill, that's why. I've had to stay in bed ever since I got home and very dull it has been. Nobody came near me except Rosa Alston, and she isn't much catch."

"I'd have come if I had known—"

"Travelling doesn't suit me," declares Miss Crease unappeased. "Especially nowadays with the carriages so draughty."

"Draughty!" I exclaim.

"That's what I said—*draughty*. There was a draught in that carriage."

"But I shut everything. It was terribly stuffy—"

"There was a draught," says Miss Crease firmly. "I could feel it blowing down the back of my neck."

"You had a fur collar."

"I had no scarf. There was a scarf in my bag, of course, but I didn't want to trouble you to get it out for me."

This surprises me a good deal.

"I wish I had," adds Miss Crease fretfully.

It is very difficult to converse with Miss Crease because I seem unable to find the right thing to say at the right moment. It is also very uncomfortable; I am beginning to get a crick in my neck from looking up at her. These circumstances, combined with the absurdity of the conversation, remind me of the conversation between Alice and Humpty Dumpty and I have some difficulty in stifling my giggles.

"I see nothing to laugh at," says Miss Crease.

"No, of course not," I reply hastily. "I'm not laughing. I'm very sorry indeed that you've been ill. I hope you're better."

"I'm better or I wouldn't be here," she replies crossly.

"How did you get there?" I enquire, for this is a mystery which has been teasing me since the first moment of her appearance.

"I'm standing upon the kitchen steps; it's very dangerous and uncomfortable and most unsuitable for a woman of my age."

The reply to this is obvious but I refrain from uttering it.

"I wanted to speak to you," she continues. "There was no other way of speaking to you. I might have written you a note of course—that hadn't occurred to me."

"Or telephoned," I suggest.

"I don't telephone," she replies shortly.

There is no suitable comment to make upon this curious statement so I make none and there is a slight pause.

"It has worried me considerably," continues Miss Crease. "I've watched you sitting in the garden every afternoon. Why don't you attend to the Maggie Motts?"

I gaze at her, speechless with surprise.

"The Maggie Motts," repeats Miss Crease loudly.

"I don't know what you mean."

"Those violas are called Maggie Mott."

"Oh, I see."

"You ought to pick off the dead ones."

"Oh, I see."

"Good gracious!" exclaims Miss Crease impatiently. "Don't you know *anything* about gardening? You'll never get a second flowering if you don't pick off the dead ones."

"No, I mean yes, I suppose I should."

"Of course you should."

"The fact is I thought the gardener—"

"Abijah Rannish is a very good gardener but you can't expect him to do *that*. You had better get onto it at once," adds Miss Crease in her usual peremptory manner.

Now that the order has been given I expect to see the head disappear and I watch somewhat anxiously, for I am aware it is easier to mount a ladder than to descend from it, but Miss Crease has not done with me yet.

"Did you enjoy your visit to Rome?" she asks, shooting the question at me so suddenly that I am slightly taken aback.

"Yes," I reply. "Yes, it was very interesting indeed. Of course I was only there for two days, but—"

"But it's wonderful what a lot of interesting things you can do in two days," declares Miss Crease. She cackles maliciously and disappears.

For a few moments I remain, staring at the top of the wall, petrified with astonishment at the startling manner in which she has vanished from view. Has Miss Crease fallen? Ought I to do something about it? I listen intently but there are no groans; there is no sound at all . . . no sound but the singing of the birds in the quiet garden.

I pick up the basket and continue my interrupted task and, now that I have recovered from the shock of her sudden disappearance, I find myself pondering upon her parting words: it's wonderful what a lot of interesting things you can do in two days.

There is a certain species of serpent which is said to have a sting in its tail.

Tuesday, 17th July

A LETTER FROM Tim arrives this morning but it is slightly disappointing. I wrote Tim a full account of all my adventures and hoped for suitable comments in reply but all Tim says in comment is, "Thank you for your nice long letter," and goes on to describe a cocktail party at the mess (and as cocktail parties are all much the same, especially in a place where the number of guests is limited and one meets the same people over and over again, the description does not thrill me to the core). It is always disappointing when one's efforts in letter-writing are not appreciated but most probably the explanation is that Tim wrote this letter in the office and had left my letter at home. The postscript is surprising: "If you like the house so much why not take it on for the whole winter?"

I gaze at Tim's postscript incredulously. Why not? Because we arranged I was to fly out to Kenya in October and spend the winter there! What does Tim mean? Is it just a sudden wild idea or does he really mean it? Does he mean I am not to go out to Kenya—and, if so, why?

Letters really are very aggravating sometimes. Especially aggravating when the writers are so far away and there is no hope of getting an explanation of a puzzle for nearly a fortnight. In a fortnight one has forgotten what one asked and the answer falls flat . . . or else, if it is something important,

112

one lives on tenterhooks for a fortnight and then finds that one's correspondent has forgotten to reply.

Very carefully I re-read Tim's letter and try to conjure up the state of mind of the writer. The letter is hastily written —that much is obvious. Perhaps it was finished with the orderly standing by, waiting to include it in the mail. Tim's letters are often finished like that. I decide to write and ask for an explanation and meantime not to worry. Tim's next letter will probably clear up the mystery.

I have just arrived at this sensible and satisfactory decision when Miss Phipps calls with my new dress. She has taken a little longer than she promised but as the garment is finished and fits me well I am pleased with Miss Phipps.

"It's just what I wanted," I tell her as I survey myself in the long mirror which is fixed to the wall in my bedroom.

"Yes," agrees Miss Phipps. "Yes, it fits nicely and the colour suits you. I thought I might have to alter it a little but there's nothing to alter. It's very satisfactory when things turn out so well. Of course you have such a good figure, Mrs. Christie. That makes it a lot easier. Some people are so difficult to fit. Take Mrs. Meller, for instance . . ."

But I have no wish to take Mrs. Meller, nor any of the other rotund clients who visit Miss Phipps, so I compliment her on her skill and tell her I shall wear the dress now and edge towards the door.

"Mrs. Meller is so fussy," continues Miss Phipps as she gathers up the paper, folds it very slowly and carefully, and packs it into the box. "You'd think a lady like that, with no figure at all, wouldn't mind very much what she looked like— I mean she could never look elegant no matter what she wore —but you've no idea the trouble she is; she brings back her things three or four times wanting them taken in here and let out there. I get quite impatient with her sometimes."

113

"What a pity!" I remark.

"Perhaps you don't know her," continues Miss Phipps. "She ought to call on you of course; she's the vicar's wife. Mrs. Barton (she was the wife of the last vicar) always called on new people. A very different sort of lady, she was. Everyone liked her—and him too. The Mellers are *not liked,*" adds Miss Phipps in significant tones.

"What a pity!" I remark. I have made this remark before but can think of nothing more appropriate.

"Then there's Miss Stroude," continues Miss Phipps as she takes a piece of string from her pocket and, very slowly and carefully, ties up the box. "Miss Stroude is much too thin to look well in nice clothes. It's an awkward angular figure, very difficult to fit. I've never had much to do for her of course —just altering things sometimes—and to tell the truth I never liked undertaking work for Miss Stroude. I remember one dress I altered for her and she was very nasty about it; she said I had spoilt it and refused to pay. It upset me dreadfully, not that I minded about the money—it was the nasty things she said. Of course I always made for Mrs. Stroude . . . and I often get things to do for Miss Crease."

Miss Phipps is a born gossip. She talks on and on, delaying her departure as long as she can. I am forced to listen to all sorts of stories about my new neighbours, some of them trivial and others scandalous in the extreme. At last however I manage to get rid of her and go out into the garden for a breath of fresh air.

The garden is "kept" by a curious gnome-like man who rejoices in the name of Abijah Rannish and comes at odd hours to do his work. Sometimes he arrives at six o'clock in the morning and I am awakened—not unpleasantly—by the whirr of the lawn mower. I have tried to make contact with him but, so far, have failed for he is a taciturn creature and avoids me whenever possible, hiding amongst the raspberry bushes when he sees me coming and, if pursued and questioned, answering with unintelligible grunts. But although he is unsatisfactory socially, he is an excellent gardener—the garden bears witness to that.

There are rows of peas and beans, there are crisp, juicy lettuces, there is a bed of asparagus (and, besides these, all the other vegetables one could ask for) and as I am extremely fond of fresh vegetables, nicely cooked, I am in clover. I like to look at them too, for to my mind a well-kept kitchen garden is entrancing and especially entrancing if it possesses a south wall with peach trees and pear trees trained upon it so that the dark brown twigs and green leaves and delicately coloured blossoms make elegant patterns. Here nature and skill mingle to produce something which is both natural and artificial but wholly delightful to the eye. Abijah's well-trained peach trees remind me of a ballet, where the natural, beautiful bodies of the dancers are trained in the artificial postures of the dance.

It is because I admire Abijah's skill and artistry that I am anxious to speak to him for it seems to me that a man who can create beauty must be interesting in himself. I want to find out about the man, to ask him where he learnt his trade, and to thank him for the pleasure I am deriving from the garden. There is nothing else I want to say; a basket of vegetables, ample for my needs, appears daily at the kitchen window and Abijah receives his pay from the owner of the house—Miss Stroude, one presumes.

Thursday, 19th July

*M*iss Crease's injunction to cut off the withered violas has disturbed my peace of mind; it is impossible to sit comfortably in the garden with the violas looking at me reproachfully from their bed. This being so, and today being cloudy and cooler, I arm myself with a basket and a pair of gardening scissors and set to work. The task is not as arduous as I expected and I am getting on quite well when the side-gate opens and Miss Carlyle appears.

Miss Carlyle is carrying a large volume under her arm (a volume which I rather suspect deals with Landscape Gardening). She hurries towards me down the path and then, as I go forward to meet her, she hesitates suddenly and stands still. I notice she is pale and breathing quickly as if something had startled her.

"Oh!" she exclaims. "Oh dear—I'm sorry! I mean I thought for a moment—but of course it was quite absurd."

"What did you think?" I ask, taking her arm and leading her to the oak seat which stands near the viola bed.

"I thought—but it was—so stupid of me."

The book which she was carrying has fallen onto the path and as I pick it up I see that it is indeed the book on Landscape Gardening.

"So stupid," she repeats. "But—but she often wore that colour—she was so fond of her violas, you know, and—and she used to pick off the withered heads. I've seen her doing it—

116

often—I used to help her sometimes. Oh dear," says Miss Carlyle, struggling to keep back her tears. "Oh dear—I don't know what you can be thinking of me—but when I saw you —and I do miss her so dreadfully." She blows her nose violently and pulls herself together. "But that's no reason why I should bother *you*, Mrs. Christie," she says valiantly. "No reason at all. I came to bring you the book on Landscape Gardening. You forgot to take it with you and I thought you might want something to read."

The matter is now explained and I forbear to offer sympathy because it is obvious she would rather I did not. Instead, I suggest tea and ask her if she will help me to make it. We go in together, set out the cups and boil the kettle. I observe with interest that Miss Carlyle is thoroughly at home in The Small House and knows exactly where everything is kept.

"Yes," she says when I comment upon the fact. "Yes, I often helped Lorna. I always felt The Small House was my spiritual home."

These words have an unfortunate association. I have always disliked them and thought them smug and self-righteous but on Miss Carlyle's lips they take a different complexion for they are uttered with innocent sincerity and express exactly what she means.

By the time tea is ready my guest has recovered her equanimity; she is ready to talk and she wants to talk about her friend.

"Lorna was so good," says Miss Carlyle. "I don't mean she was solemn and sober—she was just the reverse—but deep down beneath the surface there was a fundamental core of goodness. St. Paul says the fruits of the spirit are love, joy, peace, long-suffering, gentleness, goodness, faith. Somehow those words describe her better than any words of mine. She had absolute faith and it made her happy in spite of all the difficulties of her life. She made other people happy too. If you were feeling blue it was a tonic to see her and talk to her. Perhaps I've made her sound a prig," says Miss Carlyle. "She wasn't, of course. She was gay and amusing. We used to laugh together over silly things . . . I hope you aren't bored with all this. You *did* say you were interested in Lorna?"

"I *am* interested," I assure her. "I couldn't fail to be interested in her. The house is so beautiful and, as I told you before, I have a feeling that she likes my being here."

Miss Carlyle nods understandingly. She says, "I hope you don't mind my asking: did you get that dress from Miss Phipps?"

"Yes I did. She had the material in stock. She showed it to me and said she could make it up for me in a few days and, as I was in a hurry for something to wear, I decided to have it. Of course I didn't know—"

"Of course not," agrees Miss Carlyle. "And of course there's no reason why you shouldn't wear it. Lorna wouldn't mind."

We are silent for a few moments while the tea-cups are refilled.

"A friendship like that is an adventure," says Miss Carlyle thoughtfully. "She was so much bigger and better than I am in every way—and yet she was my friend. Nobody can take that away from me."

"Surely nobody would want to!" I exclaim.

"Miss Stroude would like to if she could," says Miss Carlyle in a low voice. "You see—but I don't want to bore you with my private affairs."

She is not boring me in the least for I am so interested in my fellow human-beings that I am practically unborable when they talk about their private affairs. I urge her to continue and at last she consents.

118

Thursday, 19th July

"I have never spoken to anyone about this, but it seems so odd that Lorna didn't mention me in her Will. I mean," says Miss Carlyle in troubled tones, "I mean—she used to talk about her Will sometimes—in a vague sort of way—but there was no Will."

"No Will?"

"Only a very old one which she made years ago when her husband died. Of course I didn't expect her to leave me anything valuable, but if she had just left me some little personal thing—a little brooch or—or something, I should have valued it so much. Of course it's very sentimental, isn't it?" adds Miss Carlyle apologetically.

"I think it's natural."

"Miss Stroude didn't think it natural. I asked Miss Stroude if she would give me some little thing that had belonged to Lorna but she refused."

"Refused?"

"It was dreadful," says Miss Carlyle in a low voice. "I couldn't tell you what she said. I suppose I had laid myself open to—to what she said—but—but it was a great shock to me."

"I hope I shall never meet that woman!"

"No," agrees Miss Carlyle with a sudden and unexpected twinkle of humour. "No, I don't think you would like her, Mrs. Christie." She rises as she speaks and says that she must go.

"Come again," I tell her as I see her off at the door. "Come whenever you like. The Small House and I will be pleased to see you."

"Really?" she asks, pausing and looking back.

"Yes, really and truly. Come and help me to pick the violas."

"I will!" she cries and runs off quickly down the path.

119

Friday, 20th July

MRS. DAULKES and the postman arrive as usual; I can hear them exchanging items of local news on the doorstep and presently Mrs. Daulkes comes in with two letters in her hand. One is from Betty, and is short but sweet; saying she is looking forward immensely to the holidays and will travel as far as London with two school friends. She can easily change and come on to Old Quinings alone. Miss Humble says it will be good for her. This relieves my mind a good deal. Miss Humble is the Head Mistress of Dinwell Hall (where Betty is at school) and what Miss Humble says is Law. There is no humility about Miss Humble. If Miss Humble says Betty is capable of changing stations in London, and travelling to Old Quinings by herself, Betty can and will carry out the manoeuvre without difficulty.

Next I turn to the other letter which is written upon hand-made paper in an unknown hand. It runs as follows:

> King William Hotel,
> London, W.
> 19th July.

Dear Madam,

Owing to the fact that my arrangements for the summer have fallen through I must ask you to vacate The Small House on 1st August. I find I shall need the house myself. I shall be in Old Quinings tomorrow morning

Friday, 20th July

and will call and see you and make the necessary arrangements about taking over the house.

Yours faithfully,
Olivia Stroude.

I can hardly believe my eyes. In fact I have to read the letter three times before I can take in its import. "Vacate The Small House on 1st August"! But how can I? Bryan and Betty are arriving next week! What am I to do? Where am I to go? I feel quite dizzy—as if the solid world were rocking beneath my feet. How can I possibly vacate the house so soon with nowhere to go? I have settled down in The Small House and although I have been here only three weeks it has begun to feel like a home. Now I am homeless again. I shall have to pack up all my belongings and leave. The prospect fills me with despair.

This sort of thing has happened to me before, of course; the wives of serving officers, who are forced to move about the world following the drum, can never be really settled. There is always the fear that people will want their own houses to live in and will give their tenants notice to leave. It has happened before and I ought to be used to it by now; but the fact is I am not used to it, Miss Stroude's letter is like a bolt from the blue . . . and Miss Stroude is coming this morning! She may be here at any moment!

Mrs. Daulkes is sympathetic but not very comforting. "Well!" she exclaims. "Isn't that just like Miss Stroude? No consideration for nobody! And you thinking you were settled 'ere till October!"

"Do you think I could persuade her to let us stay on?"

"Not Miss Stroude," replies Mrs. Daulkes. "Nobody could persuade 'er to do nothing. Very forceful, she is."

"We had better tidy up the house," I suggest.

121

Mrs. Daulkes does not take kindly to the idea, in fact she is slightly offended. She says the house is tidy already—quite tidy enough for anyone to see—and as this is perfectly true, and my suggestion was due to a feeling of panic, I smooth her ruffled feathers and retire upstairs to tidy myself.

Miss Stroude arrives shortly before eleven. I hear a car drive up to the gate and, peering from behind the dining-room curtains, I watch Miss Stroude coming up the path. Her figure is tall and angular—as Miss Phipps told me—with wide shoulders and a long neck. She is dressed in checked tweeds and a green felt hat, beneath the brim of which there juts a bony nose. I decide that I like her even less than I expected and, rushing back to the drawing room, I settle myself at the desk in the window leaving Mrs. Daulkes to open the door. A few moments later Miss Stroude walks in and glances round the room with a proprietary air.

I rise and say, "Good morning."

"Oh, good morning," she replies. "You're Mrs. Christie, I suppose. Do you mind if I pull down this blind," she adds, pulling down the blind without waiting for an answer.

"But, Miss Stroude—"

"The sunshine will fade the carpet," explains Miss Stroude. "Perhaps you will be good enough to see that the blind is drawn when the sun is strong—as it is today. Did you get my letter?"

"Yes, I got it this morning. Miss Stroude, this is going to be very difficult for me," I tell her, plunging into the speech I have prepared. "I wondered if you could possibly let me stay on here a little longer, until I can find somewhere else to go. You see I've made all my plans. I thought I could stay here until October."

"My plans have changed," replies Miss Stroude, sitting down on the sofa.

122

Friday, 20th July

"But I have nowhere to go! My son and daughter are coming here next week. How can I find other accommodation at such short notice?"

"I don't know," she replies. "I suppose you have some friends or relations who could put you up."

"Couldn't we stay until the end of August? That would give me time—"

"No, I'm afraid not."

"I like the house so much—"

"Mrs. Christie," says Miss Stroude firmly. "I didn't come here to argue with you. I came to make arrangements for taking over the house on the first of August. I can't help it if it causes you inconvenience to move. The Small House belongs to me and I intend to live here."

There is no more to be said so I say nothing.

"I shall send a man to take the inventory," she informs me. "I shall be obliged if you will give him every facility. The representative of the Electricity Board will call and read the meter. The house must be thoroughly cleaned, of course. I have engaged my own charwoman to do that. . . ."

Miss Stroude continues to enumerate the various arrangements she has made—most comprehensive arrangements— and I realise that, whatever else she may be, she is extraordinarily capable.

"There are some boxes in the attic," says Miss Stroude at last. "Would you have any objection if I went upstairs and looked through them?"

"No, of course not," I reply.

"They are full of papers," she explains. "When my step-mother died I put all her private papers away and I have a feeling there may be a valuable letter amongst them." Miss Stroude takes a bunch of keys from her bag and adds scornfully, "My step-mother was very unbusinesslike."

123

There is no need to conduct Miss Stroude upstairs to her own attic and this is fortunate for I am so shaky about the knees that it is doubtful if I could. I stand in the hall and watch her disappear from view and, as I do so, it crosses my mind that if by chance Miss Stroude should fall and injure herself severely I should not feel very sorry about it. In fact, such is my unchristian frame of mind, I should be quite pleased. Naturally I would do what I could to render first aid; I would ring up the doctor and arrange for the unfortunate lady to be removed to the hospital . . . but Miss Stroude is not likely to do anything so foolish as to fall down her own stairs, her character is much too well regulated.

Miss Stroude has no sooner vanished than the door into the back premises opens and Mrs. Daulkes announces in guarded tones that there is a cup of tea waiting for me in the kitchen.

"I wasn't going to give 'er tea," explains Mrs. Daulkes, as she drags the basket-chair up to the table and settles me in it comfortably. "'Orrible old cat—as ugly as a root—and no lady!"

It is always pleasant to hear somebody else voicing one's own opinions and this, combined with strong tea, helps me to recover.

"Impudent thing!" continues Mrs. Daulkes. "When I 'eard 'er say 'the house must be thoroughly cleaned' it was all I could do to keep silent." (Mrs. Daulkes quotes the unforgivable words in accents which are so like those of Miss Stroude that in spite of my agitation I can hardly help smiling.) "The very idea!" exclaims Mrs. Daulkes. "She's engaged old Mrs. Kempton to come 'ere and clean up after *me!*"

Obviously there is no need to give Mrs. Daulkes any information about my interview with Miss Stroude. She has heard all—whether because the walls of The Small House are thinner than I thought or because she happened to be polishing the floor in the hall while the interview was in progress.

"You're too soft, that's what," says Mrs. Daulkes. "You didn't ought to 'ave let 'er go up to the attic. 'Ow do we know what she's doing?"

"She's looking for something."

"But 'ow do we know she won't take something and then say we've stolen it?" enquires Mrs. Daulkes.

This seems unlikely to me for, although I disliked Miss Stroude intensely, I cannot see her stooping to such Machiavellianism.

"You're too soft," repeats Mrs. Daulkes. "You're too much of a lady to deal with 'ussies like 'er; it needs a gentleman. If you take my advice, you'll go and telephone to the General straight off."

"He couldn't do anything," I object.

"You'd wonder," replies Mrs. Daulkes. "The General knows what's what. 'E'd get 'er out of that attic in double-quick time."

Already it has become a habit to take the advice of Mrs. Daulkes and this piece of advice chimes with my inclination. Tony is a tower of strength and even if he can do nothing to help me it will be comforting to hear his voice.

"Straight off," says Mrs. Daulkes eagerly. "You go into the dining room and telephone and I'll keep guard in the 'all; just in case 'er 'ighness comes down before you've finished."

The manoeuvre is carried out and after a period of waiting, which seems like hours, I find myself in communication with Tony.

"Hullo, Hester," he says. "How are things going?"

Somewhat incoherently I plunge into an explanation of all that has happened. "I know you can't do anything," I tell him. "Nobody can. It's quite silly to bother you like this. It

125

was Mrs. Daulkes really. She said to ring you up . . . and of course I wanted to. She's so beastly, Tony—I mean Miss Stroude—and we don't know what she's doing in the attic."

"Don't panic," says Tony firmly.

"I'm not panicking," I reply hysterically. "It's just—the idea of packing up—and where are we to go? Bryan and Betty will be—"

"Listen," says Tony. "Will you stop panicking and listen! I'm coming *now*. I shall be there in ten minutes—not much more, anyhow. Keep the woman until I come."

"Keep the woman?"

"Keep Miss Stroude. Don't let her go until I've seen her."

"But how can I?"

"Make some excuse—any excuse—but hold onto her until I come."

"But, Tony—"

"Lock her in the attic if necessary."

The line is cut off suddenly and I realise that Tony has replaced the receiver and is on his way. This is such a cheering and encouraging thought that I am able to giggle feebly over his parting words; the idea of imprisoning that masterful woman in her own attic is ludicrous in the extreme. Tony has not seen her, of course, and unless one had seen her and felt the weight of her personality one could not appreciate the joke.

Unfortunately—or perhaps fortunately—there is no chance of trying out the desperate expedient for when I emerge from the dining room Miss Stroude is coming downstairs.

"I can't find it," complains Miss Stroude. "I've looked through two boxes and I haven't time to do more today. You haven't seen it, I suppose? It's a grey cardboard folder with some letters in it."

I reply that I have not seen it.

Friday, 20th July

"Valuable letters," says Miss Stroude. "There's a letter from Lord Byron to Mrs. Stroude's grandfather—and several others. It's most annoying. I particularly wanted the Byron letter because I know somebody who would buy it. Are you sure you haven't seen the folder anywhere?"

The question is asked in such a disagreeable way that it makes me angry and I reply that I have not looked through Miss Stroude's private papers.

"I know that," she replies. "The boxes are locked; but my step-mother was very careless and the folder might have been lying about anywhere. Of course she ought to have had the letters framed or put them in the safe. I've told her so, often."

Miss Stroude is putting on her gloves as she speaks.

"Don't go, Miss Stroude," I say impulsively.

She looks at me in surprise.

"You must be tired," I suggest. "Perhaps you would like a glass of sherry and a biscuit."

"I never drink wine," she replies, moving towards the door.

"Do come and sit down for a few minutes."

"I am going to lunch with some friends," says Miss Stroude firmly. "I shall come back another day and look through the other boxes. You have no objection I suppose?"

"No, but—but I want to show you something."

"What?" she asks, fixing me with a baleful stare.

"It's—it's the shelf in the pantry."

"What about the shelf?"

"Would you mind looking at it?" I enquire.

Obviously she minds a good deal but she has no option in the matter. I conduct her to the pantry and indicate the shelf.

127

"You see, it's loose," I explain, moving it up and down to prove my point.

Miss Stroude examines the shelf and says she can see nothing whatever the matter with it (which, as a matter of fact, is not surprising). "The shelf is meant to be loose," explains Miss Stroude. "The idea is you can take it out and wash it."

"What a clever idea!" I exclaim.

Miss Stroude looks at me with a curious expression upon her disagreeable countenance. I can see she thinks I am unfit to be loose. She has taken off her gloves to examine the shelf but now resumes them in a determined manner.

"You ought to do something about the dining-room table," I tell her earnestly. "It's wood-worm, I think."

"Wood-worm?"

"Yes—and it might spread to the other furniture if it isn't taken in time. We had a furnished house some years ago and all the furniture was riddled with wood-worm. It just fell to pieces, bit by bit."

This tragic story happens to be perfectly true but Miss Stroude is unmoved by it. She makes for the door, saying that she will have the furniture examined by a competent person when she regains possession of her house. I pursue her making various suggestions to delay her departure: would she like to wash her hands after groping about in the dusty attic? Would she like a few flowers from the garden? Miss Stroude does not bother to reply. She marches down the path, opens the door of her car and gets in.

"Miss Stroude," I cry, following and laying my hand on the door. "Miss Stroude, don't go."

"Mrs. Christie," says Miss Stroude. "I don't know what the idea is. Either you are trying to make a fool of me or else you are an extremely stupid woman, but it doesn't really matter. What *does* matter is that you vacate my house by mid-day on the first of August."

This pronouncement is merited so I cannot really complain, and I am so crushed and confused that I can say nothing in self-defence, nor can I think of any other delaying action. Miss Stroude starts up her engine and lets in her clutch.

At this moment a large shiny car approaches rapidly over the bumpy road and draws up close behind her. The road (as has been said before) is narrow and has no turning so the arrival of the newcomer blocks Miss Stroude's exit. She looks round in annoyance, and signals with her hand.

Tony immediately gets out of his car and approaches. "You must be Miss Stroude, I think," he says with a friendly smile. "My name is Morley. I was hoping to see you this morning."

"Please move your car so that I can back," says Miss Stroude.

"You aren't going away!"

"Please move your car, Mr. Morley."

"Presently," replies Tony cheerfully. "All in good time. There's no hurry, is there?"

"I am in a hurry," replies Miss Stroude.

"But before you go I want to speak to you. I should like to understand what arrangements have been made about the house."

"I have explained everything to Mrs. Christie."

"Please explain everything to me," says Tony politely.

During this exchange I have remained dumb, for I am aware that when Tony takes charge it is better not to interfere, but now I feel that I can make a small contribution to define the situation.

"Miss Stroude wants us to move out of her house on the first of August," I explain. "It's very inconvenient but it can't be helped."

"What about the lease?" asks Tony, looking puzzled.

"All this is no business of yours," declares Miss Stroude. "The matter is between Mrs. Christie and me. I have told her she must move and I have arranged everything with her. I don't know who you are nor why you imagine you can interfere in the matter. I suppose I have the right to live in my own house if I want to?"

"Not if you have let it to someone else," says Tony.

Miss Stroude looks at him down her long nose and Tony looks back at her.

"I suppose there is a legal contract, isn't there?" enquires Tony sweetly.

These innocent words are like a beam of light in a dark cellar . . . for of course there is a contract, an extremely imposing document made by Miss Stroude's own lawyer and signed by Fred Bollings on my behalf. The document is inscribed upon thick white paper, tied with pink tape, and contains all sorts of alarming and bewildering phrases such as "the party hereinafter mentioned" and "the lessee shall hold herself responsible . . ." This document was handed to me by Fred Bollings on my arrival and, after reading it through, I returned it to him and it was stowed away in his safe at the Bull and Bush. I have every reason to believe the document is still there amongst various other papers and valuables belonging to my two good friends.

My feelings are such a mixture of relief and rage and shame that I feel quite faint and am unable to follow the remainder of the conversation between Tony and Miss Stroude; in fact I do not come to myself until the two cars have

130

manoeuvred successfully and Miss Stroude's Morris is disappearing round the corner.

"Aren't you a little goat!" says Tony, taking my arm and walking me up the path.

I agree humbly that I am.

"I suppose there *is* a proper lease?"

"Yes, there is."

"I had to take a chance on that, but the moment I mentioned the word she crumpled up and there was no more spirit left in her—just like the Queen of Sheba."

"Do you think she had forgotten about the lease?"

"Goodness no, she's much too cute. Miss Stroude wasn't born yesterday. She was just trying to bounce you."

"She did bounce me," I reply. "I'm so angry about it—angry with her and angry with myself for being such a fool—that I feel quite ill. What do you think will happen now?"

"Nothing will happen," says Tony confidently. "You will stay on at The Small House until your lease is up. If she tries any more tricks we'll consult a lawyer, but she won't. You needn't worry."

Mrs. Daulkes greets us with beaming smiles and it is obvious that, once again, her domestic duties have not interfered with her pleasures.

"That Miss Stroude, with 'er long nose!" exclaims Mrs. Daulkes.

"Yes, her nose is a misfortune," agrees Tony.

"Ugly as a root," declares Mrs. Daulkes. "I said it once and I'll say it again. That's what she is—ugly—inside and out."

" 'What I tell you three times is true,' " murmurs Tony, quoting from a well-known classic.

"But you were a match for 'er," says Mrs. Daulkes admiringly. "I knew you'd send 'er packing. I said as much to Mrs. Christie. You telephone to the General, I said. It takes a gentleman to deal with that sort, I said. You telephone straight off."

"Your advice was sound," Tony assures her gravely.

"Lor!" exclaims Mrs. Daulkes, chuckling. "I never was so pleased as when I saw 'er go off with 'er tail between 'er legs!"

Saturday, 21st July

MRS. DAULKES brings Eric with her this morning because the lady who lives next door (and who usually minds Eric while her neighbour is at work) has had to go to Wandlebury to the dentist. I have heard a great deal about Eric who, according to his mother, is unusually intelligent and extremely amusing and altogether quite different in every way from other children of two and a half years old, so naturally I am looking forward to making his acquaintance.

Eric is a large child, ludicrously like his mother in appearance; his complexion is red and brown and he has the same coarse, springy hair which stands up all over his head. He is neatly dressed in a blue and white check shirt and brown corduroy shorts, white socks and brown sandals.

"This is Eric," says Mrs. Daulkes, pushing her youngest forward to be admired. "Now Eric, remember what I told you. Say, 'Ow d'you do, Mrs. Christie,' like a good boy."

Eric looks up at me gravely with two large brown eyes and says something—a much longer peroration than that indicated by his parent but absolutely unintelligible to me.

"Don't 'e speak clear!" exclaims his mother proudly.

The honest answer to this enquiry would be yes and no. Eric certainly speaks in ringing tones; he opens his mouth and enunciates the sounds he utters with exaggerated movements of his lips and tongue. One feels one ought to be able to understand every word.

"Thag moo wa, effy ammy dee," says Eric clearly.

Mrs. Daulkes smiles fondly at her offspring. "Eric's not a bit shy," she declares. " 'E'll speak to anyone. The others never would say a word to nobody when they were little. I was telling Jim about—"

"Ammy oo!" exclaims Eric with spirit. "Um ya oo tocky effy bim, thag wim foo!"

"Oh, Lor', isn't 'e a scream!" cries Mrs. Daulkes laughing heartily.

I laugh too; partly because it is obviously the right reaction and partly because I am genuinely amused. Eric's speech is like the "baby talk" of a well-known infant who does his stuff on the radio and whose remarks are interpreted by his elder sister. It is a little unfortunate that Eric has no such interpreter but it can't be helped. I feel it would wound Mrs. Daulkes if I asked for an interpretation of her son's remarks.

"Ya oo," observes Eric, looking up with large innocent eyes. "Effy wa olly bim tocky thag?"

"No, you can't, then," says Mrs. Daulkes firmly.

"Gammy ya ug. Tecky lum wimmy oy!"

"Now that's enough," says Mrs. Daulkes. "There's a limit. I'm sure I don't know what Mrs. Christie will think if you go on like that."

"Mee ug ya tocky foo wa ya!" replies her son defiantly.

"Now, Eric," says Mrs. Daulkes. "What did I tell you? I told you if I brought you to The Small 'Ouse you was to be'ave yourself proper. If I 'ave any more of your lip I'll take you straight 'ome—you see if I don't."

"Tammy goth!" objects Eric in no way cast down by his mother's threat. "Oo ga effy tocky thee wa tig moddy boo."

"Eric!"

"Gammy og, tag oddy bee thag woo."

"All right then, but I've got to get on," says Mrs. Daulkes

nodding. "You're going to be good, aren't you?" And seizing him up with a swing of her strong arms she dumps him into the basket-chair which stands near the kitchen window. "You can sit there and watch me wash up the breakfast dishes," she adds.

"Goo wa dee effy thag—ammy boo."

"I daresay, but you'll do as you're told. Mrs. Christie doesn't want *you* running all over the 'ouse and p'raps falling down the stairs. You sit there and talk to me like a good boy."

I leave them chatting happily and go upstairs to make my bed.

After a few minutes Mrs. Daulkes comes after me and says a young man has called and wants to see me.

"A young man?"

"A well set-up young feller," declares Mrs. Daulkes. "A bit pale 'e is; int'resting-looking (if you know what I mean), dark wavy 'air and brown eyes—and very nicely spoken. Quite the gentleman, 'e is. I mean 'e's not selling brushes nor nothing."

I can think of no young man of my acquaintance answering to this description.

"There now, I should 'ave asked 'is name," says Mrs. Daulkes penitently. "I never thought of it. I'll go and ask 'im."

But somehow I feel it is too late to remedy the omission, so I leave my bed half-made and go downstairs myself.

The young man is a complete stranger; he conforms in all ways to Mrs. Daulkes's description and although his clothes are a trifle shabby he is definitely "quite the gentleman."

When I go in he is standing at the window, looking out into the garden; but he turns at once and, smiling rather shyly, says he hopes I will forgive such an early call. "I wanted to thank you for all the trouble you've taken," he explains.

The most sensible thing to do would be to ask him who he is, but I have a vague feeling I have seen him before and

135

ought to know him, so I let the moment pass. Sooner or later he is sure to say something which will clear up the mystery of his identity.

"This is a delightful house," says my visitor. "I do love these big windows. I wish we could find a house of our own and settle down comfortably, but they're very difficult to find."

"Very difficult," I reply.

By this time we are sitting down; he has chosen to sit upon the cretonne-covered window-seat and he sits sideways so that he can see the garden. Abijah Rannish is mowing the lawn and this gives us a subject of conversation. We discuss Abijah and I detail his peculiarities to my guest. I tell him about the beauties of the kitchen garden and about the peach trees trained like ballet dancers against the soft pink brick of the south wall and my guest listens intelligently and understands exactly what I mean in a most satisfactory way. All this is pleasant and agreeable, but it is getting me no further and I realise I have been a fool. It is far too late now to ask the young man his name.

"Oh!" he exclaims, his eye lighting upon the copy of *Doctor Thorne* which is lying upon the little table beside him. "Oh, what a beautiful edition! May I look at it?"

"Yes, of course."

"Is it yours?" he asks, taking it up in his long slender hands and opening it.

"I wish it were," I reply. "It belongs to Mrs. Stroude—or rather it used to belong to her—but I don't think she would mind my reading it."

"Books are meant to be read. They like being read," says my visitor seriously. "I always feel sorry for books that are too valuable to be read—books with uncut pages. I'm sure they would rather be just ordinary so that ordinary people could read them."

136

Saturday, 21st July

This is my own feeling exactly and I tell him so. I tell him also that I am renewing an old friendship with *Doctor Thorne* and enjoying the experience.

"You like it better than before?" he enquires.

"Yes, it seems better when you read the story in a nice old-fashioned book with good thick paper and large clear print . . . and look at the pictures! Aren't they entrancing? Look at this one of Frank and Miss Dunstable having fun together and Lady de Courcy looking on disapprovingly! And here's one of Mr. Gazebee proposing to the Lady Augusta in a delicate manner!"

We look at the pictures together; we discuss the plot. I discover that, although I have read the novel several times and am in the midst of reading it again, my visitor knows a great deal more about it than I. He talks about it with authority and insight and is especially interesting upon the subject of Doctor Thorne. In fact he talks about the doctor as though he were a real person, known and loved and admired. Doctor Thorne is an old-fashioned practitioner but he has the right ideas. My new friend's ambition is to be the modern counterpart of Doctor Thorne with all the new and exciting discoveries of science to help him.

"Specialisation is all very well," says my new friend earnestly. "Of course we must have specialists, but the first symptoms of disease are difficult to diagnose and unless they can be diagnosed early there is much less hope of a cure. This means we must have enough doctors with a broad knowledge of medicine . . ." He stops suddenly and laughs. "I get all worked up when I talk about it," he says apologetically. "The fact is it's all so interesting and exciting to me that I can't help feeling it must be interesting to other people. Medicine is an adventure, it's a fight against the dragon of disease. Do you know Tenniel's picture of the boy fighting the Jabberwock?"

"Of course I do! 'Beware the Jabberwock, my son! The jaws that bite, the claws that catch!' "

"That's it!" cries the modern knight-errant, half-laughing and half-serious. "That's how I see the modern doctor."

Fortunately there is a copy of *Alice* in Mrs. Stroude's book-case. We find the picture and together we chant the inimitable verses:

> "One, two! One, two! And through and through
>   The vorpal blade went snicker-snack!
> He left it dead, and with its head
> He went galumphing back."

"Gorgeous, isn't it?" cries my new friend delightedly. "Gorgeous stuff! Wait till I get my vorpal blade sharpened— then off to the tulgey wood—and let the Jabberwock beware!"

We laugh together over the nonsense, but even as we laugh I am aware that it is not nonsense at all, but something fine and wonderful, and that this young man has dedicated himself like a knight of old to the service of his fellow human-beings in distress.

Presently Mrs. Daulkes comes in with a tray of coffee and biscuits and I realise it must be eleven o'clock. This brings me to my senses. I have been chatting to my new friend for nearly an hour and still I have no idea who he is. He must be about twenty-five; too old to be a friend of Bryan's and too young to be a friend of Tim's. Could I have met him in London during the hectic week which I spent with Richard and Mary? Could I have met him abroad? Have I *ever* met him—and, if not, how does he know me?

My visitor accepts a cup of coffee. The elation produced by "Jabberwocky" has vanished and we converse sanely and sensibly.

"We're very comfortable," he says. "It's a fascinating

old place, isn't it? Of course you know it well. Parts of the house must date from the sixteenth century, I should think. I love that cobbled yard, it makes one think of coaches clattering up to the door and ostlers running out to change the horses. My room is in the old part of the house and has walls at least three feet thick which makes it very quiet. There's a sort of peaceful, safe feeling about old houses, isn't there?"

"Yes—yes there is."

"I find I can work much better," he adds, stirring his coffee thoughtfully.

I gaze at my friend with dawning comprehension.

"You see, Mrs. Christie," he continues confidentially. "You see it really is frightfully important for me to get an honours degree and unfortunately I'm not particularly clever. I have to work hard. Some fellows seem to pass exams without any bother," says my new friend ruefully. "Some fellows seem to absorb knowledge like a sponge. Some fellows can work anywhere or in any conditions. I've seen people reading anatomy with the wireless going full blast. It's absolutely amazing. Gosh, I wish I could!" he adds with a sigh.

"I'm glad you find you can work—now," I tell him. It was on the tip of my tongue to say I was glad he found conditions favourable at the Bull and Bush, but I am still not quite certain.

"Oh yes," he replies. "Yes, they're most awfully good to me, especially Mrs. Bollings. She is a dear, isn't she? I really was getting desperate; you can't shut yourself up and work in other people's houses. What I wanted to do was to go off to Cornwall with a friend, but of course Mother didn't want me to do that."

"But it's all right now?" I ask anxiously; for the fact is I have become very anxious indeed that the vorpal blade should be sharpened.

"Yes," he says; but he says it a trifle doubtfully. "Yes. The only thing is I wish Mother would—I mean I wish she wouldn't *worry* about me."

"I expect it's difficult."

"Terribly difficult. Mother means so well but she doesn't quite understand. She thinks I ought to have set hours and stick to them, and perhaps she's right, but somehow I can't do it that way. People are different, aren't they?"

"Of course they are."

"She thinks I'm working now," says Mrs. Alston's son with a conspiratorial air.

It is a little difficult to find the right comment. "But you can't stick to set hours," I suggest, for as these are practically his own words it seems fairly safe to repeat them.

"No," he agrees frowning. "No, I can't. I was reading until nearly three this morning and I felt I couldn't start in again directly after breakfast. But I don't always do that. Sometimes I go to bed early and go out for a walk before breakfast and then settle down and read. I believe that's the best, really . . ." He smiles suddenly and charmingly. "It *is* good of you to listen to all this," says Edmond Alston, rising to go.

"But I've enjoyed it!"

"I know—that's what makes it so marvellous. I feel tons better. I shall go galumphing back and wade into those books. You know, Mrs. Christie, I really came just to say 'thank you' and I've stayed hours."

He walks down the path and then hesitates and comes back. "There's just one thing," he says. "I wondered . . . there's a girl who rides. I don't suppose you know her, do you?"

"A girl who rides?"

"Rides a horse," says Edmond Alston nodding and looking at me anxiously. "With fair hair—I mean the girl has fair

140

hair. I've seen her twice. She rides in the early morning before breakfast. Yesterday I opened a gate for her and she said thank you."

This seems quite natural to me (mere common politeness) but it is obvious from Edmond's manner that he thinks otherwise.

"With fair hair?" I ask in a thoughtful voice.

"Yes," he says, warming to his theme. "Slender and straight with hazel eyes and a halo of golden curls."

"Are you sure it wasn't an angel?"

Edmond laughs a trifle self-consciously.

"I *might* know her," I tell him. "I'm not sure, of course, but I think I might be able to find her."

"Mrs. Christie, you are a brick! Honestly—I mean—"

"Away with you," I tell him, laughing. "I'll see what I can do. I'll send you a message through Mrs. Bollings if I can find your angel for you."

Sunday, 22nd July

MISS CARLYLE has not forgotten her promise to come and help me to pick the violas. She arrives after lunch, when I have just settled myself comfortably in the garden to read. I have now moved my garden chair to the other side of the lawn beneath the shade of a smaller but no less beautiful beech. Here I am out of sight of Miss Crease if she happens to look out of her bedroom window. Miss Carlyle comments on the change and says Lorna Stroude always sat here—not under the other tree. She adds that if I will lend her a basket she will start on the violas at once.

I remonstrate with Miss Carlyle, for not only is this the hottest time of the day but the mere idea of stooping and bending immediately after my mid-day meal gives me indigestion.

Miss Carlyle says she forgot I was used to the tropics where, of course, everyone rests in the middle of the day. "What an interesting life you must have had!" she exclaims, sitting down on the grass and looking at me with her bright eager eyes. "You have seen so much of the world and met so many different kinds of people. I often wish I could travel. Epictetus said 'you are a citizen of the world, and a part of it,' but how can one be a part of the world unless one can travel and see it for oneself?"

"Lots of people travel and see nothing," I tell her.

Sunday, 22nd July

"Oh, I know . . . 'eyes have they and see not,' " she agrees.

My one idea at the moment is to keep my visitor sitting beside me, for if she rises and begins her task I shall be obliged to join her. It would be impossible to remain sitting comfortably in the shade and watch my visitor at work. This being so I begin to speak of my travels and my life in Kenya, hoping to keep her happy and interested so that she will forget about the violas until I have digested my lunch.

The experiment succeeds. Miss Carlyle is a very good listener (a quality which I had not expected to find in a schoolmistress). She listens entranced: not interrupting when I am in full flow but encouraging me with intelligent questions when the fount begins to run dry. I am no polished raconteuse but with such an audience hanging upon my words I gain confidence and burble on happily.

I discover that Miss Carlyle knows all the facts already, and knows them better than I. Her brain is stored with facts about Kenya. She knows about the warm damp climate of the coast and the high dry plains of the interior; she knows about the great glaciers of Mount Kenya and the tropical forests surrounding Lake Victoria. (She knows the height of the former and the area of the latter which I did not know, myself.) She knows what Kenya produces and what it exports, and she knows all about the animals and birds and plants. What she does not know is the feel of the place and the hundred and one unimportant details which make up the life of its inhabitants. What she wants to know is the effect of the place upon me.

Lying back in my chair I shut my eyes to the cosy English garden and conjure up a land so different that it scarcely seems real. It is a land of contrasts and paradoxes; there is brilliant golden sunshine and drenching silver rain; rain which

143

falls from the lowering skies in a solid mass of water and changes every little wandering stream into a rushing torrent. There are bare plains and undulating hills; there are mountains which cut the bright blue sky with their jagged contours. There are forests and jungles full of strange lush plants and teeming with beasts and birds, silent by day but waking in the darkness so that in the vast velvety stillness you can hear their eerie cries echoing through the night: the roar of a lion, the shrill scream of its prey and a hundred other voices. And in the night sky there are thousands of millions of stars, bright as diamonds. There are parts of Kenya which in an odd way remind me of the Border Country of Scotland, rolling hills of greenish-brownish grass with sheep grazing . . . but the shepherd-boys destroy the illusion for they are as brown as well-polished mahogany and scantily attired in brightly coloured rags.

The bungalow where Tim and I lived was long and low, set in a garden full of strange plants and gorgeous flowers, but we had our kitchen-garden too, and I never got used to the sight of a line of peas and homely cabbages and other familiar vegetables fraternising with the paw paw and the avocado pear. The black boys, who looked after us and made our life comfortable and leisurely, were warm and friendly children. They wore long white robes from neck to ankle and padded about noiselessly on their bare, black feet. When one spoke to them they smiled happily displaying their beautiful teeth, which looked so much whiter in contrast with their shining black faces.

Miss Carlyle is interested to hear that they spoke English fluently. Their accents and the rhythm of their speech was lilting and pleasant to the ear.

By this time I am beginning to feel like Scheherazade who was obliged to amuse the Sultan Schahriah with a thousand and one tales and my sympathy for that beautiful, talented creature—always strong—is considerably strengthened.

Miss Carlyle is insatiable. "Tell me about Nairobi," she says eagerly. "What does it look like?"

So I tell her about Nairobi, about the European part of the town with its wide streets and fine buildings and shops and parks . . . and I describe the native quarter which is dirty and squalid with little wooden shacks full to overflowing with black families. In front of these shacks, which open onto the street, you may sometimes see a charcoal fire burning and women cooking a meal. Old grandmothers sit by these fires, smoking clay pipes, and there are dozens of black naked babies rolling about in the dust. These people wear every sort of garment without regard to age or sex; you may see women with long hair, wearing nothing but a pair of trousers, and men wearing nothing but a shirt. I remember seeing a boy of about fourteen wearing nothing but a child's pinafore—his back view was very funny indeed—and I remember seeing an old black man with a white beard, wearing a girl's summer frock—quite a pretty pink and white frock with short sleeves and a flared skirt. He had very thin black legs and very large black feet and he was carrying a large black umbrella to shield him from the sun.

The afternoon wears on. The shadows of the beech trees move slowly across the lawn and still we go on talking. By special request I am now calling my new friend "Anne." This seems quite natural to me, for although she is probably a good deal older than myself she seems younger (she seems virginal, which perhaps is a strange word to describe a middle-aged school-mistress but I can find no other). Anne, I notice, has considerable difficulty in calling me "Hester" and avoids the use of my name.

Anne is an enigma to me. She is not really my kind of

person and her life has been entirely different from mine. Obviously she is very clever indeed—Tim would dub her a blue-stocking and flee from her in terror—but beneath the slightly pedantic manner I have discovered a very human person; a lonely person, brave and proud and humble, and I find myself warming to her more and more.

It is now Anne's turn to talk and I question her about her work. She tells me about the children and repeats some of the funny things they say.

"Some of them have no background," she explains. "They know nothing but what they learn at school; I try to give them a little general knowledge but it is not easy. The other day I was informed that an osteopath was a curious bird with a long bill."

"Rather a neat definition!"

Anne smiles and says, "But not the one I wanted . . . so then I asked if anyone could tell me any more about the osteopath. Winnie Seager said it had long legs and could run very fast, and Tom Rogers said it waited for you behind a tree in the jungle and sprang on your back and twisted your neck! Someone else objected strongly to the statement, saying, 'A bird ain't got no 'ands, so 'ow could it twist your neck?' Some children said it was a 'griller' others declared it was 'all over spots' . . . possibly they were confusing it with an ocelot," says Anne. "By the time we had finished, and all had said their say, the osteopath had become real and horrible to me—half-bird and half-animal with a long bill and skinny arms and a spotted hide. I could have drawn its picture. Of course I should not have let them do it; I should have stopped them at once," says Anne with a rueful smile. "But one must have a little fun sometimes or one would go mad."

"Some of the children are much brighter than others, I suppose?"

146

"They vary tremendously, not only because some are naturally more intelligent than others but also because they have better homes."

"Do many of them come from that huddle of old homes down near the river?"

Anne looks at me in surprise. "You've been there? Many people live here for years without knowing anything about that dreadful place . . . Yes, I mean dreadful. All sorts of horrible things emanate from that huddle of houses."

"You mean disease?"

Anne does not reply. Obviously she is unwilling to continue, but I have no intention of quitting the subject until I have got to the bottom of it. At last Anne is persuaded to explain.

"Well, if you must know," she says, "there are people in that old village who practise witch-craft."

"Witch-craft! But that's nonsense!" I exclaim.

"You felt there was something evil there, didn't you?" she asks.

"Yes, but—"

"Why should you find it incredible? The power of evil is as real as the power of good. There is constant warfare between them."

"But you don't really believe in witch-craft, Anne!"

She hesitates and then says, "I think we're talking about different things. Of course I don't believe in witches riding on broomsticks and turning themselves into hares, but I do believe that people can get into touch with evil forces."

"Black magic?"

"You can call it that."

"What do they do?" I ask.

"Nothing very spectacular," she admits. "But that isn't the point. The point is that these people are wicked and exert

147

an evil influence. Even if they aren't really in league with evil powers they think they are, which is almost as bad."

"But you believe they really are!"

Anne does not answer this. She says, "Whether or not I believe it doesn't matter. My responsibility is the children. If I can teach them to know God and serve Him faithfully He will give them the power to tread upon scorpions. It is a tremendous responsibility but I am sustained by the knowledge that I am led by God's hand."

Anne looks up at me as she speaks. Her eyes are clear and steadfast and she is absolutely unself-conscious. How few of us can speak of such things without self-consciousness!

"Go on," I tell her, nodding encouragingly.

"I don't know what else to say," she declares, hugging her knees and looking across the garden. "My life has made me what I am. It hasn't been easy, sometimes I have found it almost unbearable, but suffering can be transmuted into strength—as a rod is tempered by passing through a furnace —and all my hard work, all my anxieties and failures and disappointments have made me what I am. When the rod is tempered it has to be polished and made fit for service . . . everything that happens as one goes through life helps to polish the rod. If I didn't feel sure of that I couldn't go on; I couldn't face the future."

My own life seems aimless in comparison with Anne's philosophy. I have worstled through without any clear idea of where I am going. I have not been trained for any special purpose, nor do I feel that I am being used.

Anne smiles when I tell her this: "Of course you're being used," she says. "Your life has certainly been more pleasant than mine but rods can be polished in different ways and no two are alike."

"You and I are certainly very different!" I exclaim. "You're so clever and intelligent. Your brain is so—so tidy compared with mine."

Most people would have protested that this was not so and assured me that I was mistaken; but Anne, unlike most people, is absolutely sincere. She looks at me thoughtfully and says, "Your mind is undisciplined and untrained but that doesn't mean you are unintelligent."

This is true, of course. I know quite well that my mind is undisciplined and untrained, but it gives me a shock to hear the fact stated so frankly, and while I am recovering from the shock Anne goes on to say that it would be interesting to ascertain the level of my intelligence and to propose that she shall bring a book upon psychology (which she uses to grade the intelligence of her pupils) and put me through a test.

The proposal does not appeal to me at all and I say so uncompromisingly.

"But why?" asks Anne in surprise. "It would be very interesting. As a matter of fact I feel sure that your intelligence is well above the average."

"Perhaps it is and perhaps it isn't," I reply mulishly.

My visitor does her best to persuade me but without success and at last I am obliged to explain my reasons for my refusal to co-operate in the experiment. I explain my reasons as follows: if Anne discovers my intelligence to be above average she will endeavour to educate me by lending me large volumes (like the volume upon Landscape Gardening) which are unsuitable for reading in bed, and by refusing to allow me to read *The Body in the Cupboard* and other books of that ilk which I find pleasant and soothing; on the other hand, if she discovers my intelligence to be below average she will despise me for evermore. I add with absolute finality, "No, Anne, I will not be weighed and measured and put into a pigeonhole. It's better for both of us that I should remain an enigma."

She looks at me for a moment in blank amazement and then bursts out laughing. "Oh dear, you are so good for me!" she exclaims.

Tuesday, 24th July

*A*T LAST a suitable day has been found for the long-promised expedition to Wandlebury. Tony calls for me after lunch and off we go at breath-taking speed. I enquire why Tony is driving so much faster than usual.

"But I'm not," he replies in surprise. "I always drive fast when I want to get anywhere—you ought to know that."

Wandlebury is a small country town; there is a large square with a fountain in the middle and all round this square there are buildings of various degrees of antiquity. On one side there is a very ancient coaching inn called the Apollo and Boot with all the usual stables and outhouses attached; on another side stand the County Buildings and on the other two sides there are shops.

Tony parks Belshazzar in the square and announces cheerfully that he is perfectly free this afternoon and will accompany me on my shopping expedition and carry my basket. It is very kind of him. I have a feeling that I should get on much better alone, but nothing can be done about it.

The first item on my list is a pair of thick brown walking-shoes. I explain this to my companion and he replies that he knows the very place where these can be obtained and leads me across the square.

The shop is long and narrow and rather dark; there are no other customers in it but at the far end there are two girls, knitting jumpers and talking to one another earnestly the while. They pay no attention to us and, after waiting for a few moments, Tony takes the matter into his own hands.

"Sit down, Madame," he says gravely. "It was walking-shoes you wanted? I think we have just what you require."

The shelves are stacked with white boxes from floor to ceiling and Tony prowls around, taking them down and reading the lables aloud. "Glacé pumps . . . red and white strollers. Would you like to stroll, Hester? Beach sandals . . . satin slippers . . . green mules. I should hate to see a green mule so we won't open that box. Hullo, this is more like it! Brown laced shoes! Do you take size three?"

"Four and a half," I reply.

"How annoying of you!" exclaims Tony, throwing the box onto the floor, where already there is a pile of opened boxes and shoes of all sorts and sizes which he has discarded in his search. "How *very* annoying—but never mind, we'll keep on trying. You wouldn't like a navy and white court shoe, I suppose?" asks Tony, holding it up elegantly between his fingers and thumb.

"Could you recommend it for walking in a muddy country lane?"

"Well—frankly—no," says Tony sadly. "And, as a matter of fact, it's size six so it might be a little too big. Of course you could always wear a couple of pairs of thick socks for padding, couldn't you?"

At this moment one of the girls approaches. She is fat and wears a bright green jumper—obviously knitted by herself—and she looks extremely cross. "Are you wanting anything?" she asks.

"Dear me, no," replies Tony. "We're just having fun. Please don't bother about us."

"You aren't allowed to do this," declares the girl, beginning to gather up the shoes and boxes. "You're mixing everything up. It'll take me ever so long to clear up this mess."

"But I like doing it," objects Tony. "I want to see what's inside all those nice shiny boxes—all except the green mules. I don't like mules at the best of times; they're so unco-operative."

"Does the lady want mules?" asks the girl in bewilderment.

Tony is too busy opening boxes to reply. "Dinky boots!" he announces. Size four and a half, fur-lined with zip-fasteners! You can't resist Dinky boots, Hester, especially when they're exactly the right size."

"Brown walking-shoes," I murmur, struggling not to laugh.

"We've no walking-shoes," says the girl.

"No walking-shoes!" cries Tony in amazement. "But what are shoes for? Shoes are made for walking, aren't they? Calves are born and reared so that their skins can be made into walking-shoes . . ."

While he is talking Tony does not pause for a moment in his search. He opens box after box and strews them on the floor. The girl is trying vainly to sort them out and gather them up, but she is not as quick as Tony.

"I'll fetch the manager," she declares. "He'll know what to say to you. I'll go and fetch him now—this very minute."

"Yes, do," agrees Tony with alacrity. "Go and fetch the manager; I should like to see him. There are various things I should like to tell him; for instance I could tell him quite a lot about salesmanship. Perhaps he would take me in as an assistant—"

"The manager's out!"

"Oh what a pity! But I could come back and see him later."

"We haven't got any walking-shoes," declares the girl

153

in desperation. "We haven't any at all. Why don't you go away and try somewhere else?"

"Because I don't believe you," replies Tony very softly. "All those nice shiny boxes and not one single pair of thick brown walking-shoes, size four and a half! The thing is incredible! Ah, what have we here?"

Tony holds a shoe aloft. It is brown as a chestnut and has a nice thick leather sole; there is no nonsense about the shoe—in fact it is a thoroughly sound, sensible piece of workmanship which looks exactly my size and exactly what I want.

"Oh yes!" I exclaim rapturously. "Let me try it on!"

"That's not a walking-shoe," says the girl.

"Surely it isn't a dancing-shoe?" asks Tony.

"No, of course not," says the girl scornfully. "It's a Scotch brogue—that's what it is. If you'd asked for a Scotch brogue I'd have shown it to you." She pronounces the word as if it rhymed with ague, but after all why shouldn't she?

Tony kneels before me, shoe in hand. "There," he says as he takes the shoe-horn and slips it on. "How does it feel?"

"Very comfortable."

"Are you sure? No tightness across the instep?" asks Tony anxiously.

"It's perfect," I reply.

"Perfect," agrees Tony nodding. "It's neat and serviceable. You can walk through muddy country lanes without a care in the world when you're wearing that shoe. That shoe was made for you."

"I believe it was."

"Wasn't I clever to find it?"

"Very clever indeed," I reply with absolute sincerity.

As a matter of fact I feel extremely grateful to Tony, for in these days of austerity it is seldom that one finds exactly what one wants. All too often one is obliged to search high

154

and low and eventually in sheer desperation to buy something which one thinks will "do" but which rarely "does."

Tony sits back on his heels and smiles with the satisfaction of a man who has accomplished a difficult and arduous task.

"Not only clever," I tell him as I look round at the littered floor, "not only are you clever but also extremely persevering."

"It's just my nature," he replies modestly. "All my confidential reports said the same thing. *This officer is full of initiative and perseverance.* When I take on a job I like to see it through to the bitter end."

There is no more to be said. I pay for the shoes and Tony takes the parcel. We leave the fat girl standing knee-deep in shiny boxes and emerge into the square.

"She thinks you're mad," I remark.

"No," says Tony. "You underrate her intelligence. She understands quite well. I think I've taught her something." He sighs and adds: "It's hard work being public-spirited."

"But, Tony—"

"Seriously, Hester, we've got to do something about it. Unless we all take a firm stand and refuse to put up with laziness and incompetence things will go from bad to worse."

"You mean we shouldn't put up with bad service?"

"We mustn't put up with it," says Tony emphatically. "We mustn't be lazy. It's the same in a restaurant: if you're given a cracked cup or a dirty plate you should make a fuss."

"You might have reported that girl to the manager."

"I hate reporting people. I prefer to deal with people in my own way; to make the punishment fit the crime."

"You enjoyed it," I tell him.

"Well—perhaps," admits Tony, smiling.

The rest of my shopping is quickly done and we walk across the square to the Apollo and Boot where, Tony assures me, we shall get a very good tea. It is an attractive old place, half-timbered in Elizabethan style, with a painted sign hanging over the doorway. On the sign is depicted an extremely handsome Apollo clad in Grecian costume and an old-fashioned hunting boot.

"Why Apollo and Boot?" I ask as we go in . . . but Tony does not know.

The dining room is large and airy, it is full of little tables with snow-white cloths but we are the only people having tea. Tony knows the head-waiter, who has been here for years, and presently he comes over to our table in the window and chats with us. He is a thick-set man with a high forehead and a beaming smile, a benevolent creature who might easily have stepped straight out of *Pickwick Papers*.

"Edward," says Tony. "Mrs. Christie wants to know why this inn is called the Apollo and Boot. Can you do anything about it?"

"Not really," replies Edward, beaming more blandly than before. "I wish I could—that's the truth. Lots of people ask about the name, but all we can say is it's been called the Apollo and Boot for 'undreds of years. It's called that in all the old documents. There was an old gentleman used to come 'ere and he said it might have been called the Pool and Boat at one time, but that's just an idea. There isn't no foundation to it, as you might say."

"The Pool and Boat," says Tony thoughtfully.

"Yes, sir," agrees Edward. "That's what the gentleman said. He was collecting names of inns—just like some people collect stamps—and there were a lot of funny ones in his book. He let me see his book one day and very interesting it was. There was the Bat and Steeple for instance—that's down Ports-

156

mouth way—and the gentleman said it started off as the Bed and Stable."

"A good name for an inn," suggests Tony.

"Yes, sir, but very prosaic," replies Edward gravely. "Not nearly so romantic—if you see what I mean. Perhaps the lady will agree with me?"

The lady agrees.

"Yes," says Edward. "And the Pool and Boat is a poor sort of name compared to the Apollo and Boot."

"You like romance, Edward," says Tony. "Well, I don't blame you. Life would be very hum-drum without it."

"Just what I always say!" exclaims Edward, beaming from ear to ear. "You'd be surprised how much romance there is in my job—you really would. All sorts of things 'appen—interesting things. People meet each other and get engaged to each other—I've seen that 'appen more than once—and people quarrel with each other and make it up. There was a lady came 'ere last March—a very nice lady she was—and she asked me to sign my name on her Will. There's romance for you!"

"Yes," says Tony doubtfully. "I suppose there might be romance in a Will, though as a matter of fact my Will is a dull sort of affair, about a mile long and full of lawyer's jargon."

"This one wasn't. It was short and sweet," says Edward chuckling.

We have finished our tea by this time so we take leave of Edward and drive home through the leafy country lanes. We glide along slowly and smoothly which suits me down to the ground but I cannot resist the temptation to ask my companion why he is not racing along in his usual headlong fashion.

"Don't you understand?" says Tony sadly. "It's all a matter of mood. If I feel like speed I drive fast, but I always drive slowly if I don't want to get to my destination quickly. Surely that's simple enough."

Wednesday, 25th July

I HAVE INVITED Susan to come and see me this morning and have sent a summons to Edmond Alston. It is possible that Susan may not be the right angel but I have a feeling she is. Mrs. Daulkes has been told that I am expecting two young friends for coffee at eleven o'clock and, although this is all I have said, I can see from her manner that she is interested in my little party. She helps me to carry out three chairs, a small table and a rug and to arrange them beneath the beech tree— the one which is out of sight of Miss Crease's bedroom window.

"There," says Mrs. Daulkes. "That's nice. I'll bring out the coffee and biscuits when they come."

Susan arrives first. She surveys the preparations and asks who else is coming; she is also curious to know why she has been invited. I reply that she has been invited to talk pleasantly to a young man who is reading medicine and working much too hard.

"Why me?"

"I thought a little female society would be good for him."

"You could have asked Joan Meller," says Susan, who is no fool.

I agree that this might have been possible if I had had the pleasure of Joan Meller's acquaintance.

"I believe I've seen your young man," says Susan thoughtfully. "I mean when you know everybody in a place like Old

158

Wednesday, 25th July

Quinings, a strange young man sticks out like a sore thumb. If it's the one I've seen—walking about at a frightful pace with his dark hair blowing in the breeze—it'll be rather interesting to meet him. I've seen him several times when I was out riding. One day he opened a gate for me."

"Anyone would do that," I tell her.

"You'd be surprised," says Susan smiling. "Anyone doesn't open gates for horsewomen nowadays . . . besides he opened it rather nicely."

There is no time to say more (which perhaps is just as well) for at this moment the young man who opened the gate nicely emerges from the glass door of the drawing room.

" 'Ere's the young gentleman, Mrs. Christie!" cries Mrs. Daulkes, waving her duster in frantic excitement.

If there had been any doubt in my mind as to whether I had found the right angel—which of course there was not—it would have been dispelled at the sight of Edmond's face as he advances across the lawn. It is the face of a young man who sees visions. Somehow I am rather frightened at the sight of Edmond's face. I want to warn him to be careful. I want to wrap him in cotton-wool so that he shall not be hurt. I am frightened on my own account as well, and wish that I had not lent myself to this adventure. I see now that Edmond's case is not merely a young man's natural interest in a pretty girl; it is something much bigger and much more serious. What Susan's feelings are I do not know. It is too late to regret my action and to wish I had been more prudent and less impulsive. I have involved myself in the affairs of these two young creatures and the outcome is in the lap of the gods.

"We've met before, haven't we?" says Susan when the introductions are made.

Edmond agrees gravely. Today his dark hair is not blowing wildly in the breeze, but carefully brushed, and instead of his

159

usual haphazard attire he is wearing a well-pressed flannel suit.

We sit down. Edmond and I choose chairs in the shade but Susan prefers to sit upon the rug in the full blaze of sunlight. Radiance surrounds her. It is almost dazzling to look at her. She is wearing a white tennis frock; her arms and legs are bare and very slightly tanned; the sun glistens in her golden curls.

We talk about various matters—about opening gates and such-like manifestations of good-will—we drink coffee and eat little biscuits. At first the burden of the conversation is mine but presently I discover that Susan is doing most of the talking. I had intended to make some excuse and leave them to chat without the constraint of my presence (young people often get on better alone); now I have changed my mind for obviously my presence does not constrain them and besides I am responsible. This friendship must not advance too quickly.

But despite my presence it is advancing rapidly. Already they have abandoned generalities and are talking about themselves. Susan, picking idly at the grass is talking about her childhood and about the "unhappy things" she had to bear. (I know something of this, having heard it from Miss Phipps.)

"Daddy and Wanda are quite different," Susan is saying. "Daddy never wants to leave the Manor House and Wanda loves travelling, so for years and years they didn't get on very well. It made me unhappy because I loved them both and because I wanted an ordinary sort of life, like other girls, with an ordinary sort of father and mother . . . and I wanted a sister terribly much. I wanted a little sister younger than myself to play with. It's lonely being *only,* you know."

I watch her, not really listening to her words but more to the cadence of her pretty voice. I am in love with Susan myself so how can I blame Edmond for his infatuation.

"I am *only,* too," says Edmond. "My father died when I
160

was six but I remember him quite well—a big cheery man who played bears with me. He gave me a nice safe feeling. Perhaps I'm imagining the safe feeling," says Edmond consideringly. "Perhaps it was just that I felt unsafe when he had gone."

"You were the man of the family," says Susan nodding.

She is right, of course. The six-year-old Edmond was too heavily burdened and the strain on his nerves was too great. It is much easier to understand Edmond and to sympathise with his present troubles and difficulties when one knows of the troubles and difficulties of his childhood.

"Mother sold the house," continues Edmond. "That seemed the end of everything. I shall never forget my feelings when I saw the house dismantled and all the furniture carted away . . . all the things I knew . . . even my bed and the cupboard where I kept my toys. Since then we haven't had any home; we've just moved about from place to place. The only time I had any settled existence was when I was at Rugby and even then I never knew where we would be for the next holidays. Mother had nobody else except me. It used to frighten me to think of it. Sometimes it still frightens me. If we had a settled home it would be different—or so I believe."

"I think it would," says Susan softly. "I think it would make a difference if you had a settled home. It would make you feel safer, wouldn't it?"

"It's rather cowardly to want safety," declares Edmond frowning.

"But we all want it!" cries Susan. "We all want it, don't we, Mrs. Christie? We want some sort of anchor—somebody to lean on. I've got Daddy, of course. With Daddy behind me I can go forward and be as brave as a lion."

She looks at me to see if I understand—and of course I do! I can go forward and be brave for I have Tim behind me.

Presently Susan rises and says she must go. Edmond goes

too and I watch them walk down the lane together, talking earnestly. Perhaps they are arranging another meeting; it may be that they will meet by that fateful gate. Susan's horse will crop the grass while Susan and Edmond lean upon the gate and talk to one another.

It is no good worrying about them and wondering about the future. What is to be will be. I have helped them to meet, it is true, but if I had not helped them they would have met in some other way. There would have been another gate for Edmond to open. Edmond would have seen to that.

Part IV

Busy Days at The Small House

Friday, 27th July

*B*ETTY IS arriving tonight and the two boys tomorrow, and this influx provides a problem for the housekeeper. I am puzzling out ways and means of feeding my prospective visitors when Mrs. Daulkes appears, laden with parcels: rabbits, eggs, an oxtail and a pound of country butter are unpacked upon the kitchen table.

"There," says Mrs. Daulkes with satisfaction. "That ought to keep us going for a bit and Mr. 'Igginbotham 'as promised me a tongue for Monday."

"How marvellous!" I exclaim. "It *is* kind of you to take so much trouble."

"No trouble at all. It's a pleasure to do things for some people," declares my faithful Eskimo. "And 'ow could I look Mrs. Bollings in the face if we didn't 'ave enough food?"

This argument is unanswerable of course. I am aware by this time that Mrs. Daulkes is slightly scared of Mrs. Bollings and that one of her chief objects in life is to be able to meet the glance of Mrs. Bollings without fear.

The Small House is full of bustle this morning; beds are made up, furniture is polished and a magnificent cake is baked.

All day long my excitement grows and when I reach the station, twenty minutes too early, to meet Betty's train I am in a perfect fever. I walk up and down; I stand still; I go and look at the clock. Then I find a seat and sit down for a few minutes and go and look at the clock again.

"Meeting someone?" enquires the porter sympathetically.

"Yes, I'm meeting my daughter. She's coming from Edinburgh, but of course she had to go to London and change."

"Not coming by 'erself surely?" asks the porter.

"Only from London," I reply. "She is travelling with friends to London and then coming on here alone."

"You didn't ought to let 'er travel by 'erself," says the porter shaking his head reprovingly. "No, you didn't ought to. There's all sorts of 'orrible things can 'appen. Why, you can't never pick up a paper but you see something 'orrible 'as 'appened to a little girl—not nowadays you can't."

"She's sixteen," I tell him, trying to defend my callous behaviour.

"Ah, sixteen! That's a bad age, that is. That's the age they likes to get little girls—sixteen, and pretty, with fair 'air like 'er Mum—that's the kind they likes to get 'old of."

I walk away to the other end of the platform but I can't walk away from the fears which his warnings have awakened in my breast. He is right, of course—absolutely right. Why on earth was I such a fool as to allow Betty to travel from London by herself? Why didn't I go and meet her? What shall I do if she doesn't arrive? "All sorts of 'orrible things can 'appen"— yes, of course he's right. Some horrible man . . . or an accident . . . anything might happen.

164

Friday, 27th July

But at last the train arrives and Betty steps out of it and flings herself into my arms. My first impression is that Betty has not changed at all; she is as big and bouncing as ever with rosy cheeks and fair curls, but later, when I have time to look at her properly—when we are sitting together in the dining room having supper—I begin to realise that my daughter has changed a good deal. She is taller than she was eighteen months ago; her figure has lost its school-girl plumpness and her movements are more graceful and less puppy-like. She is older in other ways too; although she is still a chatterbox, her chatter is not so scatter-brained.

"This is fun," says Betty smiling at me across the table. "At first I was a little disappointed when you wrote and said you'd taken a house in England. I thought Scotland would be nicer; I know it so much better, you see. But I'm glad now. It's so different, isn't it? It looks different and it feels different and the people are the most different of all. In fact it's like a foreign country . . . and it's ages since we had a real house of our very own. I'm looking forward to seeing Bryan terribly much. I haven't seen him properly for ages."

I tell her Percy Edgeburton is coming too.

"Oh good!" says Betty. "I always liked Percy—and that will be three for tennis. Is there anybody here who would make a fourth?"

"We mustn't call him Percy," I warn her.

"No," agrees Betty smiling. "Do we call him Hedgehog?"

"We call him Perry."

"Rather nice," nods Betty. "Easy to remember. Goodness, I *am* eating a lot! Of course I didn't eat much in the train. I wasn't sick but I felt a bit queer now and then . . . you know, Mummy, I'm a bit sorry for Erica, she's awfully disappointed that we aren't going to Tocher for the holidays—she really is. I think perhaps I'd better go there for a few days on

Saturday, 28th July

*T*HE BOYS arrive soon after mid-day upon Perry's motor bicycle; which to my mind is a miraculous machine. Indeed when I see the pile of miscellaneous luggage in the hall I can hardly believe that all this, plus two large youths, has been transported sixty miles upon its ancient frame.

Betty is of the same opinion. "However did you manage it?" she enquires. "I thought you said in your letter only two people could go on the bike, but if it can take all this as well—"

"All this doesn't weigh as much as you," replies Bryan brutally.

The inference is obvious and I begin to feel a little sorry for Betty and to wonder what I shall do if the two boys go off together for expeditions and leave Betty at home; but there is no time to think of that now for the whole atmosphere of The Small House has changed. It is no longer a quiet peaceful spot but is full of movement and the chatter of young voices. People run madly up and down the stairs; the hall is strewn with caps and waterproofs, cluttered with tennis rackets and hob-nailed boots . . . and the succulent smell of rabbit stew pervades all.

"The 'ouse 'as come alive," says Mrs. Daulkes, smiling at me as she carries in the heavy tray of food.

The afternoon is warm and is spent sitting peacefully in the garden, myself in the long cane-chair and the young

167

people lying stretched out upon rugs in the shadow of the tree. Betty suggests tennis (already she has discovered the tennis club and ascertained that for a reasonable subscription anybody can join) but Bryan and Perry show no enthusiasm.

"This craze for exercise!" says Bryan wearily.

"Another day," says Perry.

"You like tennis, don't you?" asks Betty in anxious tones.

"Of course," replies Perry. "We're tired today, that's all. We had to get up terribly early, you see."

Although they are unwilling to exercise their bodies they are quite ready to exercise their tongues and I find the conversation interesting and revealing for it ranges over a wide field of subjects and, apart from a little mild banter, it is sensible and polite. They are anxious to hear about one another's doings and are content to listen as well as talk. Time was when Bryan and Betty both talked at once at the top of their voices and had no wish to hear one another's point of view.

Perry talks less than the others but what he says is worth hearing and he has a stabilising effect upon his companions. I realise that although he and Bryan are almost the same age, and have had exactly the same education, Perry has developed and matured more quickly than my son.

When they have finished talking about their doings there is a short silence.

"The Small House," says Bryan, breaking it. "Wait a minute—I know—Anthony Trollope lived here, of course. I've been trying to think where I had heard about it."

"It isn't old enough," Betty objects. "I mean Anthony Trollope was long, long ago, wasn't he?"

"He didn't live in The Small House, he wrote about it," declares Perry.

Bryan says, "Well, you *know,* of course. I won't argue

about it. I had to read one of his books once for a holiday task. It was called *He Knew He Was Right* and it was the most awful tripe—all about a man who thought his wife was carrying on with another man, and of course she wasn't at all. The whole misunderstanding could have been cleared up in a few words, but He Knew He Was Right so it went drivelling on until he'd wrecked everything. A ghastly book!"

"You haven't much use for the classics," says Perry, stating the fact dispassionately.

"They're such small print and much too long," explains Bryan. "Take *Redgauntlet*, for instance. I had to do it for my Cert—"

"*Redgauntlet* is good," says Betty quickly.

"Oh, it's a good enough yarn," agrees Bryan. "I'll grant you that—but it's far too long. It wants cutting down a lot."

"You mean you would like it re-written!" I exclaim, horrified at the thought.

"Why not?" asks Bryan. "I bet Kenneth Hardy, or somebody like that who writes modern thrillers, could make a jolly good tale of it. He could keep the plot and the characters, but make it go quicker and put some pep into it. I believe I could do it myself if I had time . . . and you needn't laugh like that," adds Bryan, looking up at me with a grin. "You don't know what I could do if I put my mind to it."

"Perhaps you could help me to make some tea," I suggest.

Bryan is quite willing to undertake the task and we are about to go in and boil the kettle when I hear the squeak of the side gate and Susan Morven appears.

"Oh bother, it's a girl!" exclaims Bryan sotto voce.

Susan advances down the path and I am interested to note that she looks much younger than usual. She is wearing a blue cotton frock and her pretty mouth is innocent of lipstick.

"This is Susan Morven," I tell them. "Susan and I met at the library . . ."

"Yes," agrees Susan demurely. "As a matter of fact that's why I've come. Miss Carlyle found a handkerchief and she thought it must be yours, Mrs. Christie."

Oddly enough it is my handkerchief—with the initials H.C. in the corner—but I feel pretty certain I did not leave it at the library all the same. The excuse for Susan's visit is a little too good to be true and the bland look in her eyes, as they meet mine, is a trifle overdone. Someday, when I get her alone, I shall find out how Susan became possessed of my handkerchief. I shall accuse the young woman of theft.

Meanwhile Susan has taken her place on a rug beside Betty and is answering a rapid fire of questions. Yes, she lives here . . . at the Manor House. Yes, she plays tennis. Yes, she is quite willing to make a fourth. No, unfortunately she hasn't any brothers or sisters, nor has she been to a boarding-school.

"I don't know why Mummy never mentioned you in her letters," says Betty in a surprised voice. "Why didn't you, Mummy? You told me all sorts of things about Old Quinings but you never said anything about knowing any girls."

This is a little difficult to answer so I rise rather hastily and say I must see about tea.

"Susan must stay to tea!" cries Betty. "Mummy, Susan must stay to tea, mustn't she?"

I agree that she must.

Saturday, 4th August

*T*HE DAYS fly past very quickly; contrary to Richard's gloomy prophesy there is plenty of entertainment in Old Quinings and Bryan and Betty and Perry seem completely happy. They have played tennis, they have been to tea at the Manor, they have gone over to Wandlebury in the bus. Occasionally Bryan suggests that he and Perry might have a run on the motor bike—"to Chevis Green or somewhere"— but for some reason or other the expedition has not yet taken place. Susan makes a fourth at tennis or, if she is not available, Joan Meller is co-opted. Betty explains that "Susan doesn't like to neglect her father, and of course she rides a lot." There is no mention of Edmond Alston nor has he appeared and I cannot help wondering what has happened to poor Edmond and whether he has been opening gates for his golden-haired angel. Mrs. Alston, who has been to see me once or twice, reports that Edmond is working very hard, but Mrs. Alston does not know everything.

Mrs. Alston is not a very cheerful visitor (my young friends vanish into thin air when they see her coming) but she is much less tiresome than Miss Stroude, who is a pest. Miss Stroude has called on two occasions and spent several hours hunting for her valuable letters in the box-room. I have not seen her to speak to (she walks in without the formality of ringing the bell) but we can hear her moving boxes about overhead. Mrs. Daulkes is of the opinion that Miss

Stroude should not be permitted to search for her letters and that the General should be summoned "to turn 'er out like 'e did before" but I do not feel justified in forbidding Miss Stroude to enter her own house and, having won the victory of the lease, I can afford to be magnanimous. It is not very pleasant to have Miss Stroude dropping in unexpectedly and I wish with all my heart that her "grey cardboard folder" with its valuable contents could be found.

In addition to these visitors we have had Tony to see us several times and of course he is always welcome. He has known Bryan and Betty since they were small children and holds the rank of Honorary Uncle. Sometimes he teases them unmercifully, but as they both have a healthy sense of humour they take it in good part and like him all the better.

Today Tony arrives soon after breakfast and is welcomed as usual with cries of delight and with enquiries as to whether he can take us all to Wandlebury in Belshazzar.

"No, I can't," replies Tony. "I'm a busy farmer."

"What have you come for?" Betty demands.

Tony sighs and says Betty's manners are hideous. He has called in for a few minutes to ask us what we think about a dance. His sister and niece are staying at Charters Towers and with so many young people about some sort of junketing seems indicated.

"Of course it will be a primitive affair—quite informal," says Tony. "It's impossible to feed one's guests properly nowadays, but we'll do what we can."

"You mean a dance at Charters Towers!" I exclaim.

"That was the idea."

"Oh, Uncle Tony, it will be gorgeous!" cries Betty in delight.

"It will not be gorgeous," replies Uncle Tony gravely. "It will be an austerity dance. And I can't think why the fact that I am giving a dance should interest you in the slightest. I said a dance, not a children's party."

"Darling Uncle Tony, you are a pet!" declares Betty rapturously. "I've never been to a real, proper, grown-up dance before. I shall have to get a new dress. Oh, joy!" cries Betty, starting to whirl round the room. "Oh, won't it be fun! Do you think anybody will want to dance with me?"

Tony repeats that it will not be a real, proper, grown-up dance and she has not been invited to it; but of course if she likes to get a new dress and gate-crash that's her look out.

"You'll dance with me, won't you, Perry?" says Betty. "And there's Bryan, of course . . ."

"Will Lady Morley like it?" I enquire (for Lady Morley is rather an alarming person in my estimation).

"Mother is all for it," replies Tony. "She is now convinced that it is entirely her own idea and is doing her best to overcome my reluctance, so you may take it as fixed."

It is very good of Tony to think of it and I tell him so. He agrees that his benevolence is phenomenal and adds that it is all the more phenomenal because he, himself, will derive no pleasure at all from the entertainment—not even the pleasure of seeing his guests eating good food. I point out that he should derive pleasure from giving pleasure to others and if he were really benevolent he would do so. Tony replies that he is not as benevolent as all that.

Bryan now chips in and says, will it be all right to come in a dinner-jacket, because he has no tails.

Perry says he has tails, but not here. Does General Morley think he should write for his tails or not? Perhaps it will be better just to come in a dinner-jacket and then he will be the same as Bryan.

Bryan says, "Will it be *soon?*"

173

Perry says, "I do hope it will be before the sixteenth, sir, because I've promised to go home."

I say, "You'll ask Grace and Jack MacDougall, won't you? They could easily come over from Biddington."

Betty says, "I know this is England but you *will* have a reel, won't you? And can we ask Susan Morven?"

Tony says, "Yes, yes, yes, yes!" and gets into his car and drives away.

In spite of all these activities I have a feeling that we are marking time and that something is going to happen. It is an unpleasant sort of feeling; like a cloud in the blue sky of our pleasant carefree existence. I have tried to track down the cause of my unease but without much success. Tim's letters are rather short and scrappy, but they come regularly and he seems well, so probably it is just that he is busy . . . and he has said no more about taking on The Small House for the winter so I have ceased to worry about that. The Small House is ideal in every way, our domestic arrangements are working satisfactorily and the young people are happy. I make up my mind that I have nothing whatever to worry about, so it is extremely silly to worry, but in spite of my good resolutions the feeling that Something is going to Happen continues to haunt me. In the evening, when I go up to see Betty in bed and say good night to her I mention it to her.

"Lots of things are going to happen," says Betty. "There's Susan's picnic to the Lion's Gorge and there's Uncle Tony's dance and then Bryan and I are going to London for our visit to Uncle Richard and Aunt Mary. These holidays are the best ever."

"Yes, of course," I agree; for what is the good of worrying Betty by telling her that my feeling about the Something is an unpleasant one?

174

Saturday, 4th August

"About my dress," continues Betty, sitting up in bed with her arms round her knees and looking at me anxiously. "I've nothing but my white school-frock, which would look frightfully silly at a proper, grown-up dance."

This is true and I agree that she must have a new dress for the dance at Charters Towers.

Betty says she thinks black velvet would be nice, or perhaps black brocade, and of course it must be a proper evening-dress with straps over the shoulders and a long full skirt. She has seen a double rope of pearls—not real ones of course—in the draper's shop in the village and they only cost five shillings.

The idea of my daughter thus attired is horrifying—so horrifying that it causes me no amusement—and I object most strongly to her suggestions.

"But I *want* a black dress!" she exclaims. "I've *always* wanted a black dress. It would make me look thinner and older."

"It would be most unsuitable."

"Mummy, please," says Betty. "Please let me. I'm the one who's going to wear it."

"I would have to see you in it."

"Mummy, listen—"

But I refuse to listen and after some argument I dig my heels in firmly and tell Betty that I will choose the dress; she can either wear it or her school-frock or, if neither pleases her, she can stay at home.

Betty is quite taken aback at this unwonted cruelty and says meekly that she is sure it will be nice; and—the point being settled—I write off to Harrods for some suitable frocks to be sent on approval.

Monday, 6th August

*T*HIS IS the day appointed by Susan for her picnic to the Lion's Gorge. The morning is not propitious but by the afternoon the clouds have cleared and the sun is shining. Betty and I travel to the rendezvous by bus, the boys having gone ahead on Perry's motor bicycle.

Much has been said about the Lion's Gorge and I must confess to a slight feeling of disappointment when it bursts upon my gaze. There are woods and paths and there are rocks with variegated heaths planted among them; a little river wanders out of the woods and into a pretty pool overhung by willows. It is very pretty of course but I had expected something grander and wilder.

Betty knows more about the arrangements than I do. "Oh, it isn't *here*," she says. "There's a waterfall higher up. That's where we're going to have the picnic."

Susan has arrived already; her little car is parked by the roadside, so also is Perry's bike, and it behoves Betty and me to climb the path by the stream and look for them. I have some slight anxiety as to whether we shall find them, for there are several paths winding in different directions, but Betty reassures me; she and Susan have both had Guide Training and a trail has been left for us to follow.

We are just starting on our quest when another car drives up and from it descends the Charters Tower party which consists of Tony, an elderly woman, and a girl.

176

Monday, 6th August

"How do you do, Mrs. Christie!" exclaims the elderly woman, advancing with a smile. "It's ages since we met, isn't it? Perhaps you've forgotten me!"

Obviously this is Tony's sister, Freda Winthrop, and of course I am obliged to say I remember her quite well and to greet her in a friendly manner; but the fact is she has changed so much that I should never have known her. The last time I saw Mrs. Winthrop she seemed little older than myself and the impression left upon my mind was of an exceedingly gay and giddy young woman with gorgeous clothes. I remember also that she behaved in a gay and giddy fashion with a handsome Naval Officer. Can this really be the same woman: this woman with the lined and haggard face, the grey and wispy hair? My consternation on beholding Tony's sister is difficult to hide and, sad to say, it is not altogether sympathetic. I have an uncomfortable feeling that if the years have done this dreadful thing to Freda Winthrop they must have taken their toll of me.

"And this is Diana," says Mrs. Winthrop, indicating her daughter who is standing behind her on the path.

Diana is older than Betty; she is a fat girl with a pretty complexion but, apart from her milk and roses, has little to recommend her. She seems uninterested in the proceedings and shows no pleasure at all at making our acquaintance.

By this time Tony has parked his car and we all set off together, Betty leading and rejoicing aloud at the various signs which have been made by Susan to guide our footsteps in the right way. We cross a rustic bridge and take a path which ascends steeply between rocks and trees. Mrs. Winthrop says several times she thinks *this* would be an ideal place to have tea, but as no hostess nor any tea is visible her suggestions fall on deaf ears.

The party thins out as we ascend; Betty's excitement in

following the trail lends wings to her feet and the Winthrops lag behind. Tony and I endeavour to keep in touch with both van and rear (this is essential for the Winthrops will get lost if we abandon them and Betty alone can lead us to the place appointed for tea); the woods resound with Tony's shouts to his sister and niece to come on, and hurry up, and with my shouts to my daughter to wait for us.

The path becomes steeper and more stony, it winds hither and thither amongst the trees. I am beginning to wonder if Betty has led us astray when we reach an open space carpeted with green mossy grass. There are the remains of a house here—a heap of large stones and a patch of nettles—beyond the ground slopes to the stream which prattles over a series of small cascades. At one side of the dell, beneath the shade of an oak, a large white cloth has been laid upon the ground and Susan, Perry, Bryan and Edmond Alston are busily engaged unpacking two large baskets.

"Here you are!" cries Susan waving joyfully. "Come and help! We've got to make a fire."

Everybody now starts talking at once; all except Mrs. Winthrop and her fat daughter who sink down upon a mossy bank with groans of fatigue.

The party is still incomplete for Anne Carlyle has been bidden and has not yet appeared. Susan seems worried about her and says she hopes Miss Carlyle is not lost in the woods. She thought Miss Carlyle was coming in the two o'clock bus and that she would join our party. If she comes in the later bus she will not know where we are. Somebody will have to go down and meet her. Meanwhile, says our hostess, there are sticks to be collected and a fireplace to be constructed. Who wants to do what?

After some argument the younger members of the party vanish into the woods to collect sticks while Tony and I set
178

to work to make a fireplace with some of the tumbled stones.

"Are you enjoying yourself, Hester?" asks Tony.

I reply in the affirmative. Picnics amuse me, especially picnics with proper fires. Vacuum flasks are extremely useful, and what we should do without them I cannot imagine, but a fire is more fun.

"Yes, if it burns," agrees Tony. "Do you remember a picnic at Loch an Darroch? It was when you were staying at Avielochan with Mrs. Loudon."

Of course I remember it, and I remember exploring the great ruined castle of the MacArbins and how we thought we saw a ghost. The scene comes back to my mind very clearly; there were towering cliffs and pine woods and a huge loch which looked cold and green. It was wild and grand and awe-inspiring—quite unlike this English beauty spot.

"This place is like a lion with a collar on," I remark as I step back and survey our fireplace with satisfaction.

"You do say the oddest things!" exclaims Tony. "But I know what you mean. This place was wild once—it was meant to be wild—but they've tamed it by tidying it up, making paths and planting heaths amongst the rocks. Yes, it's a tamed lion. Poor brute!" he adds, taking out his handkerchief and mopping his brow.

"You look hot, Tony," says Mrs. Winthrop, who has now recovered from her climb.

Tony scowls but makes no reply and I am not surprised; when one feels hot it is most annoying to be told that one looks it.

"Why is it called the Lion's Gorge?" I enquire, changing the subject.

"The lion is higher up," replies Tony. "There's a limestone cliff which is supposed to resemble the head of a lion and I must say it does bear a sort of resemblance to the King

179

of Beasts. The stream issues from the lion's mouth and falls into a deep pool beneath the lion's paws. The interesting thing about it is that the stream has a subterranean source and runs underground before it emerges from its tunnel. My cousin and I explored it once when we were boys. We did it in style with torches and a rope and we both pretended it was tremendous fun, but I was simply terrified. There's something horribly sinister about caves with water running through them—splashing and dripping," says Tony with a shudder. "There were bats and things; it was cold and dank and the walls of the little tunnel were slimy. We didn't penetrate very far—not more than a few hundred yards—and then we came to a huge, deep pool and had to turn back. How thankful I was to emerge into the good wholesome light of day! Later on Ralph had another try with one of the under-gardeners, they took a collapsible dinghy and managed to go in a good bit further. I absolutely refused to have anything to do with the second expedition, the first one was quite enough for me."

"Ralph was very brave," says Mrs. Winthrop.

This statement annoys me intensely. The unknown Ralph may have been as brave as a lion but Tony is no coward; his war record is sufficient indication of his courage . . . but of course it is no use saying anything so I hold my tongue.

The young people drift back in couples bearing bundles of wood for the fire; Betty and Perry arrive first, then Susan and Edmond. The fire is started and the kettle is beginning to sing merrily when Bryan staggers in with two enormous branches.

There is still no sign of Anne Carlyle and Edmond very nobly says he will go down and find her. Several others offer to go, though not very enthusiastically, and the matter is being debated when Anne suddenly appears. She is quite cool and not in the least exhausted by the steep climb; when asked how she found her way, she replies that although she is too old to have been a Guide herself she started a company in school and therefore knows a good deal about the mysteries of Guiding.

Although I am very fond of Anne I have a feeling that Susan has made a mistake in asking her to the picnic and this feeling is confirmed into a certainty before many minutes have passed. Poor Anne is completely out of place and has nothing in common with any of her companions (she is shy of Tony and his sister and the young people are shy of her); Susan and I, the only two who know her intimately, make valiant efforts to draw her into the conversation but without success. Anne has plenty to say upon subjects which interest her but she has no "small talk."

Quite soon the kettle boils and we all settle down to an excellent meal, but we settle down in a haphazard manner which is a little unfortunate. There are various interesting undercurrents to observe in this picnic party: for instance Tony is endeavouring to talk to Edmond, who is sitting next to him, but most of Edmond's attention is engaged elsewhere. Mrs. Winthrop has suddenly discovered that Perry is the grandson of a baronet and pulling herself together becomes quite animated. She is discussing skiing at Wengen and is doing her best to "bring out" Diana and make her take part in the conversation. Betty is perfectly happy sitting next to Susan, chattering like a magpie and bounding up to fetch the kettle and fill the tea-pot or bring a knife to cut the cake . . . and Bryan, finding himself next to Anne Carlyle, tries to talk to her, then gives it up and concentrates on the sandwiches.

When everybody has eaten their fill it is decided that the Lion must be visited and all the young people start off at once. Mrs. Winthrop says she has seen it before and will stay here and rest. She advises me to do likewise but Tony's description of the Lion has fired my ardour and I announce that I must see him. Tony is anxious to renew his acquaintance with the creature so we set off together. Anne and Mrs. Winthrop—a curiously ill-assorted couple—are left amongst the remains of the feast.

"Young Alston is a bit broody, isn't he?" says Tony as we climb the path. "Susan is an attractive creature but I don't think she's interested in the love-sick swain."

"I like Edmond," I reply.

"I never said I didn't," points out Tony.

"You implied it. Honestly, Tony, you mustn't judge Edmond by his behaviour today. He's a worthwhile person. The fact is—"

"The fact is our young friend is suffering from a severe attack of infatuation, and few men look their best under these circumstances. How unlike the male bird!" says Tony gravely. "The male bird puts on his brightest feathers to attract his chosen mate, displays himself to the best advantage and sings his sweetest songs. The male of the human species—as typified in our poor young friend—sits and gapes in a foolish manner and ties himself into knots. Our poor young friend is in a state of nervous tension and what he needs is a course of the larger mammals."

"A course of the larger mammals!" I echo in surprise.

"Alas!" says Tony sadly. "How your education has been neglected! Your friend Miss Carlyle would have understood the allusion."

"Well, I don't."

"So I perceive. It would spoil the whole thing to explain."

"Spoil the whole thing immediately, Tony."

With feigned reluctance Tony explains that an eminent doctor in *The Way of All Flesh* prescribed a course of the larger mammals for one of his patients who was suffering from nervous prostration. " 'Let him go to their house twice a week for a fortnight and stay with the hippopotamus, the rhinoceros and the elephants . . . the larger carnivora are unsympathetic . . . but with the elephants and the pig tribes generally he should mix, just now, as freely as possible.' It goes something like that," says Tony smiling.

"There's a good deal in it," I reply. "Edmond would be very much better staying in a house with a hippopotamus than with his mother. It would be more restful for his nerves."

We have not gone far when we come upon Diana Winthrop sitting by herself upon a fallen tree.

"Hullo!" exclaims Tony. "Where are the others?"

"They went on," she replies. "It's too hot for climbing. I said I'd wait till they came back."

Tony looks at his niece with an expression of disgust which almost makes me laugh, but he says nothing and we pass her and walk on.

"Perhaps she's delicate . . ." I begin in a low voice.

"Delicate!" he exclaims. "She's just lazy, that's all. Did you ever see such an uninteresting lump of a girl? Freda is a good deal to blame of course. Freda is sickening with her—spoils and pampers her and talks all the time about 'Diana's admirers.' Admirers! Who admires a lump? Oh, it's all very well for you to laugh," says Tony ruefully. "She isn't your niece. You aren't being badgered all the time to take Diana to Ascot or Henley or to some wretched dance . . . but I'm blowed if I will!"

"It's rather unkind of you."

"I've always disliked dull women," replies Tony firmly. "I told Freda her daughter was dull. Perhaps you noticed that Freda is rather annoyed with me?"

"But you're giving a dance for Diana!"

183

"The dance is for Betty," he replies.

We have now arrived at the cliff and find the rest of the party looking at it with interest and discussing whether or not it resembles the head of a lion. For my part I think it does. A mane of rough grass hangs over the lion's eyes; the stream gushes forth from his mouth and falls with a splashing sound into the pool below. All round there are little ferns growing in the crevices which give the lion's face a green and hairy appearance.

Betty, when she sees us, rushes at Tony excitedly and takes him by the arm. "Where does the stream come from? You know everything," she declares.

I am amused to see that Tony is pleased and flattered by this tribute; he teases her a little (saying that this is the rock that Moses struck and asking her if she thinks the lion's mouth is like an old-fashioned bath-tap); but on the way down he is beguiled by Betty into giving her an account of his explorations and a description of the underground ramifications of the stream. Betty hangs upon his arm and listens entranced and, as I see them together, I feel sad to think that Tony has not married and had children of his own.

When we reach the scene of the feast we discover that Anne has gone home but Mrs. Winthrop and her daughter are waiting for us and showing every sign of impatience. I watch Mrs. Winthrop's face when Tony and Betty appear and my surmise that she will not be pleased is fully justified.

Tuesday, 7th August

I ANNOUNCE AT breakfast that Grace MacDougall is coming over from Biddington for the day and bringing her twin sons, and I add that I expect my three young friends to entertain the twins.

"Oh, my dear paws!" exclaims Bryan (who has borrowed this peculiar expression from a certain sleuth in contemporary fiction and uses it when, but for his mother's presence, he would say something stronger). "Oh, honestly, Mum! You don't really mean we've got to look after those kids?"

I reply firmly that I do mean just that.

"Oh crumbs!" says Bryan. "Oh whiskers! They're ten, aren't they? What on earth do you do to amuse kids of ten?"

I reply unkindly that, as it is not so very long since he himself was ten, he must have a short memory.

Betty says, "That means we can't play tennis. Oh well, if we *must* look after them we must. What do you suppose they would like to do?"

Perry ventures the suggestion that they could be taken for a walk.

Bryan sighs heavily and says, "I expect they're just as fed up as we are."

I enquire what he means and he replies that when he was ten he hated being dragged out to see people and much pre-. ferred being left to his own devices. He then asks if Major

185

MacDougall is coming too and is somewhat disappointed to hear that Major MacDougall is too busy to come.

"What on earth do you want to see *him* for?" asks Betty.

Bryan chuckles in a secret sort of way.

"Go on," says Betty. "What's the joke? Why *do* you want to see him?"

After a little persuasion Bryan explains the mystery, saying that when he was twelve years old he wrestled with Major MacDougall and threw him under the piano, and that if he lives to be a hundred he will never forget the occasion, nor the faces of his elders. "You remember, don't you, Mum?" enquires Bryan, laughing at the recollection.

I assure him that I remember every detail clearly.

"It was that Polish soldier who taught me how to do it," continues Bryan. "As a matter of fact I had never tried it before and I was quite as surprised as my victim when it happened. I thought they'd all be furious with me, but they weren't. Dad gave me five bob."

Perry says he remembers hearing about it at the time, and he also remembers that Bryan found the trick very useful at school . . . they drift off into happy reminiscences of the time when Bryan practised the trick upon Snodgrass and various other schoolfellows much larger than himself and made them bite the dust.

Betty has ceased to listen; she remarks dreamily that she remembers holding the twins in her arms when they were babies. They were awfully sweet, but the recollection makes her feel very old.

I leave them talking and repair to the kitchen to discuss the problem of lunch with Mrs. Daulkes.

Soon after ten-thirty a small car comes bumping up the road and Grace gets out, followed by her offspring.

Grace and I have not met for years, but we have a great

deal in common and are delighted to see one another. Age has not wearied Grace. With her dark wavy hair, her creamy complexion and her slender figure Grace could pass as under thirty; but I happen to know she is a good deal more. The boys are like Grace and as like one another as the proverbial two peas; they are neatly dressed in grey flannel shorts and blue pullovers. Ian is my godson of course, but which is Ian and which Alec it is impossible to tell.

Naturally their resemblance to one another rouses comment (which, fortunately, they take in good part) but Grace says she doesn't know why people think they're alike, because in reality they're quite different.

"She's the only person we can't take in," says one of the creatures, grinning.

The first thing to decide is *what everyone wants to do.* Grace says frankly she wants to sit in the garden and talk to me.

Bryan says with reluctance, "In that case we'd better take the twins for a walk."

"Why not take them to the tennis club?" suggests Betty. "We could play and they could watch, couldn't they?"

"We might do both," suggests Perry.

Some argument ensues in the course of which it becomes fairly obvious that my three young friends are not looking forward with pleasure to the task of entertaining the twins. By the time they have decided upon a walk in the woods the twins have vanished.

"But where are they?" exclaims Betty in dismay.

"Perhaps they've gone for a walk by themselves," suggests Perry.

"But we were going to take them!" cries Bryan.

Oddly enough, now that their charges have disappeared, the three keepers seem disappointed and show an unaccountable eagerness to find the twins and conduct them to the woods.

187

"It's most extraordinary," says Betty. "They were here in the hall a few moments ago—"

"They do that sometimes," explains their mother. "They have a way of—of just fading out of the picture. One minute they're *there,* and the next they're gone. I shouldn't worry about them."

"Not worry about them!" I exclaim.

"Goodness no! They'll be all right," she replies.

"It's most extraordinary," says Betty. "I wonder whether . . ."

But Grace goes hastily into the drawing room and I, following her, find her collapsed on the sofa, giggling feebly.

"Oh dear!" says Grace. "I'm awfully sorry, Hester—but really . . ."

We both laugh helplessly, and then we apologise to one another and laugh again.

Grace says, "What a good thing we've both got a sense of humour! We'll call it quits, shall we?"

This is magnanimous of Grace for the sins of my family are the more heinous—and being older they ought to know better—but as we have a great deal to talk about we abandon the subject for others more interesting and, going out into the garden with cushions and rugs, we settle ourselves in two long cane-chairs for a real good chat.

It is delightful to talk to Grace; she is my own kind of person. Grace and I have followed the drum together; we have shared all sorts of vicissitudes and we have many common friends. Grace does most of the talking for I want to hear all the news of the regiment—which is at present stationed at Biddington—and about all the people who used to be in the regiment and are now retired. She tells me about Tubby Baxter's wedding, which was a magnificent affair. (Tubby having resisted the charms of women for years has at last fallen victim
188

to the pretty and attractive daughter of a peer.) She tells me about the Carters and about Stella Hardford, and all about their children; she tells me about Tom Ledgard and the Bensons and half a dozen more. It is ages since I heard any regimental chat and although it used to bore me a little, in the days when I heard too much of it, I find it extremely interesting now.

Time passes rapidly; I am amazed to discover it is getting on for one o'clock when the side gate opens and two small figures appear.

"Hullo!" says one of them. "We just wondered if it was nearly dinner-time, that's all."

"We've enjoyed ourselves frightfully," adds the other.

I am interested to observe that they are quite clean and tidy, for when Bryan was young and had enjoyed a morning's play he always returned dirty and bedraggled and unfit to be seen. Apparently the twins have inherited not only their mother's good looks but also her faculty for looking at all times as if she had "come out of a band-box."

"What have you been doing?" I enquire.

They look at one another and smile.

"Tell us, Ian," says Grace encouragingly.

Thus adjured, Ian (one supposes) takes from his pocket a small pile of silver and says, "We earned it."

"For the tank," explains Alec. "You see, Aunt Hester, we're collecting money for a proper tank for our gold-fish. It will be more fun for them than a bowl that they have to swim round and round in, all the time."

"We helped the man to deliver parcels," says Ian. "The other man, who usually helps him to deliver them, was off duty today, so we offered to help and he took us round in the van. It was fun."

"He's an awfully nice man. His name is George and he has twins—only they're girls—and he gave us sixpence each."

"But you've got three shillings there," says Grace.

"That was Miss Crease," replies Alec, who, although the younger, seems to be the leader of the couple.

"It was rather funny," says Ian smiling.

"We played a joke on her," says Alec, smiling too.

Grace does not know Miss Crease so she is not as surprised as I am.

"I'll tell you," says Alec, sitting down on the grass and preparing to entertain us with his tale.

"We'll both tell you," declares Ian, doing likewise.

"It was like this, you see. George said Miss Crease was an old terror, so we thought we'd play a joke on her."

"We often play jokes on people," puts in Ian.

"Well, you see, there were two parcels for Miss Crease, so Ian took one and I took the other. She was sitting in the garden in a chair."

"I went first," announces Ian. "I said 'Are you Miss Crease?' and she said, 'Yes.' So then I said, 'Here's a parcel for you. I'm helping the man deliver them because the other man's ill.' She was terribly ugly," says Ian shaking his head sadly. "Terribly ugly—but quite polite. She said, 'Thank you,' and she asked my name, and then she asked me to get a ball of wool that had rolled under a bush (she was knitting a sort of scarf with terribly ugly pink wool) so I got it for her. Then she said she liked boys, especially when they were clean and tidy and nicely behaved, and she gave me a shilling and I said 'Thank you' and went away."

"Then I went," says Alec giggling. "I went up to her and said, 'Are you Miss Crease?' and she said, 'What do you mean? You know perfectly well who I am.' Oh, it was rich!" exclaims Alec. "But I didn't laugh at all. I said, 'Well, are you? You see

190

I've got a parcel for Miss Crease, but I must know if you're her before I give it to you. George said so.' "

"I was listening!" declares Ian, rocking himself backwards and forwards in delight. "I was hiding behind a bush, listening!"

"So then," continues Alec. "So then she got a bit ratty and said, 'I suppose this is your idea of a joke! How dare you make fun of me! You're a very naughty little boy . . .' and she went on like that—awfully ratty, she was! Then Ian came out of the bushes and we stood in front of her like Tweedledum and Tweedledee with our arms round each other's necks —not saying anything but just standing."

"It always makes people laugh when they do that!"

"Miss Crease laughed and laughed!"

"She laughed till she choked!"

"It *was* funny!"

"And then she said, 'I suppose you think you'll get another shilling? Well, it's worth a shilling.' "

"And then she said, 'Which of you did I give the shilling to?' and Ian took it out of his pocket and showed it to her."

"So then she took another shilling out of her bag and said to Alec, 'I suppose you think I should give this to you?' and Alec said, 'Yes.' And then she laughed again and she said, 'Well, I shan't, because it says in the Bible, "To them that hath shall be given," ' and she gave the other shilling to me."

"Then she said to me, 'I suppose you think that isn't fair?' and I said, 'Well, it isn't fair, is it? But it doesn't matter because we always go shares.' She didn't say anything. So then we both said, 'Thank-you-very-much-and-good-bye,' and we came away."

"You're awful," says Grace chuckling. "Aren't they awful, Hester?"

I agree that they are awful.

Ian says, "But, Mummy, does it really say in the Bible, 'To them that hath shall be given'?"

Grace replies that she rather thinks it says, "Unto everyone that hath shall be given . . . but from him that hath not shall be taken away even that which he hath."

"But, Mummy, it isn't fair, is it? And how can you take away things from a person who hasn't got them?"

Grace says, "Ask your godmother. That's what godmothers are for." Which in my opinion is rank treachery.

Fortunately at this very moment Mrs. Daulkes opens the window and shouts, "Dinner's ready!" (this being her usual manner of announcing meals) and the twins leap to their feet and cry with one voice, "Hurrah, we're simply starving!"

By this time the others have returned; and, as they have been playing tennis all the morning, they have recovered their good humour and are interested to hear of the twins' activities.

Bryan says quite seriously, "You know there are all sorts of things you could do."

"Oh yes, we know," agrees Alex. "We're always thinking of new things."

"Can you think of anything really smashing?" asks Ian hopefully.

Four large eyes gaze at Bryan while he endeavours to think of a really smashing joke to be played upon an unsuspecting world by identical twins . . . but Bryan can think of nothing.

"Sometimes it doesn't work," says Alec. "I mean you have to think it out very carefully."

"Tell them about The Run," Ian suggests.

Alec giggles. "Yes, well, it was at school. There was a cross-country run and they put me down for it. I hate runs," says Alec emphatically. "And it was a beastly hot day—so we made a plan. Ian started off with the others and then fell out

192

and I waited near the end and came in with them. Of course I didn't *win;* that would have been cheating," says Alec virtuously. "I just came in about ninth. Everything seemed okey doke until we were sent for by Old Shirley. He's the headmaster of course."

"We knew we were for it then," says Ian with a sigh. "It's never anything *nice* when Old Shirley sends for you to go to his study."

Alec continues the tale: "Old Shirley was smiling in a funny way and he said, how was it I had started off for the run in dirty gym shoes and come in with clean ones. He said it was careless. He said it ought to have been the other way round. He said if I'd started off with clean ones and come in with dirty ones he wouldn't have noticed."

"He's so awfully noticing; we call him Sherlock," says Ian.

Grace says he is a man of many names. She and Jack usually refer to him as Shylock.

"So then," continues Alec, determined on rounding off his tale. "So then he said carelessness was a serious crime and he would have to punish us for it, and we both got whacked."

Bryan says it was jolly bad luck, that's what he thinks, and Perry agrees, saying runs were a blight; he always got out of them when possible and he wishes he had had a twin.

All is now gas and gaiters and plans are suggested for the afternoon.

"Could we take them to see the Lion's Gorge?" suggests Betty.

"Oh yes!" cries Alec in excitement. "That would be marvellous."

"I don't think it would be very interesting for them," says Bryan. "It's a long way and we'd have to go in the bus."

"Oh do let's!" exclaims Ian. "We'd love it . . ."

193

"We must start home directly after tea," says Grace.

"Well, what time is it?" enquires Alec.

Bryan looks at his watch and says it is two o'clock.

"Alec means what time does it happen," explains Ian.

"Yes," nods Alec. "What time do we have to be there?"

"Any time," replies Betty.

"Oh, do let's go!" cry the twins in unison.

Everyone now starts talking at once; Grace saying there is no time, Bryan saying they would not enjoy it, and the twins asserting that they *simply must see the lions.*

"There aren't any lions," says Perry, shouting above the din.

"No lions!" exclaims Alec in amazement. "But I thought Betty said we could see them having a gorge."

The matter takes a little explaining and the twins are more than a little disappointed when all is made clear.

"Oh well," says Alec looking very crestfallen. "If it's only an old rock . . . you see, I thought Betty said would we like to see the lions gorge . . . and of course it would have been fun."

"We saw them at the Zoo, gorging like anything," adds Ian. "The keeper gave them great chunks of meat on the end of pitchforks and they growled and tore them to bits. It was thrilling."

As there are no lions to be seen and the afternoon is warm and sultry, it is decided to abandon all idea of an expedition. Grace and I return to our chairs at one end of the garden and our five young friends recline on rugs at the other end; the fact that they are in full view of Miss Crease's bedroom window does not worry them. Grace and I still have plenty to say to one another but, in spite of my preoccupation, I notice that there is a good deal of talk and laughter going on in the other group and I have a feeling that various ideas for new and daring jokes are being suggested to the twins by their elders.

We see our friends off after tea. In spite of the unfavourable start the day has been a success; so much so that when we are all seated at the supper-table Bryan suggests we should ask them again.

"Again?" I ask, hiding my amusement beneath an expression of surprise.

Bryan chuckles and says, "They remind me of when I was a kid."

Perry nods, "Yes, me too. It's awfully amusing to hear that prep-school talk again. What fun we had at Nearhampton!"

"It *was* fun," agrees Bryan. "You know, Hedgehog old boy, one didn't really appreciate it at the time. It's only when one looks back . . . no responsibilities, that's the secret. I mean you didn't even have the responsibility of working. You were *made* to work and you did as little as you could. You never *thought* about work. Knowledge was shoved into you without your having to bother. All you thought about was rugger or cricket; all you worried about was whether you would get into the Second Eleven."

Perry says, "Do you remember those feasts we had in the dorm after lights out? And how we ragged about and had idiotic jokes with our pals and yelled our heads off? Then one of the prefects came and said, 'What a filthy row! Shut up, you little brutes.' I began to feel old when I became a prefect," adds Perry smiling ruefully.

"You were beastly smug," declares Bryan. "Lord, how I hated you that term!"

"My responsibilities were very heavy," says Perry laughing.

The conversation continues on these lines. Anybody

would think my companions were middle-aged at least.

"Forty years on," I tell them.

"That's the Eton Song!" exclaims Bryan in surprise.

"Yes I know: 'Forty Years On, growing older and older'; it just came into my mind when I heard you and Perry talking about your lost youth."

"Well, but it *is* lost. We shan't ever be ten again."

Betty has been silent, but now she says, "When I'm married I should like to have twins, just like Ian and Alec."

Thursday, 9th August

*I*T IS wet this morning; the rain drizzles down in dreary
fashion and the trees are droopy and despondent. No
tennis is possible so my young friends put on their waterproofs and sally forth to do the shopping. No sooner have they
gone than Tony arrives and I can see from his face that something has disturbed him.

"Look here, Hester," says Tony, taking me by the arm
and dragging me into the drawing room. "I've just heard—
I mean Freda heard yesterday—Freda went to tea with Mrs.
Meller, the vicar's wife. Apparently there's some garbled
account of our meeting in Rome all over the village."

"Oh, I've known that for ages."

"You knew!" he exclaims.

"It's Miss Crease, I expect. She said something about
Rome one day. Of course she watches me like a hawk."

"How does Miss Crease know about Rome?"

"Through Mrs. Alston," I reply. "Mrs. Alston called at
the pensione and spoke to Signora Scarlatti—"

"Damn the lot!" exclaims Tony with concentrated ferocity. "Signora Scarlatti, Mrs. Alston, Miss Crease and Mrs.
Meller . . . and all because I flew over to Rome and took you
out to dinner!"

"Does it matter?"

"Not to me," he replies. "I was afraid you would be
worried."

"But it's all so silly."

Tony walks to the window and looks out at the drizzling rain. "I know it's silly," says Tony. "The only thing is supposing one of these charming old ladies thinks it her duty to write to Tim?"

"Tim knows all about it."

"Tim knows!"

"Yes, Tim likes me to write and tell him everything that happens, and especially anything amusing, so of course I told him what we did in Rome."

"Great Scott!" exclaims Tony.

"Why? I mean why shouldn't I?"

"No reason at all—as long as he doesn't—take it the wrong way."

Tony's gravity alarms me a little, for it is unlike Tony to be serious about unimportant matters; and, now that I think about it, I begin to wonder whether Tim *has* taken it the wrong way. Perhaps Tim was not amused at my amusing account of all that happened in Rome: of how Tony was shown into my bedroom by mistake and how we braved the vultures and went out to dinner together, of my attempts to absorb spaghetti in the manner of the Romans and finally of our walk back to the pensione in the dark and the Signora's ecstatic welcome.

"What did Tim say in his letters?" asks Tony after a few moments' silence.

"Nothing much," I reply uncomfortably. "I mean he has been too busy to write long letters. Of course I haven't told him about the gossip. I thought he might be annoyed."

"Annoyed!"

"Angry, then," I suggest, amending my statement.

"He'll be rabid," declares Tony. "If I know anything about Tim he'll be absolutely rabid; and his rage will descend, not upon Miss Crease and Co., but upon me."

198

Thursday, 9th August

"Why should it?"

"Because I'm the world's prize fool," says Tony.

There is a short but pregnant silence.

"All the same he had better be told," says Tony at last. "He had better be told the whole story from beginning to end. I'll write to him myself and explain everything."

"Don't worry him too much!" I exclaim. "Don't make too much of it! It's horrible to be worried over things that are happening far away. You can't talk it over and explain and everything seems a hundred times worse . . ."

"I'll be careful," says Tony, looking down at me and smiling.

When I accompany my guest to the gate I am surprised to see no large shiny car waiting there.

"I parked Belshazzar in the square," says Tony nonchalantly.

His casual air does not deceive me. "No, Tony!" I exclaim. "No, I don't like that. When you come to see me please come in your car and leave it at the gate as usual."

"Yes," says Tony thoughtfully. "You're right of course . . ."

"And please come whenever you feel inclined," I tell him. "I don't care a button for those old cats and I'm very proud of your friendship."

He looks at me with an odd sort of expression and says in an odd sort of voice that he is proud of being my friend.

There is silence for a few moments after that, and then Tony says in quite a different voice, "That old cat next door is looking at us out of her window. It would be fun to kiss you, but I suppose that's out of the question."

"Quite out of the question," I reply. "I shouldn't dream of allowing you to kiss me—not even to please Miss Crease."

"I was afraid you wouldn't," says Tony with a sigh.

Saturday, 11th August

*T*HIS IS the day appointed for me to do the flowers in church and, as Betty has signified her desire to help me, we take a basket and a pair of scissors and go out into the garden to cut them. Oddly enough I have never been asked to do this before—neither has Betty—and we are both somewhat elated at the privilege and the responsibility which has fallen to our lot.

"It will be nice seeing them when we go to church to-morrow," says Betty happily. "We'll know we've done them, I mean. Do you think those white campanulas would be nice? Do you think we could put some of those lovely pink snapdragons with them? Or must they be all white?"

We are still considering the matter very seriously when Mrs. Daulkes comes out of the house with a letter in her hand.

"It's from Mrs. Meller," explains Mrs. Daulkes. "The youngest Meller boy brought it on 'is bike. I told 'im 'e'd better wait for an answer, but 'e said no answer was required. If it's to ask you to go round collecting for the organ *just you say no.* You've plenty to do without trailing round the village collecting for the organ."

But the letter is not to ask me to collect for the organ, it is to tell me that I am not to do the flowers . . . and, although Mrs. Meller does not state the reason in plain words, she makes it quite clear that she considers me unfit to arrange the altar vases and has changed her plans accordingly.

Saturday, 11th August

It is foolish to feel hurt and disappointed; it is even more foolish to feel ashamed. I remind myself that I have done nothing wrong, so why be ashamed? I have known for some time that the ladies of Old Quinings were shaking their heads over my friendship with Tony and it has not worried me; why should it worry me now? Why should I suddenly feel sick and shaky? It is a mistake, that's all. It is a very small thing. It will be all the same a hundred years hence—nay, it will be all the same one year hence. There is nothing to worry about. I decide that I am not ashamed, nor upset, and only a very little annoyed with Mrs. Meller and her cronies for their stupidity.

But Betty is still busy cutting flowers. She is intent upon her task, her bright head stooping over the beds as she looks at each one and carefully selects the best—and only the best—for their high destiny. I have got to disappoint Betty, which is a cruel thought, and the longer I leave it the worse it will be.

I call to Betty and tell her we are not to do the flowers after all.

Betty looks up and comes towards me. "Not to do the flowers?" she asks in amazement. "But why?"

"There's been some mistake," I reply, looking at the letter in my hand, for it is impossible to meet Betty's straight honest gaze and lie to her. I hate lies at any time (even the lies which are commonly called white) but to lie to Betty is unbearable.

"Some mistake?" she asks. "You mean somebody else is doing them?"

"Yes."

"What a pity! I've picked such a lot and they're so beautiful!"

"Yes, I know."

"We'll do them next week," says Betty comfortingly.

201

"No, I don't think so. Mrs. Meller doesn't ask us to."

"You mean we're not to do them at all?"

"Mrs. Meller doesn't mention that."

Betty looks at me. "Oh well," she says. "It's—it's disappointing but it can't be helped. Don't worry, darling. Don't look so awfully worried about it. We'll get out all the vases and have a grand show in the house. That will be nice, won't it?"

"Yes, it's a lovely idea," I reply.

Betty puts her arm through mine and squeezes it. "I know you're disappointed, darling," she says. "I am, too, of course, but it doesn't matter *really*, does it?"

"No, of course not."

"It isn't an important sort of disappointment."

"No, of course not."

"Darling," says Betty anxiously. "Darling, you aren't feeling sick or anything, are you?"

"No," I reply smiling at her and returning the pressure of her arm. "No, I'm perfectly all right. Let's go and get out the vases and arrange the flowers together."

Just for a few minutes Betty and I have changed places; she has been the sensible elder and I the child. It is comforting to lean upon her sympathy and kindness . . . and I am comforted.

Sunday, 12th August

MY THREE young friends go off to church without me. It surprises them a little that I do not want to go, and Betty asks anxiously if it is because I am disappointed about the flowers? I assure her that it is not. This is true, for the prohibition to arrange the flowers is merely symptomatic of Mrs. Meller's feelings, and it is her feelings about me which prevent me from going to church. It would be impossible to fix my attention upon the service with Mrs. Meller sitting just behind me; her eyes boring into my back and her mind thinking unkind thoughts about me . . . and for all I know Mr. Meller may share her views. I shall go next Sunday, for by that time I shall have recovered from the shock. Today I cannot go.

There is very little to do in the house (we are having a cold lunch and salad from the garden) and, having made the necessary preparations for the meal, I decide to go for my favourite walk by the river. The day is silver with a layer of thin cloud obscuring the sun and everything is very quiet and peaceful. I walk along immersed in thought and, if the truth be told, feeling a little unhappy. There is nobody about, not a creature to be seen; some of the inhabitants of Old Quinings are sleeping, others have gone to church; it is not until I reach the fallen tree beside my special pool that I see another human being.

Anne Carlyle is sitting upon the tree gazing at the river and it is obvious from her pose that, like me, she is deep in

203

thoughts and not very happy ones. I watch her for a few moments and note the droop of her thin shoulders . . . and wonder whether I should speak to her or not. Perhaps she has come here seeking peace and solitude and my advent will be unwelcome.

At that moment Anne looks up and sees me, and her sad face brightens to a smile.

"Mrs. Christie!" she exclaims. "I thought I was the only wicked person!"

"Two wicked people! But I thought you were going to call me Hester."

"I forgot," says Anne blushing. "There are so few . . . somehow I don't make friends easily, and I have no relations. In fact I have just been thinking I could drop out of life very easily. There would be—no ripples," adds Anne with her eyes on the pool.

"Anne!"

"It's ungrateful, isn't it? I have a great deal to make me thankful, and usually I am thankful and contented. But today is my birthday and although the twelfth of August has no significance and is just like any other day in the year I am foolish enough to feel it to be a milestone." Anne smiles at me rather shyly and adds, "I was sitting on the milestone reckoning up all the miles I have travelled and feeling a little anxious about the miles in front of me when you found me."

It is difficult to know what to say and even if I knew what to say it is doubtful whether I could say it. Perhaps it is foolish to attach importance to the day upon which one was born, but the celebration of a birthday is a pleasant custom. Tim and Bryan and Betty—and others as well—remember my birthday and make it happy. How sad—how unbearable it would be if there was nobody in the world to give one a loving greeting on one's birthday morning!

Sunday, 12th August

In view of what Anne has said it is impossible to wish her the usual birthday wish, so I kiss her—which surprises and embarrasses her considerably—and wish her happiness.

When this small ceremony is over Anne changes the subject abruptly by asking why I am not at church, adding hastily that if I do not want to reveal the reason there is no need for me to do so. But this new friend of mine is sympathetic and I need a confidante so, after a little hesitation, I tell her the whole story.

Anne listens in silence—she is an excellent listener—and when I have finished the silence continues. I glance at her anxiously and begin to wonder whether it was a mistake to tell her; she is a nun-like creature and perhaps she is shocked.

"Poor Mrs. Meller!" says Anne at last.

"Poor Mrs. Meller?" I repeat in bewilderment.

"So narrow-minded, so mistaken in her judgment!"

"Mistaken, certainly," I agree. "It's dreadful that anyone could think I was so wicked."

"Not wicked, surely."

"Mrs. Meller thinks so."

"Yes, because she is a foolish, narrow-minded woman. Love should be free," says Anne calmly.

"Love should be free!" I echo in amazement.

"Perfectly free," declares my nun-like friend. "I have thought about it a great deal and the more I think about it the more I realise the beauty of true love. It is quite wrong that any woman—or any man—should be tied by marriage. In an Utopian State love would be free."

"But, Anne—"

"Of course I appreciate the difficulties," she continues thoughtfully. "And perhaps in our present state of partial civilisation it would be impossible to abolish the tie of marriage . . ." She goes on to expound her ideas on the subject with earnest sincerity, quoting various Great Lovers of classical fame—amongst them Sappho, who threw herself from the promontory of Leucadia into the sea for love of Phaon:

> "Thence injured lovers, leaping from above,
> Their flames extinguish and forget to love."

Naturally she does not omit to mention Abelard and Héloise and Hero and Leander, who counted the world well lost for love. She sweeps on through the centuries; she speaks of Romeo and Juliet, of Lord Nelson and Emma Hamilton and a host of other Great Lovers whose names I have never heard . . . and from all these examples she draws the conclusion that Cupid should reign supreme and the course of True Love should always run smooth. It is obvious that she has studied the subject and given it much thought and her erudition is amazing.

Several times I endeavour to interrupt Anne to explain that I do not share her views, but without success . . . and somehow this reminds me of another conversation on the same subject but in very different surroundings; my conversation with Signora Scarlatti. It is very strange to discover that Anne and the Signora share the same views. Two more different women it would be difficult to imagine yet both are apostles of "Free Love." Stranger still is it to discover that, whereas I was not really shocked to hear these views propounded by the Signora, I am definitely shocked to hear them propounded by Anne. I am so shocked that for some minutes my brain refuses to function, but after a little I realise that Anne holds these astounding views because she is absolutely innocent—and ignorant. In theory she knows a great deal about love, in practice nothing. The Signora's case was the opposite.

Fortunately I am not hampered by the necessity of trying

to explain myself in a foreign language. "Listen to me!" I exclaim, breaking, without ceremony, into her account of the love of Paul and Virginie. "Listen to me, my dear Anne. You know nothing whatever about it."

"I know nothing about it!" she cries in bewilderment.

"You don't know what you're talking about," I explain. "The kind of love you're talking about is very wonderful no doubt, but when you've been married for over twenty years you love one another in quite a different way. You're partners in the game of life, you're necessary to one another. It's a far bigger thing than—than physical attraction which does not last."

"But in many cases—"

"No, it does not," I tell her. "It may develop into the other kind of love—the kind I'm talking about—or it may die a natural death. Only time can tell which of the two things will happen."

"But, Mrs. Christie!" exclaims Anne. "What about Robert Browning and Elizabeth Barrett? They were Great Lovers all their lives!"

"They loved one another—which is quite a different thing."

Anne does not believe me. She is a romantic and her fairy tales satisfy her and give colour to her drab existence . . . and, as it is now getting late, I rise and tell her I must go home and cook the potatoes for lunch.

"You are funny," says Anne.

"Potatoes are important," I reply. "Love fades and dust hath closed Helen's eye but potatoes go on forever. I do them in the pressure cooker so they don't take long."

Anne laughs—which is what I intended her to do—and we walk home together in amity.

We talk about Miss Stroude as we walk home. Anne has

seen the Byron letter, but has no idea of its present whereabouts. She is very angry when she hears that I have been directed to pull down the blinds and shut out the sun so that it shall not fade the carpets.

"I wouldn't do it if I were you," says Anne earnestly. "The house was built as a sun-trap—that was Lorna's idea; it was built so that every room should get as much sunshine as possible. It would be interesting to know whether Miss Stroude has any right to tell you to pull down the blinds. You might ask a lawyer."

I agree that I might, but add that it would be of little use for I am so frightened of Miss Stroude that I am bound to obey her behests.

Tuesday, 14th August

HITHERTO BETTY has taken singularly little interest in clothes (she likes them to be comfortable and to give her complete freedom of movement and, if these ends are attained, she does not care how they look) so it is a surprise to me to find how thrilled and excited she is over her new party frock. Her eyes are bright and her cheeks even pinker than usual when the box arrives from Harrods and we carry it upstairs to my bedroom and unpack it on the bed. Harrods has done us proud. There is a pale green silk, trimmed with ruchings; there is a blue and pink in pretty pastel colours and there is one with a white satin bodice trimmed with rose-buds and a full skirt of white net.

Betty tries them on and regards her reflection in the mirror with delight. "I'm really very pretty," she declares.

The surprised tone of her voice amuses me for it seems strange that my daughter has reached the age of sixteen without being aware of the fact.

"I like the green best," she continues. "It's more grown-up."

My preference is for the white and I point out that white is recognised as the correct wear for the young.

"That's an old-fashioned idea," says Betty.

"The white one suits you better."

"But I like the green one best."

It is unfortunate that she should like the green one best

because she looks adorable in the white, with the pink rose-buds, and I am determined that this is the one she shall have. I remind her that I am choosing the frock and, incidentally, paying for it.

Betty glances at me enquiringly and gives in at once. I can see she thinks it good policy to propitiate me. "Oh well," she says. "Of course it's lovely. If I hadn't seen the green one I would have been absolutely thrilled with it. I like the green one because it is such a lovely colour; but if you like the white one . . ."

"It suits you best," I explain. "People don't wear clothes because they are attractive to look at or because they like the colour. They choose clothes to suit their personalities and to enhance their appearance. The white one is *you*."

She puts on the white one again and again she examines her reflection. "Yes," she says with a sigh. "Yes, it does enhance my appearance. I'm a babyish-looking person, that's the trouble. I wish I were like Susan; the green one would suit *her*."

The new dress is a secret between Betty and me. It is a feminine secret. Bryan and Perry have been kept in ignorance of our doings.

"They won't care," says Betty. "Men aren't interested in clothes. I don't suppose they'll even *notice* I've got a new frock."

My ideas upon the subject are different and when Betty is ready for the dance, arrayed in all her finery, I decide that only a blind man could fail to be impressed. Perhaps I am partial—mothers sometimes are—but to me Betty is a radiant vision, a personification of spring.

Bryan and Perry are ready first and are waiting for us in the drawing room when we appear . . . and it is obvious from their expressions that my ideas have been right and Betty's wrong.

"Gosh!" exclaims Bryan looking at his young sister in amazement. "Gosh, you've got a new dress! My hat, you're quite good-looking!"

These compliments from a brother are the height of admiration and I feel convinced that if Bryan is so impressed others will be stunned.

Perhaps Perry is stunned for he says nothing.

"It's pretty, isn't it?" says Betty, turning round slowly. "Mummy chose it for me."

"It's very pretty," agrees Bryan. "It isn't very serviceable, of course."

"I don't intend to climb trees in it," declares Betty with a smile.

Bryan does not comment upon this statement. He is still looking at her with critical appreciation. "You really are *quite* pretty," says Bryan. "It's a pity you don't take more trouble with your appearance on ordinary occasions, you know."

"Betty always looks pretty," says Perry.

This remark is the first Perry has made, but Bryan and Betty are too intent upon their argument to hear it.

"I do take trouble," declares Betty indignantly. "Nobody can look nice in a gym tunic or a school coat. I don't go about in baggy trousers, anyway."

Bryan ignores this jibe, which, to be fair, is quite unmerited for Bryan is rather particular about his appearance. "You've got lipstick on," he says. "I think you'd look a lot nicer without it."

"Oh, I thought it looked rather nice!"

"You aren't the type to wear lipstick," says Bryan gravely. "Susan wears it."

"My dear girl, Susan is different. You'll never look like Susan if you live to be a hundred."

This curious statement seems to convince Betty. "Oh," she says. "Oh well—I'll lick it off. It's got quite a nice taste."

She licks it off and Bryan completes its removal with a corner of his handkerchief.

We are now ready and, as the taxi is waiting for us, we set off.

Charters Towers is ablaze with lights, there are lights in every window and the front façade of the palatial building is flood-lit. I look at it with interest as we drive up to the door for I have not been here for more years than I like to remember; in fact not since Tim and I spent an uncomfortable weekend here and Tim rode in a Point to Point. Let me hasten to add that in the matter of creature comforts the weekend was luxurious in the extreme, it was my self-consciousness which made me uncomfortable. The other guests all knew one another well; they were hunting people, rich and carefree. My hostess was alarming in the extreme, and Tony—who was then a major in the regiment—was in some ways even more alarming. Since then much water has flowed beneath the bridge; I have knocked about the world and overcome my shyness; since then I have come to appreciate Tony for what he is (a true friend in good or bad weather) and the flippant manner which he uses to disguise his benevolence has ceased to deceive me.

Tony is welcoming his guests in the hall and has a few words for everyone. Some he welcomes in a dignified manner, others with banter and ribaldry.

The drawing room has been cleared of furniture except at one end where there is a Persian carpet and a few comfortable chairs. Here Lady Morley sits enthroned and I realise we are expected to greet our hostess—or allow ourselves to be greeted—and move on. The room is very long, with six tall windows; at the other end it opens into a large conservatory full of brilliant flowers. One corner of the room has been roped off for the band, the members of which are settling themselves and starting to tune up. A number of guests have arrived before us and are standing about on the shining parquet floor talking and laughing gaily. The scene is set and to my mind it is a brilliant setting; Tony's warning that it would be "a primitive affair" seems unwarranted.

Most of the other guests are complete strangers of course and I am looking about, somewhat at a loss, when I am addressed in honeyed accents by Mrs. Winthrop. She looks even older tonight, having chosen most unwisely to wear a gorgeous gown of gold brocade.

"Mrs. Christie, how delightful to see you!" she says. "I hope you were none the worse for that picnic."

I am about to reply in suitable terms when I realise that Mrs. Winthrop requires no answer and that her enquiry as to my well-being is a mere formality.

"And Perry!" exclaims Mrs. Winthrop, looking over my left shoulder. "How nice to see you again! I'm so glad you were able to come. How is your grandfather?"

Perry replies that his grandfather is quite fit.

"Good!" cries Mrs. Winthrop. "Splendid! I expect he's looking forward to seeing you . . . here is Diana! I don't know if she has any dances left—mothers aren't supposed to ask—but you must have a little chat, mustn't you?" Mrs. Winthrop laughs in an artificial manner and produces her daughter (in much the same manner as a conjuror produces a rabbit from a hat) and Perry has no alternative but to smile and ask Diana for a dance.

This explains the cordiality and at the same time reminds me of my duties. I ought to be finding partners for Betty of course; though, as I know nobody in the room, the task will not be easy.

I look round anxiously but Betty seems to have vanished.

"If you're looking for Betty, she's over there," says Bryan pointing to a cluster of black-clad figures at the other side of the room. "She's in the middle of *that*. It's rather comic, really. I hope it won't give her a swelled head to have all those chaps milling round wanting to dance with her . . . it's just as well Perry and I booked our dances with the kid before we came in."

The crowd is increasing every moment and the buzz of talk waxes louder and louder. The Alstons have arrived, so have the MacDougalls. Susan is here, looking very lovely and ethereal in jade green silk. She makes her way towards us through the crowd and is greeted with enthusiasm by Bryan and Perry.

Susan is accompanied by a tall handsome man with grey hair. "This is Daddy, Mrs. Christie," says Susan. "He doesn't dance but he wants to talk to you."

Mr. Morven smiles. "You've been so kind to Susan," he explains. "Perhaps we could have a chat later."

The matter is arranged and Mr. Morven moves on.

Anne Carlyle has come; I can see her standing at the door looking slightly dazed as if she had been transported here by black magic and was wondering where on earth she had got to. Tony suddenly appears at my elbow and says he has welcomed all his guests and how many dances can he have.

"Three if you like," I reply.

"Does that mean six?" he enquires.

I tell him it means three exactly and add that I am now too old to dance all the evening but intend to sit out and talk to the other chaperones.

Tuesday, 14th August

"Don't be so silly," says Tony. "You've come here to dance, and dance you shall." He produces several partners for me and then moves on to do more introducing as behoves a considerate host.

Soon after this the band begins to play and the company begins to dance.

Somewhat to my surprise I discover that all my young male friends want to dance with me: Bryan and Perry and Edmond Alston, who would be better employed dancing with their contemporaries, will not take "no" for an answer; when I point out that girls have been provided for them they reply to the effect that they are doing their duty by the girls.

It is fun to dance with Bryan and I am glad to find he dances extremely well. He seems surprised that I am a competent partner and when our waltz is over says regretfully that if he had known I could dance like that he would have booked another with me. It's too late now because his programme is full . . . unless he cuts out that Winthrop girl who is the dullest, dreariest thing and the world's worst dancer. I reply firmly that it is extremely bad form to cut dances and anyhow she is Tony's niece.

After that I dance with Jack MacDougall, who spends his whole time talking about the twins, bewailing the expense of their education and the fact that, although this costs the earth, the twins seem to be unappreciative of their opportunities. I have not seen Jack for years but I remember he was always grumbling about something (if he was not grumbling about the regiment and the incompetence of his senior officers he was moaning about the rate of promotion or Grace's inability to cope with domestic problems). The years have not changed Jack, he still must have some grievance or he would not be happy, but it seems a pity that his present grievance should be directed against his sons. I tell Jack that I liked his sons, and enquire whether Jack appreciated his educational opportunities when he was ten years old.

Jack says, "Oh!" in a rather surprised voice and then adds, "but in those days school fees were only about a third of what they are now."

This answer confirms my opinion that men, not women, are the illogical sex.

Edmond is not a good performer and after we have circled the room twice he suggests we should sit out the remainder of the dance, so we find two chairs in the conservatory and light cigarettes. I have been looking forward to a chat with Edmond, for he and I got on very well before and found plenty to say to one another, but tonight he is not in good form and conversation is difficult. Edmond sits forward in his chair and gazes at the large red and white tiles which form the floor of the conservatory, and presently he breaks into my monologue to ask if I think dancing is important.

"Important?" I enquire.

"I mean," says Edmond. "I mean I can't dance. You noticed that, of course. You can't expect girls to dance with you if you can't dance well."

This statement is so true that it is difficult to find a reassuring answer. It is all the more difficult when Perry and Susan sweep past the door of the conservatory amongst the throng of other dancers. Their steps seem to suit exactly and obviously they are enjoying themselves. I look at Edmond and realise from his face that he has seen them too.

"I suppose one could learn," says Edmond miserably.

"Of course you could learn!"

"If I had time . . ." says Edmond.

"But you've got to work, and that's much more important than dancing."

"I know," he agrees. "It's just sometimes—one feels—but of course you're right, Mrs. Christie."

"How is the work going?"

Edmond is silent for a few moments and then says impulsively, "If only Mother would leave me alone it would be easier."

"But I thought your mother—"

"Oh, I know!" he exclaims quickly. "Mother is awfully kind. I ought not to say anything . . ."

Edmond hesitates, and in the pause I remember the hippopotamus.

"Awfully kind," repeats Edmond, "and of course I appreciate all she has done; but sometimes I wish she hadn't given up all her visits to come here and be with me. It's dull for her, you see."

"Yes, I know, but—"

"I really ought to have gone to Cornwall."

"Why don't you go now?"

"Oh," says Edmond, twisting his thin hands together. "Oh yes—but—but things are difficult. I ought to, of course, but I can't go away now. I know I ought to—but I can't."

There is no time to say more; another dance is starting and I have promised it to Susan's father. I am sorry to leave Edmond for I have a feeling that if we had longer together he would confide in me.

"Come and talk to me some morning," I tell him as I rise.

"Yes, I'd like to," he says. "Only I usually read in the mornings. I usually go out early, before breakfast."

"Come any time that suits you."

Mr. Morven does not want to dance; he suggests refreshments, which he has discovered are to be had in the dining room, and as we have heard about one another (though not too much) and have a good deal in common we fall quite naturally into conversation.

Suddenly I realise that somebody is standing beside me and, looking up, I behold a friendly face wreathed in smiles.

"Symes!" I exclaim in delight.

"Yes, Mrs. Christie," says Symes. "Yes, it's me. I wondered if you'd remember me; it's a long time since Donford, isn't it? Yes, I'm still with the General. I'm with him in a private capacity now of course," says Symes grandly.

I explain to Mr. Morven that Symes was Tony Morley's batman and that Symes and I have shared various experiences, grave and gay.

"That's right," agrees Symes. "Making up those parcels of wool at the Depot and shooting on the moor—and that day when the Gerry plane came down; that was a bit of all right, wasn't it?"

This is not how I would have described the incident and I am about to say so when Mr. Morven, who has been listening with interest to the conversation, chips in and asks if he may be told about it. Symes is only too pleased to oblige and gives him a short but spirited account of the shooting party on the moor, describes how the "Gerry plane was pranged" and its occupants made prisoners. Mr. Morven is suitably impressed by the recital but says the war seems so long ago that it sounds like a fairy story.

Although I have not thought of Symes for years the sight of his pleasant open face takes me back to those far-off days and I remember all about him. I remember the photograph he showed me—though not the name of the sitter—and I enquire somewhat tentatively if Symes is married.

Symes says he is and he isn't, if I know what he means . . . and then, seeing that obviously I do not, he explains

218

that he and "Miss Gertie Ebb" *did* get married but that it did not last long.

"She took up with another chap when I was in the desert," says Symes cheerfully. "It was a bit of a blow at the time but it was just as well in the long run. Gertie was a smart girl; she'd always lived in London and she liked a gay life—shops and pictures and all that. She wouldn't have liked it here, Gertie wouldn't—too quiet—and I wouldn't have left the General, not for nobody. So it was just as well we got it over when we did. Now, what are you going to have, Mrs. Christie? A nice bit of tongue and salad is what I would recommend."

Mr. Morven and I accept the recommendation; we eat tongue and salad and drink hock-cup. I tell him how much I admire Susan and he tells me that Bryan is a fine lad and Betty quite adorable and, although we feign a proper modesty about the attractions of our offspring, it is obvious that we each think the other has excellent taste. We are getting on famously when Tony appears with thunder on his brow and says, there we are! and do I realise this is his dance?

"My dear fellow, I *am* sorry!" exclaims Mr. Morven. "It is entirely my fault. I had no idea another dance had started. Mrs. Christie and I have been discussing our children and the time passed like lightning."

Tony murmurs something about pistols for two and coffee for one—at dawn—and sweeps me away.

This unceremonious behaviour is unlike Tony and, as we dance, I tell him he was rude to poor Mr. Morven.

"Rude to poor Mr. Morven!" echoes Tony scornfully.

"Well, you were."

"This is my dance and it's nearly over and I didn't know where you had gone."

We finish the dance in silence and retire to an alcove beneath the stairs. Tony is still cross and, as it is unthinkable to quarrel with him, I tell him in contrite tones that I am very sorry I forgot his dance. But, far from being pacified, he becomes crosser than ever and says he wishes he had never thought of giving this wretched party.

"Tony!" I exclaim. "But what on earth is the matter? You know perfectly well I don't care a pin for Mr. Morven."

This seems to sooth him considerably. "It wasn't altogether Morven," says Tony. "I mean he was just the last straw which upset the apple-cart."

"I suppose you mean the last apple which broke the camel's back?"

"Something like that," he agrees. "The fact is I was alarmed. I hunted high and low for you . . . and then I saw you sitting there with Richard Morven, having a good time!"

"Alarmed!"

"I thought you had gone home or something. I thought —perhaps—somebody had said something—to upset you."

For a moment I am completely bewildered and then light dawns. "I suppose you've been talking to Mrs. Meller?"

"No, to Miss Carlyle."

The implications of this simple statement are extremely complicated, but what strikes me most forcibly is the humorous possibilities of a conversation between Tony and Anne Carlyle and I begin to laugh.

"What's the joke?" enquires Tony. "I had to talk to the poor soul. She seemed so—lost. She was frightfully shy at first and then, quite suddenly, she wasn't shy any longer and said the most amazing things."

I am laughing uncontrollably by this time and, laughter being infectious, Tony begins to laugh too.

"I suppose it *is* funny," he admits. "I mean she's such a mousy little creature that it's quite startling when she airs her very broad-minded views. Oh well, if you think it's funny that's all right. *She* said you were unhappy and upset and that people were being unkind to you. She seems very fond of you," adds Tony with a surprised inflexion in his voice.

"You find that surprising, Tony?"

"Well—yes, if you want the truth!"

Tony is now himself again. He teases me about my friendship with Anne Carlyle, asking what we talk about when we are alone and refusing to believe me when I tell him we discuss witchcraft and the art of Landscape Gardening and the benefits of travel. Presently he says, "I must go. I'm dancing this with your beautiful daughter; she kept it for me. Wasn't it sweet of her?"

I look at Tony to see if this is a joke but he is perfectly serious.

"She's ravishing," adds Tony. "It's a delight to look at her."

"Wasn't she ravishing yesterday?" I enquire.

"Oh!" exclaims Tony. "But yesterday—"

"Yesterday she wasn't dressed in satin and net and rosebuds," I tell him. "That makes all the difference, doesn't it?"

"No, of course not," he replies smiling. "At least . . . I suppose it shouldn't . . . I must fly!"

After this I talk to Lady Morley for a little and find it difficult, for Lady Morley has always been an alarming personage. She is no less alarming tonight, dressed in black velvet and lace, glittering with diamonds and seated upon an old oak chair which, with its high straight back and carved arms, resembles a throne.

We talk at cross purposes for a few minutes and I am beginning to entertain a suspicion that Lady Morley has mistaken me for someone else when suddenly she says, "Do you know that Mrs. Christie?"

I am struck dumb.

"Everyone's talking about her," continues Lady Morley. "Some silly nonsense about her and Tony. Freda says the woman is here tonight."

"Yes," I murmur helplessly. "Yes, but there's nothing—I mean—"

"Do you know her?"

"Yes, of course. I mean—"

"Point her out to me," says her ladyship in peremptory tones.

For a moment I am tempted to point out somebody else to Lady Morley and make my escape, but this course is fraught with peril for obviously Lady Morley must know most of her guests. The only other course open to me is to treat the matter as a joke, so I point to myself and endeavour to smile.

"What do you mean?" she asks in surprise.

"I'm Hester Christie," I tell her. "I'm so sorry I didn't introduce myself. I thought you knew me."

"You're Mrs. Christie?"

"Yes."

Lady Morley does not apologise for her mistake, nor is she the least embarrassed at having made it. She raises her lorgnettes and looks at me. "How strange!" she says.

Fortunately the band begins to play "God Save the King" and I am rescued from my predicament. I collect my family, we all say good-bye and go home.

Betty is so exhausted with her night of pleasure and dissipation that she goes to sleep in the car with her head on my shoulder. She has to be awakened when we arrive at The Small House and put to bed like a baby. As her head touches the pillow she murmurs sleepily that she wishes Uncle Tony would have a dance every night. It's been simply gorgeous.

Wednesday, 15th August

WE ARE all tired after the dance. I am awakened by Mrs. Daulkes shouting lustily beneath my window and I rise very reluctantly and go down to open the door. The others sleep like tops until nearly lunch-time, when they appear looking fresh and fit and perfectly restored.

Perry is leaving tomorrow and although I am very sorry he is going I have not tried to persuade him to stay. It is natural that his grandfather should want to see him and it is right that Perry should go. As this is the last night of Perry's visit we are going to have a special supper with cold chicken and ham and a chocolate pudding with jam sauce.

Everything has been prepared by Mrs. Daulkes and I am in the kitchen putting the finishing touches to the repast when Perry appears at the door. He explains that Bryan and Betty are still playing tennis but he thought he would come back early.

"You have your packing to do," I suggest.

"Yes," agrees Perry, sitting down upon a kitchen-chair and looking at me with his clear hazel eyes. "Yes, I've got to pack, but it won't take long."

"Did you have some good sets?" I enquire.

"Yes," replies Perry. "Yes, very good sets. Susan was there."

Obviously Perry wants to tell me something and finds it difficult . . . but I have no idea what it is so I cannot help him. Perhaps the best thing is to talk vaguely and give him confidence. "I'm glad Susan was there," I tell him. "It makes a better game, doesn't it? And she's such an attractive creature, so pretty and amusing."

"Yes, I suppose she is," agrees Perry doubtfully. "The fact is I don't know much about girls. Perhaps it's because I've always been with men. I don't remember my mother at all . . . and Grandfather is a bit of a recluse."

It is difficult to know what to say to this, so I say nothing.

Perry leans forward with his hands between his knees and, as I am standing above him at the table, I can see the parting in his thick glossy hair. "You know," says Perry slowly in his low deep voice. "You know the funny thing is I don't see much attraction in girls . . . except one . . . and attraction isn't the right word for what I feel about her. I mean it wouldn't matter what she looked like. I'd love her just the same."

This confidence touches me profoundly. This is the real Perry speaking from his heart and I realise that although he is so young in years his feelings are mature—for these are not the words of a boy. Perhaps it is Perry's nature to feel deeply or perhaps his strange lonely life has developed his character and made him older and more thoughtful than his contemporaries.

"Yes," continues Perry. "She's beautiful to look at, of course, and I'm glad. But that isn't why I love her. I love what's inside her beauty. I love herself. I expect you know the old song, Mrs. Christie; it's by Thomas Moore and it describes my feelings exactly . . ." He hesitates for a moment and then says in his low deep voice:

"Believe me, if all those endearing young charms
    Which I gaze on so fondly today

Were to change by tomorrow and fleet in my arms
  Like fairy gifts, fading away.
Thou would'st still be adored as this moment thou art
  Let thy loveliness fade as it will . . ."

Perry looks up to see if I understand . . . and of course
I do. I understand because I have always wanted to be loved
like that, but somehow I think it is a rare sort of love. Perry's
adored is fortunate and I hope she realises her good fortune.

"That's how I feel," continues Perry. "That's how I've
always felt."

"Do I know her, Perry?"

He raises his eyes and gazes at me in amazement. "It's
Betty," he says in a bewildered voice. "I thought you knew! I
mean it couldn't be anybody else."

"Betty!"

"Yes, of course!"

"But, Perry, she's just a child . . ."

"Oh, I know that," says Perry hastily. "She's far too young.
You needn't worry. I promise faithfully I won't say anything.
It's easy to promise that, because I don't want to say anything.
Betty hasn't the slightest idea of what I feel about her and I
don't want her to know. It would be dreadfully wrong to waken
her too soon."

"You're both very young . . ."

"Yes," agrees Perry in a doubtful voice. "Yes, I suppose
that's true. I mean—of course it's true. I've got to make good
before I can think of marriage. I don't *feel* young," says this
strange young man. "I feel as if I had lived a long time . . .
but I expect you're laughing at me."

"No," I tell him. "No, I'm not laughing, Perry."

"I've loved Betty for years," he continues. "Ever since I
came and stayed with you at Donford. I've never loved anybody

225

else and I never shall. That's all, really. I just wanted you to know." He rises and adds, "I thought—I thought it was the right thing to tell you—the honourable thing."

"Perry!" I say rather desperately. "Perry, wait a minute. It's such a surprise. I never thought for a moment—"

"Of course not," agrees Perry.

"It wasn't until the other night at the dance that I realised Betty was beginning to grow up."

"But that made no difference! Of course I know she looked perfectly beautiful at the dance and everybody was raving about her; but that made no difference to me—none at all. I do want you to understand."

"Yes, Perry. I think I do understand."

"She's Betty," says Perry, as if that explained the whole matter—which perhaps it does.

"Oh, Perry!" I exclaim. "You are a dear, dear boy. I'm very, very fond of you."

"Good," says Perry with his shy smile.

I stretch out my hand and he takes it. Somehow I feel as if we were making a solemn pact; I have no idea what the pact is, but Perry knows. "You'll tell me when the right time has come," says Perry confidently.

There is a little silence.

"I know what you're thinking," he declares. "You think I may get tired of waiting."

"Well, perhaps I was thinking something like that."

"I shan't, ever," he says—not making a promise but stating a fact. "I shall be there. I shall wait until Betty is ready and then ask her to marry me. It's quite simple."

Yes, it's quite simple. Dear, good Perry. I realise that if Betty, when she is ready, should want to marry Perry I could ask for nothing better for my darling child.

Perry has gone to the door but now he comes back. "You

won't worry, will you?" he says. "I know there are difficulties. She may fall in love with someone else. I've got to take that risk, of course."

"Betty loves you!" I exclaim.

"Oh, I know," he agrees smiling rather sadly. "She loves me nearly as much as she loves Bryan, but that's no use at all."

There is no more to be said. We understand one another perfectly.

There is no more to be said, but there is a good deal to be thought. I find some difficulty in completing the arrangements for supper. I find myself standing with a dish in my hand and no idea as to what I intended to do with it. I find my thoughts racing back to the time when Betty was a tiny baby and then racing forward to the time when—perhaps— Betty may have a tiny baby of her own. I find myself smiling . . . and the next moment my eyes are full of tears. It is rather silly to feel like this, because it is all so vague and Perry and Betty are little more than children. Nothing may come of it. Betty is fond of Perry in a sisterly way but that does not mean she will fall in love with him; Perry—in spite of all he has said—may change his mind. But somehow I don't think he will.

Thursday, 16th August

MISS STROUDE turns up this morning and, as Perry is on the verge of departure and we are busy cutting sandwiches for him and helping him to pack, she is even less welcome than usual. Mrs. Daulkes, who has brought me the news of her arrival, suggests that she should be told to go away straight off, but unfortunately I am not the stuff heroes are made of.

Contrary to her usual custom Miss Stroude has asked to see me so I go down to the drawing room and find her standing in the middle of the room looking more than usually disagreeable.

She says, without any formal greeting, "I must find that folder, Mrs. Christie."

"I wish you could," I reply in heart-felt tones.

"The letter is valuable."

"Yes, you told me that before."

"It is a letter written by Byron to my step-mother's grandfather."

"Yes, I know."

"I must find that letter," says Miss Stroude firmly.

"I wish you could," I repeat.

Miss Stroude glowers at me. She says, "I have been through all the boxes in the attic so it must be somewhere else —somewhere in the house. As I told you my step-mother was careless and untidy so it may be anywhere. I intend to search the house thoroughly. You have no objection, I suppose."

"N-no," I reply doubtfully. "At least—"

"I shall start at once," declares Miss Stroude firmly. "The folder must be found today. The gentleman who wants to buy the Byron letter is going back to America on Monday so there's no time to be lost. Perhaps you will be good enough to inform your charwoman that I have your permission to search the house."

"Y-yes," I reply doubtfully. "But the only thing is—"

"Thank you," says Miss Stroude.

Mrs. Daulkes takes the news badly but we are all so busy running about the house and collecting Perry's belongings and helping him to lash them firmly onto his ramshackle steed that Miss Stroude is left to search in peace. I can hear her in the drawing room, opening and shutting drawers and moving the furniture, but it is merely a background noise and does not worry me. Presently Perry announces that he is ready to depart; we all go out and wave as he bumps slowly down the road—Bryan and Betty race him to the corner shouting, "Good-bye!" and "Come back soon!" and other less conventional valedictions.

When he has gone I return to the house and meet Miss Stroude coming out of the dining room with a grey cardboard folder in her hand.

"You've found it!" I exclaim.

"This is the folder but the letter isn't here," replies Miss Stroude in furious tones. "The Byron letter! It's gone! Where has it gone?"

"I know nothing about it."

"The folder was there," says Miss Stroude, pointing to the book-case. "I took out all the books and the folder was there; it had slipped down behind the books—or somebody had hidden it deliberately."

"Why should anybody—"

"Why, indeed," interrupts Miss Stroude. "Why should the folder have been hidden—unless the letter had been taken out of it."

"I don't know what you mean."

"The book-case was locked. Who unlocked it?"

"I did," I reply. "The key was in the little brass bowl."

"You unlocked the book-case," says Miss Stroude in cold hard tones. "Perhaps you saw the folder. Perhaps you took the letter out and slipped the folder down behind the books."

"Are you accusing my mother of being a thief?" demands Bryan, who has come into the hall while we have been talking, and is now standing in the open doorway. He is very red in the face and breathing quickly, but whether these symptoms are due to rage or to the fact that he has raced Betty all the way back from the corner it would be difficult to say.

Miss Stroude is somewhat taken aback. She says, "No, of course not. I was only asking your Mother if she had seen the—"

"You're quite sure?" asks Bryan. "You're *quite* sure you weren't suggesting that my mother had taken your beastly letter?"

Miss Stroude seems quite sure.

"Because," says Bryan, "because if you *were* suggesting anything like that you've got to reckon with me, and I know *exactly* what to do about it."

The threat, though vague, sounds most alarming . . . and as a matter of fact Bryan's looks are sufficiently alarming to terrify any but the stoutest heart. Miss Stroude says she must go, and moves towards the door.

"Good-bye," says Bryan, standing aside to let her pass.

Miss Stroude says nothing.

230

Thursday, 16th August

We watch her walk down the path, get into her car and drive away. Then we look at each other and heave sighs of relief.

"Bryan," I enquire in hesitating tones. "What—what would you have done?"

"Done?" says Bryan. "Oh, you mean what would I have *done?* Gosh, I don't know! I mean you can't take a woman by the scruff and throw her out, can you?"

We have got rid of Miss Stroude but I cannot get rid of the exceedingly uncomfortable feelings which the disappearance of the wretched letter have aroused in my breast and I spend some hours hunting for it in all sorts of probable and improbable places—including places where I know it cannot possibly be.

Bryan pretends to be scornful about the matter and assures me that the letter is not in the house at all. Nobody in their senses would leave a valuable letter kicking about the house. The letter is in the bank, says Bryan, or else it as been sold without Miss Stroude's knowledge, or perhaps there never was a letter at all and Miss Stroude is kicking up all this fuss to annoy us and to make us leave The Small House before our lease is up.

"Yes," declares Bryan. "That's what it is. She wants us out of the house. She tried one way to get us out, and now she's trying another. She thinks we'll get so fed up that we'll pack and go. That's what it is. Mark my words."

Bryan's theory sounds far-fetched to me and I have a suspicion that he does not believe it himself; a suspicion which is considerably strengthened when I discover him taking all the books out of the book-case in the dining room and ruffling through the pages.

"Oh!" exclaims Bryan when he sees me come in to lay

the supper. "Oh, I just thought—I mean you never know. Things *do* get shoved away in books sometimes."

I tell him that already I have been through all those books and the Byron letter is not there.

"Oh!" says Bryan in disappointed tones.

Friday, 17th August

"I MUST GO to London for a few days," Mrs. Alston says. We have met in the chemist's, where I am buying some soap and Mrs. Alston is endeavouring to obtain some especially strong form of antiseptic bath-powder.

"You see," continues Mrs. Alston. "You see I must have some clothes for Scotland. I *must* have a tweed coat. Yes, I've made up my mind to go to Scotland after all. I don't know whether Edmond will come or not; he doesn't seem to know *what* he wants to do—it's very worrying—but I've decided to go myself. I really can't bear this place any longer. Don't you think I'm right?"

The question is a little difficult to answer but fortunately the young man in the chemist's has succeeded in unearthing a tin of the antiseptic bath-powder and at this moment returns with it triumphantly, so there is no need to answer.

"Yes, that's it!" cries Mrs. Alston. "I'll have two tins. I want it for the bath," she explains, turning to me. "You see several other people use the bath, so I always wash it thoroughly before Edmond uses it. I don't think Mrs. Bollings is very pleased about it, but I can't help that. I have to look after Edmond—not bothering him, but just watching him carefully. He has always needed care and of course he's all I've got. Edmond and I are alone in the world," adds Mrs. Alston pathetically.

233

"You have no relations?" I ask; not because I want to know but because I must say something.

"No relations at all. We have always been everything to each other . . . and, as I say, I have to look after him. I watch what he eats, of course; I know exactly what suits him and what doesn't. I like him to have a clean pair of socks every day —and a clean handkerchief. I once read that a used handkerchief is a very dangerous source of infection. I look after Edmond in all sorts of little ways. It's the little things that matter."

Poor Mrs. Alston! I remember Edmond's cry: "If only Mother would let me alone!" and I decide that it is quite terrifying when people misunderstand one another so completely. My sympathies are with Edmond (for I am aware that it would drive Bryan mad if I ran after him all the time forcing clean socks and handkerchiefs upon him and insisting that the bath must be disinfected before he used it) but I can spare a little sympathy for Mrs. Alston as well.

"Little things like that matter, don't they?" she asks.

It is obvious that she wants reassurance. She wants me to tell her that little things matter and that Edmond is fortunate in having such a good mother . . . but how can I reassure her?

"Men don't like being fussed over," I tell her.

"Oh, but I never *fuss!*" she exclaims. "I just *watch* Edmond and do things for him unobtrusively. For instance this morning at breakfast he said he would have a kipper—and of course I know kippers don't suit him—so I just got up quite quietly and went and told Mrs. Bollings to bring him an egg instead. Things like *that*," says Mrs. Alston earnestly. "You see what I mean, don't you?"

"Yes," I reply, for I see exactly what she means. I look at

her and wonder whether it would be any use trying to make her understand how maddening undue solicitude can be. I decide that it would not. It is Mrs. Alston's nature to be unduly solicitous and, as she has reached her present mature age without realising how extremely annoying she is, it would be hopeless to try to change her.

"Perhaps you think it's rather unkind of me to leave Edmond here and go to London?"

"You must get clothes . . ."

"Yes, I really must. And I thought . . ." Mrs. Alston hesitates and then continues in confidential tones. "I *do* want Edmond to come to Scotland with me; it would be so good for him to have a complete change of air . . . and I thought if I went to London for a few days, and left him here alone, he would realise how much I do for him. I mean he would miss me, wouldn't he? You see what I mean?"

"Yes," I reply, nodding. "Yes, I think you should go."

"Do you think it's very naughty of me?" asks Mrs. Alston smiling archly.

"It's worth trying."

"He's *rather* selfish," she explains. "He really is just a *tiny* bit inconsiderate . . . besides it really would be so good for him to come to Scotland."

My parcel of soap is now ready so I take it and escape.

Bryan and Betty are going to London tomorrow; they are looking forward to ten days of gaiety with their uncle and aunt but I can see they have qualms about leaving me alone. They cannot understand why I refuse to shut up The Small House and come with them—as I have been invited most cordially to do—and it is all the more difficult for me to explain my reasons because they are so mixed. Perhaps my chief reason is that I do not want to exchange the peace and quiet of The Small House for the rush and bustle of Wintringham Square but there are various other reasons as well.

Betty goes to bed as usual and when I go up to say good night to her she puts down her book and hugs me.

"I wish you were coming," she says. "It will be fun. But all the same I'm awfully sorry the last three weeks are over."

"You're coming back," I remind her.

"I know," she agrees. "But the last three weeks are over. We can't ever have them again."

This feeling is well known to me (past pleasures can never return; we go on to other pleasures but they are different) but it seems strange that Betty should have discovered this truth, for to the young it is the present that counts.

"It's been lovely," continues Betty, as she draws up her legs to make room for me to sit down on her bed. "It's been almost perfect. Perry is such a dear, isn't he? Somehow or other he seems like one of the family; he fits in so well."

"Yes," I agree. "We're all very fond of Perry. Aren't we?"

"Do you think he likes me?"

"I'm sure he does."

"I think so too," agrees Betty, smiling happily.

Whether this is good or bad—from Perry's point of view —it would be difficult to say. Betty is sitting up in bed in her favourite attitude, with her arms round her knees; she is wearing pale blue pyjamas of the recognised school pattern and, with her round rosy cheeks and fair tousled hair, she looks about ten years old. She returns my gaze frankly and her blue eyes are honest and innocent as the eyes of a very small child.

"Yes, I think he *does* like me," says Betty seriously. "I think he likes me especially—not just as one of the family."

I wait for more—half-hoping, half-fearing to hear it—

Friday, 17th August

but no more is said about Perry. We talk for a few minutes about arrangements for tomorrow and then Betty yawns and rubs her eyes. I leave her to her slumbers and go to bed myself.

Part V

The Wind Changes

Saturday, 18th August

*H*AVING SEEN Bryan and Betty off to London I return to
The Small House and endeavour to busy myself with
domestic affairs, but somehow domestic affairs seem
unimportant. The house is quiet and empty in spite of the
activities of Mrs. Daulkes . . . even Mrs. Daulkes is quieter
than usual and her dustings and polishings are unaccompanied
by song. At my solitary lunch, which consists of a cod steak and
a dish of salad, I think of Bryan and Betty and Richard and
Mary having lunch together in Wintringham Square. There
will be chatter and laughter, plans will be made for the afternoon—what a gay meal it will be! Why was I so foolish as to
refuse to go?

My feeling of loneliness and bereavement is unexpected
for I enjoyed my quiet life in The Small House before Bryan
and Betty and Perry descended upon me and stirred me up. I
remind myself of this and decide quite firmly that I am being
very silly; I shall enjoy it again. I shall resume my routine; I

shall read and knit and sit in the garden and go for walks as before. This afternoon I shall sit in the garden of course . . . so I finish my lunch quickly and selecting a book at random from the ill-starred book-case I go out and settle myself beneath the tree.

The book I have taken is *The Wind in the Willows* which is an old favourite of mine; I know it well, having read it to Bryan and Betty, and also for my own amusement. Although it is a book beloved of children there is much in it that children cannot appreciate; there is much in it to entertain and instruct an adult mind. Today, however, *The Wind in the Willows* fails to charm me for, like Martha, I am troubled about many things.

I am troubled about Tim. I have not heard from him this week which is very unusual. Is he ill, I wonder, or is he angry and upset. Perhaps I should not have let Tony write to him. Perhaps he has taken the silly gossipmongering too seriously. In addition to my worries about Tim I am troubled about the Byron letter; I am worried about Edmond (who has not yet been to see me); I am unhappy about Anne.

The worst of it is that I can do nothing about any of these worries; it is impossible to get into touch with Tim and find out what he is thinking; the Byron letter cannot be found, and my two friends, Edmond Alston and Anne Carlyle, must worstle through their difficulties without my aid, for it is not in my power to help them.

Mrs. Daulkes now appears attired for the road in a long green coat with a fur collar which she wears without regard to the weather or the temperature. She approaches saying she is just off and will be here on Monday as usual and adds that the General's car is at the gate and she'll put him in the drawing room.

"That'll cheer you up," says Mrs. Daulkes kindly.

This annoys me slightly which is most unreasonable because of course she is right; I need cheering up and Tony's visit is welcome.

Tony is in the drawing room when I go in. He smiles and says he has come to cheer me up and adds that I look as if I needed it. He thinks I ought to have gone to London, it would have done me good. I am lonely, that's what's the matter.

"It isn't at all," I reply somewhat tartly. "I'm perfectly happy alone—if everything is all right."

Tony's face changes and he asks anxiously what has gone wrong.

I review my various troubles and decide to tell Tony about Miss Stroude and the missing letter and, as he has been told nothing about the matter before, it makes quite a long story.

"A Byron letter," says Tony thoughtfully. "Yes, I daresay she might get quite a lot for that. Where can it be?" His eyes rove round the room as he speaks.

"Do you expect to see it hanging on the wall?" I enquire with bitter irony.

"N-no," he replies. "But still—I suppose you've looked in the drawers of that bureau."

"Your supposition is correct."

"Don't bite me," he says smiling. "I was only trying to help. Sometimes there are secret drawers in those old Chippendale bureaux and—"

"Tony!" I cry, leaping from my seat.

We approach the bureau together. We open the flap. We feel it all over. We tap it and press it and shake it but without result.

"No," says Tony with a sigh. "No. Sorry to have raised your hopes. The fact is I've got a bureau something like this and it's got rather a neat little secret drawer . . . but this one hasn't, or else its secret is too cunning to be found."

But I have not given up hope. "Let's take out all the drawers and examine it thoroughly," I suggest.

The top drawer is full of my own belongings, writing paper and envelopes and bills. We take it out and put it on the sofa. Tony puts his hand into the space and brings out a piece of crumpled paper.

"The letter!" I exclaim, seizing it from him in triumph.

But it is not the letter, it is only a half sheet of azure notepaper, dirty and creased, covered with large and rather illegible writing and with the address, THE SMALL HOUSE, OLD QUININGS printed in the top right hand corner. I am so disgusted with it that I crumple it up and throw it into the waste-paper basket.

"Hold hard!" says Tony. "Let's see what it is. I'm rather an inquisitive person." He retrieves it from the waste-paper basket and smooths it out carefully.

"What is it?" I enquire.

"You remember what Catherine Morland found in the secret drawer?"

"A washing list."

"Exactly."

"It's a washing list!"

"No," says Tony slowly. "No, I think it's a Will!"

"You think it's a Will!" I exclaim incredulously. "What nonsense, Tony! It can't be a Will."

"Why not?" he enquires.

To me a Will is an imposing document, neatly typed upon parchment and fastened with pink tape. That dirty, dog-eared, crumpled piece of notepaper is not my idea of a legal document. I explain this to Tony, but he replies quite
242

seriously that there are Wills and Wills; he has a feeling that this piece of paper may be a perfectly legal document.

We read it together:

THE SMALL HOUSE
OLD QUININGS
Wednesday 28th March, 1951.

This is the last Will and Testament of me Lorna Stroude of The Small House, Old Quinings, which I make this 28th day of March, 1951, and whereby I revoke all previous Wills and Testamentary dispositions.

1. I hereby appoint my friend Richard Morven to be the executor of this my Will.
2. I give all my property real and personal to my dear friend Anne Carlyle at present residing in The School House, Old Quinings.

Signed by the testator in the presence of us both present at the same time who in her
presence and in the presence
of each other have hereunto   Lorna Stroude
set our names as witnesses.

Edward Shanks, waiter at The Apollo and Boot,
Wandlebury.

Amy Ward, chambermaid at The Apollo and Boot,
Wandlebury.

"Do you realise what this means?" exclaims Tony.

"But it *can't* be a proper Will. It isn't even typewritten—"

"All the better. It's in Mrs. Stroude's own handwriting, or so one supposes. Is there such a thing as a *Whitaker's Almanac* in the house?"

There is no copy of the reference book in the cupboard but eventually we discover one beneath the table where the telephone stands; it is a 1948 edition and contains all the information we require. According to Whitaker Mrs. Stroude's last Will and Testament is in perfect order.

Until now I have not believed that it was possible, but now I begin to believe and my excitement grows; it grows all the more quickly when a rough draft of the Will is discovered by Tony between the leaves of the book. This proves that we are not the only people who consulted Whitaker on the subject of Wills.

Tony is excited too. "This is fun!" he exclaims. "My goodness, this is absolutely staggering! I wouldn't have missed this for worlds . . . our long-nosed friend will be as sick as mud, won't she? No more striding into the house and pulling down the blinds! It isn't her house—nor her blinds!"

"Tony, are you sure?"

"And the joke is," says Tony laughing delightedly, "the cream of the joke is that the whole thing is entirely her own fault. If she hadn't made herself so unpleasant we should never have found it."

"She might have found it herself . . . someday."

"Yes, and then what? I wonder," says Tony. "I wonder what she would have done!"

"What do we do next?" I enquire, for as a matter of fact I am concerned not so much with Miss Stroude's displeasure as with the good fortune of Anne Carlyle. Dear Anne, it is like one of her own fairy-tales come true!

Tony does not answer my question. Instead he says, "I suppose you've noticed that it's witnessed by our friend Edward Shanks of the Apollo and Boot. He told us about it that day—do you remember?"

"It was one of his romantic incidents!"

"Of course. What a pity we didn't ask him who the lady was! It just shows, doesn't it?"

"Shows what?" I enquire.

"Shows that one should turn every stone and leave no avenue unexplored," replies Tony smiling. "The fact is I was beginning to get slightly bored with the romantic Edward, so I shut him up and we came away without hearing his story."

This is true of course but I doubt if Edward would have told us the mysterious lady's name and, even if he had told us, we could have done nothing until the Will was found . . . but these conjectures are getting us no further so again I enquire of Tony what we shall do.

Tony considers our next move seriously and then says he will write a short account of how and where we found the document. We will both sign it in the presence of each other and put it in an envelope, together with the Will and the rough draft. We will address the envelope to Richard Morven and seal it with a big red seal.

All this is done in due order and when the envelope is ready Tony puts it in his pocket and says he will now proceed to the Manor House with all speed and deliver it personally.

"Don't say a word about it to anyone," he adds as I see him off at the gate. "We want to make certain it's absolutely watertight."

Sunday, 19th August

THE MORNING is mild and wet and windy. It is one of those unpleasant English summer days which have nothing to recommend them. In the garden the dripping trees thresh about wildly and the flower-petals are scattered and lie soiled and sodden upon the ground; but I have made up my mind to go to church and to church I shall go. Neither the inclement weather nor Mrs. Meller shall keep me from going to church. I am uncomfortably aware that this is not the right spirit in which to attend divine service, but I feel it is better and more courageous to attend divine service in the wrong spirit than to stay at home.

Susan and I arrive at the lych-gate at the same moment and, as we have arrived early, we chat for a little before going in. Susan wants to know if Bryan and Betty went to London yesterday as was arranged, and she lets fall the information that the Mellers are away too: "So there is nobody to play tennis with," adds Susan rather sadly.

"Have they *all* gone?" I ask anxiously.

"Yes, all of them," replies Susan. "They've gone to Wales for three weeks holiday."

Although I am sorry for Susan, bereft of all her young companions at one blow, I cannot be other than delighted on my own account.

"We're having Mr. Grace this morning," Susan continues. "He's the vicar of Chevis Green and *such* a dear old

man. Mr. Meller is very clever of course, but sometimes he
makes you feel hot and angry; I think it's because *he* gets hot
and angry. Mr. Grace talks to you as if he loves you. Come and
sit in my pew, Mrs. Christie," adds Susan. "I'm all by myself
this morning; Daddy has gone over to Wandlebury on some
mysterious business of his own. He wouldn't tell me a word
about it, but went off in the car looking frightfully important
and pleased with himself. Aren't men funny?"

There is no time to say more for the "hurry-up-bell" has
begun to ring, so we go into church together and sit in the
Manor pew.

The service is beautiful; we have all my favourite hymns,
and Mr. Grace (who is like my idea of Santa Claus but without
a beard) talks to us as if he loves us, just as Susan said. He
retells the story of the Good Samaritan, making it new and
fresh and applicable to modern life. We can all be Good
Samaritans, says Mr. Grace. There are plenty of people in
trouble who need a friendly hand—or even just a friendly
ear—and he knows the desire to help is *there*. We would all
be Good Samaritans if we were not too shy, too afraid of interfering or of appearing to interfere in the affairs of our
neighbours. He tells us that Good Samaritans are brave and
that the bearing of one another's burdens brings its own
reward, here and now, for it will lighten our own burdens
and give us happiness.

It may not be a great sermon, but it is uplifting and
comforting and gives one food for thought.

"Isn't he a lamb?" says Susan as we come out together into
the damp churchyard and the drizzling rain. "Isn't he an
absolute pet? He has made me feel good and brave and happy.
I want to go and do something for somebody straight off."
She smiles at me as she makes this statement (for Mrs. Daulkes's favourite expression has become a joke to us all). Susan's

smile is a lovely thing to see. Susan's smile is like a ray of sunshine in this damp and drizzly world, and I should like to tell her (if I were not too shy) that she can lighten the burdens of her neighbours by smiling at them.

The day passes without any news from Tony about Mrs. Stroude's Will, but at least I know that something is being done about it. Obviously Mr. Morven's visit to Wandlebury, which roused Susan's curiosity by its mysterious nature, is connected with his duties as executor.

All day long the rain continues to fall—it is one of the longest and wettest Sundays I can remember—and it is still raining when I go upstairs to bed; I can hear the drops pattering with dreary monotony on the cupola. Bed is the best place in this sort of weather and I have just settled down comfortably with *The Wind in the Willows,* to read myself to sleep, when the front-door bell rings.

Can it possibly be Tony arriving at this hour of night? And, if not Tony, whom? Shall I get up and answer it or pay no heed? But the bell goes on ringing and its persistence alarms me, for it seems unlikely that anybody would ring the door-bell and go on ringing it at this untimely hour unless the news they brought was important.

At last I rise and put on my dressing gown and go down to the door. My visitor is Edmond Alston.

"Oh!" says Edmond in a dazed voice. "Oh, had you gone to bed? I'm so sorry—is it late? I didn't look at the time. I just—wanted to see you, Mrs. Christie."

I take him into the drawing room and turn on the electric stove. Now that I see him properly I realise that he is wet to the skin. In fact he looks as if he had been in the river. His cap, which he is squeezing nervously between his hands, is like a sponge; water is dripping from his jacket and oozing from

248

his shoes. Edmond seems quite unaware of his condition and for a moment I entertain the unworthy suspicion that he has had too much to drink . . . but I am soon undeceived.

"I'm sorry," he repeats, sitting down near the stove. "But you said to come and see you. I didn't look at the time. I've been walking. I'm afraid my shoes are muddy. I went for a walk."

"You got lost," I suggest.

"No," he says. "At least—yes, I suppose I did get lost. I don't know where I went."

His shoes look as if he had been walking through ploughed fields.

"You're tired, Edmond. You're working too hard," I tell him.

Edmond laughs bitterly and says. "Working! I haven't done any work for days!" He gets up and walks to the door and back and then stands still in the middle of the room. "I'm in love," he says.

This announcement is made by Edmond as if it were a startling piece of news . . . and he looks at me as if he expected me to be absolutely staggered by it. He is so intense, so serious and has such a wild and distracted air that it is impossible to treat his announcement lightly and, as I do not know how else to treat it, I remain dumb.

"Yes, I'm in love," says Edmond. "It's absolute hell." He sits down and gazes at me with imploring eyes. "What am I to do?" he asks.

For a few moments there is silence and then he repeats, "What am I to do? I can't work, I can't sleep. I read and read and when I get to the bottom of the page I have no more idea of what it's all about than the man in the moon . . . and it's so frightful, because the only way I could ever hope to— to have anything to offer Susan is by getting an honours degree

. . . and there isn't the slightest chance—I'm done—life is absolutely hopeless."

"No, no!" I tell him. "You must take one thing at a time. Go to Cornwall as you intended (it will be easier for you to work when you're there), concentrate on passing your exams and then you'll have something to offer Susan."

"Oh yes," agrees Edmond miserably. "Yes, I know that's wise advice; but even *then*—even if I passed—there's still Mother. I haven't told her anything and I don't think she suspects anything or she wouldn't have gone to London but —but I'm all she's got, you see."

"Edmond!" I exclaim. "Mothers can't stand in the way of their sons' happiness. She wouldn't want to, I'm sure."

"I'm all she's got," repeats Edmond. "She keeps on saying it all the time . . . and if she thought there was anyone else . . . I mean if she knew about Susan . . . not that there's anything to know about Susan, because of course I haven't said a word to Susan. How can I? But if Mother had the slightest idea of what I feel about Susan it would be awful. I don't know *what* Mother would do. Mother has nobody but me. She keeps on saying it all the time—saying we're alone in the world and nothing matters to her except me—talking about how she's going to make a home for me and how happy we shall be together—just the two of us, she says. She keeps on about it all the time—harping on it—saying she understands me so well, saying she doesn't mind about anything else except me. And of course it's true. She thinks of me all the time, doing things for me, watching me. If only she wouldn't!" cries poor Edmond. "If only she'd leave me alone! It's driving me mad! It's too much—it's such a burden—I can't bear it! I know it's awful coming to you like this, but you've been so kind and understanding and I must talk to somebody."

"Yes of course," I tell him. "I'm glad you came."

Sunday, 19th August

"I don't know what to do," says Edmond, twisting his hands.

"What does Susan think?"

"Susan!" he exclaims. "I haven't said a word to Susan. How could I? It wouldn't be right. We meet and talk but— but just about other things. Susan is wonderful, she's as far above me as the stars, she's so much better than I am in every way. She's so beautiful—beautiful inside as well as outside— and so brave and good and noble. She's clever too—and very funny sometimes—dear and funny and sweet. Oh, Mrs. Christie, I'd die for Susan willingly; I'd face mad bulls; I'd do anything on earth to save her a moment's unhappiness. I don't think I can go on living without Susan, without seeing her and talking to her. We meet each other and talk nearly every morning and I just crawl through the hours in between. I know it's wrong to go on meeting her, because nothing can come of it—nothing—it's quite hopeless. I'm in a sort of trap and there's no way out. Everything goes round and round. I think about it and think about it and I get nowhere. That's why I can't sleep—because all the time I'm trying to find a way out . . . but it's hopeless. There's no hope anywhere and my head aches so frightfully. You'll think I'm mad, coming to you like this and talking like this. Sometimes I think I am going mad . . . sometimes I think it would be nice if I could just lie down and die and not bother about anything anymore."

Poor Edmond! It is difficult to know how to help him. I am terribly sorry for the creature. I can understand exactly how he feels—and understand all the better because in some ways Edmond is like me. People of strong, bold character can cut their way out of a tangle, but Edmond cannot—and neither could I. To make matters worse it is obvious that he is on the verge of a complete breakdown. What he ought to do is to consult a doctor; but it would not be much good to tell him that. All I can do is to assure him that I understand and sympathise.

"Yes," he says wretchedly. "It's awfully kind of you. It does help a bit. You see, don't you? I mean of course I owe Mother a lot and I don't know what she'd do if I let her down —and of course I shall let her down, anyhow, because I haven't a hope of passing my exams. Even if I go away and never see Susan anymore—"

"Listen, Edmond," I beseech him, breaking into his dreary monologue which, I can see, is starting all over again. "Listen to me and I will tell you what to do. You will go straight home and take off your wet clothes and have a hot bath and go to bed. I will give you two pink tablets which will make you sleep. Meanwhile I shall think about it and try to find a way out."

"There's no way out," Edmond declares. "There isn't, really. I've thought about it for days . . . but still . . . it's awfully good of you. I don't know why you should bother."

"Because I understand."

"Yes," says Edmond. "Yes, I know."

"And you'll do what I tell you?"

"Yes. Yes, I'll do it."

"Remember," I tell him. "A hot bath—tablets—bed. I'll come and see you tomorrow."

"Yes, I will, really," says Edmond nodding.

He goes off with the tablets in an envelope and I retire to bed.

Monday, 20th August

*I*HAVE SPENT such a wretched night, worrying about Edmond, that I am late in getting up and Mrs. Daulkes arrives before I have had my breakfast. She asks anxiously if I am poorly and adds that I look very poorly indeed; she thinks I should go back to bed straight off and have a nice rest. For once I refuse to take her advice for I have promised to go and see Edmond this morning, and, although I can think of no way out of his troubles, I must keep my promise. The fact is I am very uneasy about Edmond. He was in such a desperate frame of mind that there is no knowing what may happen.

In addition to this I have my own worries for there was no letter from Tim on Saturday (not even one of his miserable air-mail letter-cards) and I am aware that I cannot hope for a letter until the end of the week. The idea that Tim may be feeling angry and upset has become a cloud in the sky. Sometimes I forget about it for a while . . . and then if I am tired or sleepless the cloud grows bigger and darker and the world seems shadowed by it. I have noticed before that, when one has an indefinite trouble like this, ordinary life goes on during it in a perfectly ordinary manner. One goes about one's ordinary business; one talks, laughs, orders food and has one's bath. In fact there are very few crises or disasters that upset the tenor of ordinary everyday life.

When I have finished toying with my breakfast Mrs.

253

Daulkes wants to know about food and suggests a nice rabbit for lunch.

"A nice rabbit stewed with onions," says Mrs. Daulkes in persuasive tones. "That would be a nice change, wouldn't it? Or a nice bit of boiled cod with parsley sauce?"

In my present condition both suggestions sound equally revolting, but Mrs. Daulkes is so kind and so worried about my wan appearance that I pull myself together and say a nice rabbit would be nice and will she ring up the butcher and order it straight off. This delights Mrs. Daulkes—as I knew it would—for Mr. Higginbotham is an old school-friend of Mrs. Daulkes's and a telephone conversation between the two, especially if it be on the subject of tails or kidneys, is always enlivened by a little mild banter.

Mrs. Daulkes is still engaged upon the telephone when the front-door bell rings and, opening the door, I find Mr. Morven on the step.

"It's very early for a call," says Mr. Morven apologetically. "But Susan said you were an early bird and I know you will be delighted to hear my news so—"

"Hush!" I whisper, pointing to the dining room.

Mr. Morven nods understandingly.

I lead him into the garden—fortunately the morning is fine—and explain that Mrs. Daulkes has an insatiable curiosity about everything that goes on, and if we talk inside the house she will probably glue her ear to the keyhole. I add that the odd thing is she seems unaware that this behaviour is un-ethical.

"Daulkes," says Mr. Morven thoughtfully. "She must be Jim Daulkes's wife, of course. He drives the station motor-lorry. It's a good steady hard-working family. Jim's father was under-gardener at the Manor for years; then he married one of the housemaids and, as we had no cottage for them, I

254

recommended him to Lord Ponsonby as head gardener. He did exceedingly well, as I knew he would. They had three children, George and Jim and Elsie—yes, Elsie was the girl's name—a nice little thing with fair hair. George went to sea, Jim is still here—as you know—and Elsie has a good post in Wandlebury. I don't know much about Jim's wife, she wasn't an Old Quinings girl, but if she is anything like the rest of the Daulkes family you can rely upon her."

This little bit of old English squire-ishness enchants me. It enchants me all the more because Mr. Morven looks the part of country squire. His grey hair, his fine eyes, his benevolent smile and his tall erect figure, clad in well-cut riding breeches and a grey tweed coat, all fit the part to perfection.

We sit down together on the oak seat near the viola bed. Mr. Morven smiles and says in a stage whisper, "Are we alone?"

I reply that we have as much privacy as we can hope for. It is possible, of course, that Miss Crease may bob up from behind the wall.

"Miss Crease!" exclaims Mr. Morven, looking at the wall with apprehension. "Great Scott! Of course that's her garden!"

"We can talk quietly," I tell him.

We talk quietly. Mr. Morven says it's all very exciting. The Will is as sound as a bell. "I thought it was," declares Mr. Morven. "I know a little about these things and when Morley showed it to me I was fairly sure it was in order. But yesterday, just to make certain, I went over to Wandlebury and saw Mr. Tyler, who is a very competent lawyer. I caught him coming out of church," says Mr. Morven with a slightly shame-faced smile. "The old chap didn't mind. He was interested. He advised me to get hold of the two witnesses, which was an easy matter. Everyone knows Edward, the head-waiter at the Apollo and Boot, and the chambermaid was still there, so I saw her too. They both remembered Mrs. Stroude and remembered witnessing her signature. She had told them it was a secret and that she didn't want anybody to know. Although they didn't say so, I expect she remunerated them handsomely for their trouble. I asked them why they didn't come forward when they heard of her death and they said they had never thought of doing so. Mrs. Stroude had told them it was a secret." Mr. Morven sighs and adds, "Very stupid, but I suppose one can't blame them."

"You explained?"

"Oh yes—but it took a good deal of explaining. At first they were determined not to open their mouths, but eventually I managed to make them understand that Mrs. Stroude did not intend them to keep the matter secret forever, but only until her death, and that unless the Will could be proved her wishes could not be carried out. After that it was plain sailing; if necessary they are prepared to go into court and swear that they witnessed the signature . . . but it won't be necessary. Olivia Stroude would be quite mad to take the matter to court. Mr. Tyler says no lawyer would look at the case."

"Then it's true!" I exclaim.

"It's true," agrees Mr. Morven smiling at me. "Anne Carlyle will get everything—not a fortune, of course, but enough to make her comfortable. I'm very glad about it not only because Anne needs the legacy and Olivia does not— Olivia is comfortably off already—but also because I was worried when I heard Lorna had left no Will. As a matter of fact I had every reason to believe she had made a Will. Some little time ago she asked me if she might name me as her executor and gave me to understand that she intended to make provision for Anne Carlyle. I told her that she ought to get somebody younger as her executor—her life was as good as mine. She said no more—Lorna never spoke about her ailments—but I suppose she must have known that her heart was in a bad condition."

Mr. Morven pauses and sighs. Then he continues: "When Lorna died and no Will was found—except the old one which she had made fifteen years ago—I was surprised and distressed. I knew Lorna well. She was not the sort of person to say one thing and mean another. I made a few discreet enquiries but I couldn't do anything about it. I had no status; I had absolutely nothing to go on but a few casual words. All I could do was to write to Olivia and tell her that I knew Lorna had intended to make a Will and that she wanted Anne Carlyle to have something. I suggested a small annuity and pointed out that this would cost very little and that it would make a great difference to Anne. I said I was sure she would want to carry out Lorna's wishes. . . . It was foolish of me, I suppose," adds Mr. Morven ruefully.

"Miss Stroude was rude to you?" I enquire.

"Exceedingly rude," replies Mr. Morven. "I don't think I ever received a more unpleasant letter."

As our feelings about Miss Stroude are similar we spend a few minutes discussing her; then we discuss the Will and the manner in which it was found. Mr. Morven says Lorna Stroude was very unbusinesslike and any papers she had were always in a mess. He knows, because he used to help her with business matters.

"The drawers of that bureau of hers were always bursting with papers and letters," says Mr. Morven smiling.

I suggest that it is a mistake to be unbusinesslike but Mr. Morven says, "Lorna was a womanly woman." And it is obvious that he thinks the fairer sex is all the fairer for having no business acumen.

"But the Will is all right?" I ask anxiously.

"Yes, yes! There is no doubt about that. There are various formalities to be observed before it can be executed but I shall hurry them up. Meanwhile I thought perhaps you would tell Anne."

"Me!" I exclaim.

"I thought perhaps you would—break it to her."

"But surely it's for you to tell her!"

"I couldn't," he replies. "I simply couldn't face it. If you feel you can't undertake the task it must be done by letter . . . but I hope you will do it, Mrs. Christie. It's bound to be a shock—a pleasant shock of course, but still a shock—and ladies can do these things more tactfully." This last remark has an old-fashioned flavour, but the squire is an old-fashioned gentleman so it sounds quite natural upon his lips.

After a few moments' thought I decide to accept the assignment for it will be better for Anne to hear of her good fortune from me than through the medium of a lawyer's letter. I promise to break the news gently and to stand by while the recipient adjusts herself.

"Good!" says Mr. Morven with a sigh of relief; and he takes out a large white handkerchief and wipes his brow.

I am now anxious that Mr. Morven shall go, so that I can visit Edmond and see how he is feeling, but Mr. Morven does not go. He talks vaguely about one thing and another, repeating himself several times and showing various other signs of mental stress. Then, suddenly, when I have almost screwed myself up to the point of pushing him out, he looks at me and says, "Mrs. Christie, you know that young man of Susan's, don't you?"

I gaze at Mr. Morven, speechless with astonishment.

"You know him and like him, I believe," urges Mr. Morven.

258

"Yes," I reply a little breathlessly.

"Susan said you did. Susan has told me the whole story. She tells me most things, thank God."

"What did she tell you?"

"Everything," he replies. "She's engaged to him—at least she considers herself to be engaged. I gather he hasn't proposed to her, but Susan intends to marry him quite soon." Mr. Morven smiles at my astonished looks. "It seems a little odd to me," he admits. "But of course I'm very old-fashioned. Susan says so. What ought I to do, Mrs. Christie?"

"What ought you to do?" I repeat stupidly.

"Yes," he says nodding. "You see my wife is away at present and I find myself at a loss. I thought perhaps you would be kind enough to advise me what I should do. I wondered if you had any idea of what the young man felt about it."

"He would die for her with the greatest of pleasure!"

"He told you that?"

"With his own lips," I reply, smiling a little at the recollection of Edmond's distracted condition. "He said he would face mad bulls for Susan, that he would do anything on earth to save her from a moment's unhappiness."

"That sounds satisfactory," says Susan's father smiling back at me. "The only thing is he hasn't asked her to marry him."

"Because he has nothing to offer."

Mr. Morven nods. "I see," he says. "But that can't be helped. Susan intends to marry him. As a matter of fact I like him myself. He has been to the Manor House several times and I found him very agreeable indeed—a young man with good manners and an attractive personality—but even if I had disliked him it would not be the slightest use for me to object. Susan has made up her mind. Don't mistake me," says Mr.

Morven hastily. "Susan is always charming to me; I have absolute confidence in her judgment. We understand one another perfectly. Susan is a delightful companion and is very fond of me, I know. If I offer her advice on any subject she listens most respectfully and then explains with the greatest patience why her way is so much better than mine."

I cannot help laughing.

"Yes," agrees Mr. Morven. "Yes, I know it sounds funny but it's perfectly true and I feel sure you will be faced with the same problem when your daughter is a few years older. In this matter, for instance," continues Mr. Morven with his slightly wistful smile. "In the matter of this young man I pointed out to Susan that she was very young to think of marriage, that Alston was studying for his medical degree and that any talk of an engagement might upset him. I suggested that everything should be left in abeyance until he had graduated. Susan said I was wrong and that he would settle down to work more comfortably if the matter were settled."

"I believe he would."

"You think so?"

"Yes, but the only thing is . . ." I hesitate, for this is delicate ground.

"How to settle matters?" suggests my visitor.

"That would be easy," I reply. "No, Mr. Morven, the chief obstacle—if you aren't an obstacle—"

"I am *not* an obstacle," declares Mr. Morven, interrupting me. "I thought I made that clear. I couldn't be an obstacle if I tried, and I don't intend to try."

"Well then, the chief obstacle is Edmond's mother."

Mr. Morven's face changes. "His mother! Do you mean to tell me that any sane woman would object to my Susan as a wife for her son!"

"No, of course not," I assure him. "Susan is a darling.

You know I love Susan. But unfortunately Edmond's mother isn't quite sane where her son is concerned."

"Mrs. Christie—"

"It's no use your being angry."

"Angry!" he exclaims in surprise.

"It's no use," I repeat. "Being angry will get us nowhere. If we're going to do anything about it we must face the facts. Mrs. Alston is a possessive mother and will fight tooth and nail to prevent Edmond from marrying anybody."

"Oh, I see," says Mr. Morven.

"Mrs. Alston must be removed," I tell him.

"Removed!" exclaims Mr. Morven in alarm.

"I don't mean we must poison her—just send her away."

"Of course," agrees Mr. Morven in relief. "Yes. As a matter of fact she has gone to London, hasn't she?"

"She'll come back."

"Yes . . . but Susan wants everything arranged before she returns," explains Mr. Morven. "And that brings me back to where I started: what am I to do?"

"You've been sent to arrange it?"

"Yes," says Mr. Morven uncomfortably.

There is a short silence. The sun is shining brilliantly and the birds are singing madly in the garden. Mrs. Daulkes is singing too; the dulcet strains of "The Deserted Maiden" come wafting out of the open window of my bedroom and across the lawn.

"She has a good voice," says Mr. Morven.

"I know," I reply. "But that's not the point. You've been sent on a definite mission and you're wasting time. You had better go and see Edmond now, and ask him if his intentions are honourable."

Mr. Morven smiles. "Wouldn't that be rather old-fashioned?" he enquires.

"It will be very old-fashioned," I reply.

He rises and stands looking down at me. "I suppose it would be no good asking you to do it, Mrs. Christie?"

"No good at all, Mr. Morven."

"One couldn't expect it," says Mr. Morven sadly and he goes away.

As there is now no need for me to visit Edmond—his case being in other more capable hands—I spend the rest of the morning in domestic duties. The Small House looks different in my eyes, it looks happier and brighter. Perhaps the house knows that in future it will belong to somebody who appreciates its beauties, or perhaps it is merely due to the fact that I have pulled up all the blinds and the sun streams in, glittering on the brasses and gleaming richly on the polished furniture.

The nice rabbit appears for lunch and I partake of it with appetite. Mrs. Daulkes says I look a lot better and most probably it was "a touch of liver." Apparently she sometimes suffers from this curious complaint herself.

Tuesday, 21st August

*I*T IS most unusual for Annie Bollings to leave the Bull and Bush, and quite unheard-of for her to quit her post in the morning, so when I see her hastening up the front path with a large covered basket on her arm (and note that it is not yet eleven o'clock) I have a sinking feeling that something has gone wrong. But, like so many premonitions, this one is false; Annie is all smiles.

"Now that She's gone I'm freer," explains Annie. "You knew She'd gone to London, didn't you? Well, this morning I suddenly felt a bit fed up with everything," says Annie cheerfully. "I just thought—well, what a waste! It's a case of so near and yet so far. I never seem to get a chance of coming along to see you, and when you come to the Bull I never have a moment to sit down. So I just left the lunch to the girl—she's improving a lot—and out I came! Oh, good morning, Mrs. Daulkes!"

"Good morning, Mrs. Bollings," replies my faithful henchwoman who has just appeared with a tray of coffee and biscuits.

It amuses me to observe that Mrs. Stroude's finest china and my very best drawn-thread-work tray-cloth have been produced for Annie's benefit; I rather think it amuses Annie too, for a faint smile curves her lips as her eyes fall upon the tray-cloth. She knows it well of course; Time Was when she produced it for highly favoured guests, and she washed and ironed it with tender care in the days of long ago.

"I'm not sorry She's gone," continues Annie. "The fact is she was a nuisance, really. Not that she complained or asked for things much, but you just felt she was there, looking at you and watching you. It wasn't a nice feeling. She did things in the house, too. Fred said I ought to be pleased at her helping —making her bed and washing the bath and all that—but I'd rather she'd left things alone. The place feels quite different now that she's gone. I don't know how to describe the feeling I had about her except that I felt she was there all the time."

"How is Mr. Alston?" I enquire.

"He's all right," she replies. "He'd be much better if She stayed away—that's the truth."

"He isn't lonely without his mother?"

"Not him. He isn't the sort to be lonely, besides he's got good friends. Yesterday Mr. Morven came for him and he spent the whole day at the Manor. He's sweet on Miss Susan, you know," adds Annie confidentially. "I don't wonder, either. Miss Susan is as pretty as a picture."

"How did he look?" I ask anxiously.

"Mr. Alston? Oh, don't you worry, he was nice and tidy. He can smarten himself up when he likes." She smiles and adds, "He was working hard at his books when I came out and he called to me from the window that he would be out to dinner. 'Oh,' I said. 'Out to dinner? I wonder where you're going. It wouldn't be to the Manor by any chance?' So then he laughed and said, 'Whatever makes you think *that*, Mrs. Bollings?' He's quite fond of a joke."

All this sounds very good indeed and I heave a sigh of relief. Of course there will be trouble when Mrs. Alston returns but I have a feeling that Susan, backed up by her father, will be more than a match for Mrs. Alston.

"It's getting late," says Annie, glancing at the clock and

picking up her basket. "I'll have to get on, I'm afraid. I'm taking a few things to that poor Miss Carlyle."

"Miss Carlyle!" I ask, following Annie to the door.

"The school-mistress," explains Annie. "She's ill in bed with earache, the girls tell me, and there's nobody to do a thing for her. I thought she might fancy a bit of cold chicken and a few eggs."

My heart misgives me and I feel very guilty for I have not seen Anne for a week—not since the dance at Charters Towers. I have been thinking about her of course but I have made no attempt to see her; at first because I was so busy and afterwards because I was afraid I might let out the Great Secret prematurely. Anne, as I already know, is an intuitive person and it would have been difficult for me to talk to her with the secret on my mind. I realise now that although my motives were good their results have been bad and my poor friend has been neglected.

"You wouldn't know her," Annie is saying. "She isn't the sort of lady you would have anything in common with—very clever she is, by all accounts."

The unintended insult amuses me. Annie is quite innocent of offence and of course she is perfectly correct—Anne Carlyle is not my sort of person at all—but, curiously enough, this fact does not prevent us from being good friends; indeed it seems to give spice to our friendship.

I explain to Annie that I know Miss Carlyle quite well and if she will wait until I change my shoes I will accompany her on her mission; and I add that if we find the patient uncomfortable I shall bring her home with me to The Small House.

"Bring her here!" exclaims Annie in amazement. "But who'll look after her?"

"I shall," I reply.

Anne Carlyle is here, in The Small House, but she still has no idea it is her own. It was a little difficult to move her, for she is an independent person, but Annie and I accomplished it between us and she is now upstairs comfortably tucked up in Betty's bed. Doctor Berry is with her, examining her ear, and I am waiting in some trepidation for his verdict.

This is my first introduction to Doctor Berry, but I know him by sight having seen him tearing about the village in his small sports car. Tall and spare with bushy eyebrows and blue eyes, deeply sunken in bony sockets, he is not the sort of man who could be overlooked or easily forgotten; somehow, although I have discovered that he has no trace of accent, I am fairly certain he is a Scot.

"No need to worry," says Doctor Berry as he comes into the drawing room. "Miss Carlyle has a small abscess in the ear—probably due to some local infection—it is causing pain and deafness but I've prescribed some drops which will help, and it should clear up in a few days."

"You don't think it did her any harm to move her?" I enquire anxiously. "She seemed so uncomfortable and forlorn."

"Forlorn describes her well," agrees Doctor Berry. "Mrs. Stroude was her only friend."

"Mrs. Stroude's death was a great shock to her."

"Yes, it must have been. Mrs. Stroude was my patient and I had been attending her for a very serious heart condition but she preferred that nobody should be told about it and of course I respected her wishes. She had no relations except her step-daughter and there was no reason why *she* should be told. I did suggest that Miss Carlyle might be warned but Mrs. Stroude wouldn't hear of it; she hated being fussed over."

"Mrs. Stroude knew about it herself?" I enquire.

"She knew she might die at any moment," replies Doctor

Berry in a low voice. "I don't think it worried her at all. She was a deeply religious woman and believed implicitly in an afterlife of pure happiness. It was a privilege to know Mrs. Stroude—or so I felt."

There is nothing to be said, or at least I can find nothing, and after a little pause Doctor Berry pulls himself together and smiles at me.

"Now for Miss Carlyle," he says. "We've got to do our best for her. I'm very glad to think she has found a new friend. It was a masterly move on your part to kidnap her. I don't know how you managed it for she's a very determined little person."

"I just—kidnapped her. There's no other word for it I'm afraid. I sent for a taxi, packed her into it and brought her here. When I found she hadn't seen a doctor about her ear I sent for you."

"Quite so," agrees Doctor Berry.

"Of course she made all sorts of objections and said she didn't want to be a nuisance, but I took no notice. I felt I couldn't leave her there with nobody to look after her. It was very high-handed of me and as a matter of fact I felt a bit worried about it afterwards. I'm rather apt to get carried away and do things without thinking them over properly."

"You leap before you look?" suggests the doctor.

"I see now that I should have sent for you first, before I moved her."

Doctor Berry chuckles. "Well, if that's all your worry, I can set your mind at ease. In my opinion a few days of rest and good food and pleasant company will do her all the good in the world." He hesitates for a moment, looking at me with his keen blue eyes.

"Is there something else?" I enquire.

"Well—yes," he says doubtfully. "It's difficult sometimes

267

for a doctor to know how much to tell. But I think I'll risk it. The real trouble is that our patient is undernourished. That's at the bottom of the whole thing. Nowadays people who live alone are often undernourished. This doesn't mean they're starving of course, it simply means they aren't getting enough of the right kind of food. I should imagine Miss Carlyle takes very little interest in what she eats," adds Doctor Berry thoughtfully.

"She's more interested in food for the mind," I suggest.

Doctor Berry laughs. "No doubt that's true; but the older I get the more I realise that you can't separate the mind and the body; they react upon each other. The mind affects the body; the body affects the mind. In this case for instance . . ."

"Yes?"

"I have a feeling that Miss Carlyle is worrying about something."

"Her ear?"

"Yes, of course; but even after I had told her there was nothing seriously wrong I felt she was still anxious. If you could find out what's troubling her and get her to talk about it frankly I think it would help."

I promise to do my best and after giving me some instructions about drops for Anne's ear the good man takes his departure.

It is not difficult to make Anne talk. When I go up she is waiting for me, her eyes fixed upon the door.

"What did he say?" she asks anxiously. "He told me it was an abscess and would clear up in a few days but you must tell me honestly. What did he say to you?"

"Exactly what he said to you."

"But he was a long time with you. He's just gone."

"He was explaining about the drops for your ear."

"Oh dear!" exclaims poor Anne. "What a nuisance I am!

268

Tuesday, 21st August

You shouldn't have brought me here! I can't help fussing. Supposing it affects my hearing? A school-mistress *must* be able to hear. If I can't go on teaching what will become of me? There is no other work I could do."

I sit down upon the bed and look at her. Perhaps it is natural that I should be reminded of Betty, for this is Betty's bed, but there is more to it than that. Anne's eyes are the same bright-blue as Betty's and have the same honest, innocent gaze.

"You understand, don't you?" she continues earnestly. "This queer dull feeling in my ear has been going on for days."

"Why didn't you go to Doctor Berry before?"

"Because—because I was a coward," says Anne blushing. "I was afraid of what he would say."

"Well, now you know. He said it was a temporary thing and would clear up in a few days."

"Yes," she agrees. "Yes, I know, and I was so relieved. But then I had a feeling he wasn't being quite open with me and that there was something else. Are you sure it won't leave me deaf?"

"Quite sure. I've told you what he said."

"And there's nothing else the matter with me?"

"Nothing that rest and good food won't cure."

Anne sinks back on her pillows with a sigh. "Rest!" she says. "But the Christmas Term begins in three weeks, and I feel so . . . done."

For a few moments I hesitate. Shall I tell her now? Shall I tell her that she need not worry about the Christmas Term, nor any other term, but can rest as much as she likes, here, in her own house? Shall I tell her now or wait until tomorrow when she has had a night's sleep? The difficulty is I do not know how she will take the news.

"What is it?" asks Anne with a sharp note of anxiety in

269

her voice. "You're hiding something from me, Mrs. Christie!"

"Well—yes," I reply smiling. "But it's a pleasant Something. You know I'm rather sorry for those children in your school. Can you always tell if they're hiding something from you?"

"A pleasant Something?" asks Anne, ignoring the red herring.

"Very pleasant."

"I can't think of anything. What is it?"

"A legacy."

Her eyes widen and she looks at me with dawning comprehension. "You mean . . . Lorna!" she exclaims.

I nod, and rising quickly I go over to the window and arrange the curtain. When I look round my patient is sitting up in bed.

"Tell me quickly!" she cries. "The Will has been found!"

Wednesday, 22nd August

A NNE SMILES at me when I take up her breakfast and admits to having slept all night.

"It was those tablets," she says. "I didn't expect to sleep; there was so much to think about."

"There's plenty of time to think," I reply.

The day passes slowly. Every now and then I look in to see my patient and I find her lying quite still looking out of the window at the tops of the trees and the cloudy sky. She does not want to read nor to listen to the wireless; she asks for nothing and her desire is to give me as little trouble as possible. Unfortunately the desire to give me no trouble gives me more, for I am unused to such a good patient (my own family, when confined to bed, demands constant attention) and I have an uneasy feeling that anyone who lies perfectly still and quiet without visible means of entertainment must be seriously ill. Her appearance alarms me too. She looks different. She looks younger and more vulnerable. It is as if her shell had softened.

When I take up her supper I tell her that I am going to send for the doctor.

"Dear me, no!" exclaims Anne. "I'm much better. I shall get up tomorrow. It's quite ridiculous for me to lie here and for you to toil up and down those stairs."

"I've been a little worried . . ."

"I know," she agrees. "I'm sorry to have been a worry,

but I've had to do a lot of readjusting. I've had to think things out and it hasn't been easy. At first I felt that I shouldn't accept the legacy. I felt it was too much. I wanted some little thing from Lorna, a token gift to show she had remembered me."

"But she wanted you to have the house!"

Anne nods. "Yes, I see that now. I see that I must accept it because she wanted me to have it . . . so that's settled. But even when I had settled that there was a great deal of readjusting to be done. All my life I've been on my own. I've had to fend for myself and fight for what I wanted. Now I can let go. Now I need not worry about the future. You don't know how wonderful it is."

"Perhaps I can guess."

"I doubt it," she says thoughtfully. "The future has always been a burden to me. I tried not to think about it, but sometimes I couldn't help wondering what I should do if I were ill and unable to work."

Anne looks at me and I nod. "Yes I understand," I tell her. "I realised what you were feeling that day when I found you near the river, sitting on a milestone."

"I'm sitting on another milestone today, but it's a much more comfortable one. I've been looking back and looking forward and thinking about the present too. Can you wonder that I didn't want to read or talk or listen to the wireless! My mind has been turned upside-down in the most extraordinary way. Everything seems different—"

"You look different, yourself."

"Well of course! What did you expect!" exclaims Anne laughing. "I'm quite different. I'm not the same person at all. Yesterday I was the village school-marm; today I'm Miss Anne Carlyle of The Small House."

I rise and make her a little curtsy.

Wednesday, 22nd August

"But it isn't only that," says Anne hastily. "That's just fun. It's more important to know that Lorna thought of me with affection and wanted me to have her house. The Small House meant so much to her, you see. She loved it."

"She wanted you to have it—because she knew you would love it and appreciate it."

"That makes me very happy," says Anne. "Of course I shan't give up my work. I enjoy teaching and I know I can give the children something worthwhile. Lorna wouldn't want me to be idle. But I can do my work more comfortably and I can help the children—some of them need clothes and books."

"You can travel," I suggest.

"Of course! I can go abroad during the holidays! I can go to concerts! I can buy all the books I want!" Her eyes are very bright and her cheeks are flushed with excitement at the thought of the pleasures in store. "All the books I want!" she repeats in delight.

"If you go on like that you'll send up your temperature," I tell her in admonishing tones.

"Who cares!" she exclaims. "And you needn't pretend to be so stern. You're almost as pleased and excited as I am. Dear Hester, I owe it all to you!"

It is interesting to notice that this new Anne calls me by my name and does it quite naturally, without thinking.

"Yes, I owe it all to you," she repeats emphatically. "If it hadn't been for you—"

I interrupt her to explain that she owes nothing to me and I remind her that I threw Mrs. Stroude's Will into the waste-paper basket. I add that if Tony Morley had not been an inquisitive sort of man it would have been put out with the salvage.

"Oh, but—" begins Anne, somewhat dashed.

"You're a romantic," I tell her. "You like fairy stories."

"I!" cries Anne. "What nonsense! I'm extremely realistic. In this matter for instance; the Will would never have been found if you hadn't been searching high and low for the Byron letter. It was entirely—"

Anne begins to laugh.

"Entirely what?" I ask.

"Oh Hester, how funny! I suppose it's my letter, isn't it?"

The fact that Miss Stroude's "valuable letter" does not belong to her at all seems excruciatingly funny to us. Perhaps we are over excited and slightly hysterical, but it is some time before we can control our mirth . . . and even after the laugh is over I keep on giggling feebly when I think of the hours Miss Stroude spent in the box-room searching feverishly.

"I shall get up tomorrow," declares Anne. "That laugh has completed my cure. Besides I want to go all round my house and gloat over it. My house! It's almost incredible!"

"Do you want it soon?" I ask. "Would you like me to make other arrangements?"

"No, of course not! I want you to stay here as long as you can. I'm going on with my work and naturally I should like you to be here. It's completely selfish," says Anne when I begin to thank her. "If you're here I know The Small House is safe and happy . . . and I can come and see it when I like."

Saturday, 25th August

*Q*UITE OFTEN during my varied life I have thought how very pleasant it would be to have a guest who would always be there when I wanted to chat, but would vanish into thin air when I did not. Anne is as near this ideal guest as it is possible for a human being to be. She does not actually vanish of course—that would be too much to expect —but when I am busy or disinclined for companionship she curls herself up in a large chair and reads for hours without moving. She possesses the power of concentration which Edmond coveted when he said he knew "fellows who could read anatomy with the wireless going full blast." Anne's only fault, from the point of view of a hostess, is that she does not appreciate good food; but in these days of austerity this peculiarity is not always a disadvantage. Although it is a little disappointing to see her eating the breast of a chicken without proper appreciation it is gratifying to see her eating boiled cod without distaste.

It has been agreed that Anne is to remain here until Bryan and Betty return from London and, as their visit has been extended, so has hers. Her ear has cleared up and she is looking a great deal better; Doctor Berry is pleased with her—and also with me.

This afternoon I leave her curled up in a chair and set off to the village to do the shopping. The day is cloudy and there is a definite feeling of approaching autumn in the still, damp air. There are a few early chrysanthemums to be seen in Miss Crease's garden and Miss Crease herself is pottering about with a basket, cutting off the withered blooms from her rose-bushes.

Miss Crease calls to me and waddles to the gate. "Mrs. Christie! Why have you never been to see me?"

"I didn't think you would want me to come," I reply. Today I am feeling bolder than usual and quite suddenly I make up my mind to take the bull by the horns. "In fact I thought you would rather I stayed away," I continue, fixing her with an unwinking stare. "You've told your friends all sorts of stories about me—stories which are quite untrue."

"I can say what I like," declares Miss Crease. "I told you that the first time I saw you."

"You can say what you like." I agree. "But if you say horrible things about me you can't blame me for not coming to see you."

"Oh!" exclaims Miss Crease in surprise.

I leave her standing there and walk on. Somehow I am rather pleased with myself, for this is quite definitely a victory; not only a victory over Miss Crease but also over my own cowardice. I see now that I should have tackled Miss Crease before. I should have walked up to the bull and seized it by the horns instead of sitting back and pretending I did not notice its antics. Like all bulls—and bullies—Miss Crease should be firmly handled.

It is just as well I have something to cheer me on my way for there is still no letter from Tim. I had expected one this morning by the nine o'clock post and was disappointed when all I received was a bill. The letter may arrive by the afternoon post, it may be waiting for me at The Small House when I return. If not, I have made up my mind to send Tim a cable and ask why he has not written.

276

Saturday, 25th August

The butcher is my first port of call. As has been said before he is a friend of Mrs. Daulkes's. He has kept some liver for me and promises me a piece of stewing steak Monday, which is exceedingly good of him . . . but I want a bone as well, and as animals nowadays seem to possess no bones my request must be led up to in a diplomatic manner. I explain that Miss Carlyle is staying with me at present, that she has been ill and the doctor says she must be fed up. Mr. Higginbotham knows this already of course—everybody in Old Quinings knows it—but he pretends it is news to him and makes all the proper enquiries. When I have prepared the ground carefully I bring out my request.

"A bone!" says Mr. Higginbotham looking at me sadly.

"To make soup, you know."

"Why not buy a tin?" he suggests. "Save you a lot of trouble, that would. Bones need boiling."

"You haven't got one to spare?"

"I'll try," says Mr. Higginbotham. "I will, reely."

This being settled we chat pleasantly together for a few minutes as is the custom in Old Quinings. It would not be comme il faut to hurry out of the shop without a pleasant chat.

The door of the shop is partially blocked by the carcase of a sheep, so it is impossible to see out clearly; one can get a glimpse of people passing—a hasty glimpse and no more. While I am chatting to Mr. Higginbotham several people pass and amongst them a tall man in a Burberry who looks a little like Tim. He is just about Tim's height and strides along in the same loose-limbed manner. This has happened to me before—not once but many times—and occasionally I have been deceived by the chance resemblance. Today I am not deceived but only saddened for how lovely it would be if Tim were really here! But Tim is thousands of miles away in Kenya and the reason for my illusion is not difficult to discover: I have been thinking about Tim so much that his image is in my mind.

"Well, that's 'ow it is," says Mr. Higginbotham ruefully. "If I could sell you a nice leg o' mutton there'd be nobody better pleased than me. I'd tie it up with ribbings and deliver it at The Small 'Ouse with my own 'ands—believe it or not, Mrs. Christie."

I assure Mr. Higginbotham that I believe it implicitly.

Saturday afternoon is a busy time in Old Quinings; the pavement is thronged with pedestrians and there are a good many cars of various shapes and sizes to be seen. Susan's car is drawn up outside Wiggs, the baker's, and as I cross the street its owner comes out of the shop with Edmond in tow.

"Mrs. Christie!" cries Susan waving wildly. "Mrs. Christie, we were on our way to see you. We're engaged! Well, of course you know all about it, don't you? But I wanted to tell you properly and show you my ring."

"Isn't it marvellous?" says Edmond, looking at me with a dazed expression. "Isn't it simply marvellous?"

I congratulate them and tell them how pleased I am; and these conventional expressions of good-will are more than usually sincere. Not only am I very fond of them both but I think they will suit one another well.

"You'll help, won't you?" says Susan, looking at me imploringly. "I mean you'll go on helping? Please say you will."

This somewhat mysterious request from a newly engaged young woman is no mystery to me. I am aware that I am being enlisted in the battle between Edmond's mother and Edmond's future wife and, as I am deeply involved already and heart and soul upon the side of the younger generation, I promise to do all I can.

Edmond is now busy putting parcels into the car so it is possible for Susan to speak more frankly.

Saturday, 25th August

"She doesn't know yet," whispers Susan. "He can't make up his mind to tell her. He thinks we should wait till she goes to Scotland and then write. It seems a bit—I mean I feel it would be braver to tell her. What do you think?"

The problem is somewhat difficult but after a moment's thought I tell Susan that I think she should wait and announce the news by letter.

"Oh bother—that's what Daddy says!" exclaims Susan.

The squire is a sensible man in my estimation and I am glad to hear his opinion on the subject coincides with mine. I explain my reasons for counselling delay: namely that Edmond should be spared as much as possible on account of his impending examinations.

"Oh, there's bound to be a row," says Susan with a sigh. "I just feel I'd like to get it over quickly."

At this moment Mr. Wiggs emerges from his shop; he and I have been particular friends ever since the day of my adventure in the old village.

"I beg your pardon, Mrs. Christie," says Mr. Wiggs with old-world courtesy. "Please excuse me for interrupting your conversation. I just wondered if you had seen the gentleman, that's all."

"Seen the gentleman!" I exclaim.

"A tall gentleman—very sunburnt he was," explains Mr. Wiggs. "I would say he was a military gentleman. Called in to ask the way to The Small House. I told him he must—"

But at these words light breaks; I abandon Mr. Wiggs and Susan and run. I tear madly across the street, heedless of the traffic; I turn the corner into the lane and putting on a sprint arrive breathless and dishevelled at the gate of The Small House . . . and there is Tim standing upon the doorstep.

"It *was* you!" I cry rushing up the path and hurling myself into his arms. "I thought it was—but I knew it wasn't—because you were in Kenya."

"But I'm not in Kenya, I'm here!" cries Tim, crushing me in a bear's embrace.

"But, Hester, I *did* write to you," says Tim when the first excitement of our meeting has died down a little. "I wrote and explained everything. As a matter of fact *there* is my letter!"

And there, without doubt, is his letter in the wire basket which is fixed to the front-door.

"How funny!" exclaims Tim, taking it out and looking at it. "How awfully queer to see it again! You won't want it now, of course."

"Of course I want it!" I cry, seizing it out of his hand.

We laugh again. We have done nothing but laugh and exclaim and carry on like a pair of lunatics for the last five minutes. No sensible word has been said and I still have no idea as to why Tim has arrived so suddenly and unexpectedly.

"Need we stand in the hall?" asks Tim. "It's a nice hall of course, but I've been travelling for the last two days. If there's any hot water I should like a bath. Bath first and then some food if possible. I didn't wait to have a meal in London; I came straight here by the first train."

"Yes, of course! Oh, I forgot . . ."

"What?" Tim enquires. "Nothing wrong is there? Bryan and Betty all right?"

"Perfectly all right. They're in London with Richard and Mary having a very gay time. It was just—I suddenly remembered my guest."

"Guest!" exclaims Tim in disgust. "Oh, I say, Hester! You don't mean to say you've got somebody staying in the house!"

Saturday, 25th August

My guest is still reading. Incredible as it may seem she has heard nothing of the tumult and, when awakened from her trance, she gazes at Tim with a dazed and horrified expression and scrambles to her feet.

"I must go!" cries Anne. "I had no idea—I'll go home at once!"

"Nonsense, Anne!" I exclaim.

"It isn't nonsense! Of course I must go. You won't want me."

Tim was slightly annoyed to discover a strange woman in the house, but his heart is melted by these expressions of dismay. He assures Anne that we are old married people, inured to one another's charms, and have no wish to be alone on the evening of our reunion. I add my reassurances to his and after a good deal of persuasion Anne agrees to postpone her departure until tomorrow morning.

"Poor little soul!" says Tim as we go upstairs together to see about his bath. "You do manage to pick up the oddest creatures, Hester."

"What's odd about her?"

"Everything," says Tim vaguely. "In fact I've never seen anything the least like her before. Who is she?"

"A friend of mine, and incidentally the owner of The Small House."

Tim is mollified. "Oh well," he says, "if she's our landlady that's different . . . but I thought you said in your letter that Miss Stroude was an absolute fiend? That little creature seems quite harmless."

"It's rather a long story . . ."

"Then it must wait," says Tim firmly. "I'll have my bath and then we can talk our heads off."

Tim seizes his sponge from his suitcase and vanishes into the bathroom and as I still know nothing of his plans, nor how he has managed to escape from his duties and fly home to his family, I take his letter out of my pocket and, slitting it open, unfold the sheets.

20th August.

Dearest darling Hester,

I am so sorry my letters have been scrappy but I have been most awfully busy—also various things have been happening and I did not want to say anything to you until I could tell you definitely what was what. I knew you would worry if I told you that I might be sent here or there or I might not, so I thought it best to wait. Quite soon after you left I got a signal from the War House posting me to Korea to take command of the 2nd Battalion vice Meredith who was being invalided home. This gave me a bit of a jolt coming out of the blue, all the more so because as you know I am up to the eyes in the Defence Schemes for East Africa. It seemed pretty sickening to have to hand over the whole thing to some other bloke to finish and as a matter of fact it would have been difficult for another bloke, however capable, to take over the job at a moment's notice. The General was not a bit pleased when I showed him the signal; he looked at it and said, This Shall Not Be—or words to that effect. I could not tell you the exact words of course. So he Took Steps and the posting was cancelled. Rather fun to be a General and throw your weight about like that! All these things took time and, as I said before, I did not want to worry you until I knew exactly what was going to happen. It was difficult to write with all this on my mind and not mention it and I expect that is why you found my letters a bit unsatisfactory. Now for the great piece of news. There is to be a conference in London about the

Defence Schemes and I am to attend it to explain what
is being done here. I shall be flying home—not sure yet
which day—and of course I shall come straight to Old
Quinings. Isn't it marvellous! As regards future plans
it is difficult to say. The conference may last some time
and then I can take my leave which might be made to
stretch over Christmas. I wondered if we could stay on at
The Small House, could we? Of course you must do as
you think best but the house sounds very attractive and
personally I would rather be comfortably settled than
move about from pillar to post staying with friends and
relations. About your letters—of course I appreciate
them! I laughed like a drain at your description of the
Roman pensione and Tony being shown into your room
by mistake—and your interview with the Signora, her
excitement and your feeble efforts to explain! I can
imagine the whole thing and just wish I could have been
there; but of course if I had been there it would not have
happened! No need to fuss about those old cats gossiping.
I expect they have nothing else to do in a sleepy little
village like Old Quinings. It will die a natural death
when I appear upon the scene. I meant to write to Tony
but there is no time. The orderly is waiting to include
this in the out-going mail. You can tell Tony the news
and thank him from me for all he has done. He really
is a good friend—none better—and I am thankful he is
there to keep an eye on you. It is grand to think I shall
be seeing you soon—simply gorgeous (as Betty would
say).

No more now—Wilkins is pawing the ground—
    Oceans of love, my dearest, from Tim.

My heart is very light as I fold up the sheets. All my